PRAISE FOR EDWARD BUNKER

'Edward Bunker is among the tiny band of American prisoner-writers whose work possesses integrity, craftsmanship, and moral passion . . . an artist with a unique and compelling voice.'

William Styron

'. . . Quite simply, one of the great crime novels of the past 30 years . . .'

James Ellroy

'Bunker writes in straight-ahead, unadorned prose and, refreshingly, he refrains from excessive psychologizing and sentimentalizing . . . a rough-hewn memoir by a rough-hewn man.'

The New York Times Book Review

'It's easy to see why Bunker has acquired such diverse admirers as Quentin Tarantino and William Styron . . . What distinguishes Bunker from other crime writers is his ability to convey the compassion dormant within his violent criminals without resorting to excess luridness, sympathy, or moralism.'

Publishers Weekly

'Bunker shoots straight – his direct and transparent prose captures the 'primacy of violence' that defines life in the slammer.'

Kirkus Reviews

'Bunker is a true original of American letters. His books are criminal classics.'

James Ellroy

'Edward Bunker writes about   asts with a passion and insight th   ose to the bone.'

mes

PRAISE FOR *NO BEAST SO FIERCE*

'. . . The most compelling quality of *No Beast So Fierce* is that, solidly rooted in his own experiences, it explores the nature of the criminal mind with almost blinding authenticity. Bunker is obviously a man of unusual gifts honed under circumstances that would destroy most men . . .'

Los Angeles Times

'. . . A gripping and harrowing read . . .'

Daily Mail

'. . . The best first person crime novel I have ever read . . .'

Quentin Tarantino

'*The Animal Factory* joins Solzhenitsyn's *One Day in the Life of Ivan Denisovich* and George Jacksosn's *Soledad Brother* in the front rank of prison literature . . . a stone classic.'

Time Out

PRAISE FOR *LITTLE BOY BLUE*

'A scalding experience – and a literary triumph in the tradition of Dreiser, Farrell and James Jones. This is an important book . . .'

Roderick Thorp

PRAISE FOR *DOG EAT DOG*

'... The "angel dust" of crime fiction: thrillingly violent and addictive, surging with exhilaration and fear ...'

The Evening Standard

'Mr. Bunker has written a raw, unromantic, naturalistic crime drama more lurid than anything the noiresque Chandlers or Hammetts ever dreamed up.'

The New York Times

'Bunker is a true original of American letters. His books are criminal classics.'

James Ellroy

PRAISE FOR *MR BLUE*

At 40 Eddie Bunker was a hardened criminal with a substantial prison record. Twenty-five years later, he is hailed by his peers as America's greatest living crime writer. Those who know and understand these things become hushed at the mere mention of his name. Some call him simply, The Man ...'

The Independent

'... compulsively readable piece of real-life southern Californian noir ...'

The Saturday Times

'... a classic of criminal pride and indignation ...'

The Times

Also by the same author

No Beast so Fierce
The Animal Factory
Little Boy Blue
Mr Blue
Stark
Death Row Breakout

no exit press

This edition published in 2016 by No Exit Press,
P.O.Box 394, Harpenden, Herts, AL5 1XJ
www.noexit.co.uk

A CIP catalogue record for this book is available from the British Library.

978-1-84243-754-4 (ePub)
978-0-85730-114-7 (Print)

2 4 6 8 10 9 7 5 3 1

Printed in Great Britain by Clays Ltd., St Ives plc

To Bill Styron, Blair Clark, and Paul Allen
friends and advisors

Introduction

by William Styron

Is it true that for a writer there should be no area of experience that is off limits to his imagination? As a novelist who has ventured far afield into alien territory, I have always felt that it is a writer's prerogative to deal with places and events of which he does not necessarily have firsthand knowledge. The imagination is sovereign and its power, almost alone, according to my theory, should be able to transform any subject into something wondrous, if the writer is good enough, so that his world will appear more real to the reader than the world of a writer who may have total familiarity with his milieu but possesses a lesser talent. Certainly there are examples of these triumphant forays into terra incognita. Stephen Crane had no acquaintance whatever with warfare, yet his portrayal of the horrors of combat in *The Red Badge of Courage* remains one of the great fictional accounts of the Civil War or, indeed, any war. Its author never set foot in Africa, yet *Henderson the Rain King*, Saul Bellow's novel of the Dark Continent, shimmers with authenticity.

Is there any region of experience, then, where the intrusion of a writer unfamiliar with its realities should be discouraged? Once again I was about to say no, but in fact I believe there is such a place, and that is the modern American underworld, the landscape inhabited by the hardened criminal. This is a province of our society so remote from the happenings of the middle-class book reader, a place so corrupt and violent, populated by human beings so grotesquely and unpredictably different from you and me, that its appalling contours and the behavior of its denizens can be portrayed only by a writer who has been there. Edward Bunker has been there.

A little over twenty years ago, Bunker, who was then approaching forty, was set free from prison after serving nearly continuous confinement in state and federal institutions since the age of eleven. During the years after his release, in his role as witness to the Los Angeles underworld, Bunker has produced a series of tough, gritty, painstakingly crafted narratives that has revealed better than any contemporary novelist the anatomy of the criminal mind.

Like so many criminals Bunker was the product of a dysfunctional, alcoholic family. Growing up in Los Angeles as an adolescent in the years following World War II, he fell into a pattern of petty crime that led to his being sent to a reformatory. After his release at the age of sixteen he resumed a criminal career that was considerably more hazardous, involving as it did professional shoplifting and drug dealing. An arrest on drug charges earned him a year in the Los Angeles county jail, from which he promptly escaped. He was caught and given two concurrent sentences of six months to ten years in San Quentin. He was of course still only a teenager. It was while he was in San Quentin, where he served four and a half years, that Bunker diverged in his behavior from that of most young convicts and acquired a passion that eventually saved his life—although his salvation would come only after many more years behind walls. He discovered books. He became a consecrated reader, ransacking the prison library in his newfound hunger for the printed word; his enthusiasm turned him into an aspiring writer who scribbled indefatigably away in his cell, with immense pleasure though with no success in publication.

When Bunker was released on parole from San Quentin, at the age of twenty-three, he entered a phase in his life whose grimly frustrating nature would provide a key to his later work. In *No Beast So Fierce*, Bunker's powerful first novel published many years later, the theme is that of a young ex-convict—attractive, promising, eager to make his way in society—whose prison record is enough by its very existence to cause doors to be shut unremittingly in his face. Like his fictional protagonist, Bunker tried desperately to adapt himself to the new straight world, making countless efforts to get legitimate jobs, but the shadow of San Quentin was too baleful and persistent: Society had locked him out. He turned to crime once more (masterminding robberies, extorting pimps and madams in a protection scheme, forging checks), was caught, convicted, and sent to San Quentin again with a sentence bearing a fourteen-year ceiling. This was Bunker's longest continuous sentence and he served half of it. They were seven agonizing years. He has described this period as one of near madness (a profoundly rebellious streak caused him more than once to suffer the terrors of The Hole—solitary confinement), but his furious love affair with the written word, which kept him reading and writing, provided a kind of spiritual rescue and also, in concrete terms, four unpublished novels and dozens of short stories. He emerged again from behind bars, with a hunger to succeed as a writer of fiction.

But it should be no surprise, given the fate of so many ex-convicts in America, that Bunker's new freedom was short-lived. Once more his prison record was a curse. After writing over two hundred applications for legitimate jobs and receiving not a single answer, after walking the streets until his feet blistered, after responding to ads week after week only to be turned away, Bunker headed out again on the crime route. He burglarized a safe in a bar and was captured after a high-speed automobile chase. He made bail while awaiting trial but was then seized by what would appear to be euphoric over-confidence: He decided to rob what he has described as a "prosperous little Beverly Hills bank." Unaware that his car had been wired with a beeper by narcotics agents, who thought he was on his way to a drug deal, the heavily armed Bunker was trailed to the bank, where he was caught at gunpoint and badly beaten. He was tried on federal charges, sentenced to six years, and transported to the McNeil Island penitentiary on Puget Sound in Washington.

At McNeil Island, Bunker's insurgent spirit once again got him into trouble. Enraged at being housed in a ten-man cell, he went on strike and for his defiance was sent to the nation's most fearsome lockup, the maximum-security prison at Marion, Illinois. There, despite monstrous handicaps and restrictions, he displayed his invincible scorn for the system by continuing to write fiction. And it is the writing, of course—the dedicated, passionate writing—that eventually saved Edward Bunker.

No Beast So Fierce was accepted for publication while Bunker was awaiting trial for the Beverly Hills bank robbery, and was published in 1973, during his incarceration at Marion. The book received generally fine reviews and gained its author widespread attention, adding to the luster he had already gradually acquired as a brilliantly outspoken literary convict who had written eloquent essays about prison life and prison conditions in such journals as *Harper's* and *The Nation*. By the time his second novel, *The Animal Factory*, was completed in his cell at Marion, Bunker's reputation in the vast national prison cosmos shone so brightly that it plainly contributed to his final parole.

This last release was in 1975. Since then he has lived the life of a peaceable citizen, settling in his native Los Angeles where he has married, fathered a son, and has continued to write fiction (his third novel, *Little Boy Blue*, appeared in 1982), while also pursuing a successful career as a screenwriter. In 1978, a remarkably powerful (though mysteriously neglected) film version of *No Beast So Fierce*, with a script by Bunker, was produced under the title *Straight Time*, starring Dustin Hoffman in a taut, superbly focused performance as a prototypal Eddie Bunker. The character is a desperate ex-convict whose decent aspirations are thwarted by a society bent upon denying such men their right to rehabilitation and redemption.

In Bunker's novels the failure to achieve redemption is joined by another motif: the wretched abandonment of our children. This theme, obviously derived from Bunker's own bitter and brutalizing experience, reoccurs throughout all his fiction, and in *Dog Eat Dog*, his fourth novel, the outcast protagonist is Troy Cameron. Like Bunker, he is a reformatory graduate, and as one follows his progress through this raw, unrelenting, sometimes terrifyingly brutal narrative, tracking his lawless spree in the company of two other reform school alumni, Diesel Carson and Mad Dog McCain, one perceives that the subtext in the work, as in all of Bunker's writing, is that of the perpetuation of violence and cruelty. For Bunker, crime is nurtured in institutional cradles and those who are abused and spiritually mutilated in their earliest youth, whether within the family or in the foster home or the reformatory, grow up to become society's bloody marauders. *Dog Eat Dog* is a novel of excruciating authenticity, with great moral and social resonance, and it could only have been written by Edward Bunker, who has been there.

Prologue
1981

"Hup, two, three, four! Hup, two, three, four. Column right . . . march!" The monitor called the cadence and bellowed the command. The thirty boys of Roosevelt cottage marched in step through the summer twilight. Each affected a demeanor of extreme toughness. Even those who were really afraid managed to hold up the meanest mask they could. Faces were stone, eyes were icy, mouths that seldom smiled would sneer easily. In the underclass fashion of the moment, they pulled their pants absurdly high, virtually to their chests, and cinched their belts tight. Although they kept in step, each had a stylized swagger. They marched like a military academy, but were inmates of a California reform school. Aged from fourteen to sixteen, they were among the toughest of their age. Nobody got to reform school for truancy or writing on walls. It took several arrests for car theft or burglary. If it was a first offense, it was armed robbery or a drive-by shooting.

Situated thirty miles east of downtown Los Angeles, the state school was located on the earliest tract maps of the area, when L.A. had a population of 60,000 and farmland was cheap. Once, the reform school had resembled a small college. Sweeping lawns and sycamores framed buildings that resembled manor houses with brick walls and sloping slate roofs. A few of the old buildings still remained, empty relics from the age when society believed the young could be salvaged—back before the days when kids packed MAC—back when Bogart and Cagney were tough-guy role models. They only killed "dirty rats," invariably with a snub-nose, up close, not "spray and pray."

The marching boys halted while The Man unlocked the gate to

the recreation yard. As they marched inside, he counted them. The yard was formed by a chain-link fence topped with rolled barbed wire. The Man nodded to the monitor. "Dismissed" yelled the monitor.

The neat ranks disintegrated and formed clusters by race. Chicanos were half the total, fifteen, followed by nine blacks, five whites, and a pair of half-brothers, one of whom was Vietnamese while his half-brother was a quarter Native American, a quarter black and half Vietnamese. The half brothers glared at the whole world with baleful challenge.

The Chicanos and two of their white homeboys from East L.A. headed for the handball court, a free-standing wall that allowed a game on each side. The blacks picked sides for half-court basketball.

The three remaining whites came together and began to pace the length of the yard next to the fence topped with barbed wire. One of them wore new black oxfords, identical to U.S. Navy issue. The shoes were issued to be broken in a week before parole. It was Saturday and Troy Cameron was being released on Monday morning.

"How many you got left?" Big Charley Carson asked. At fifteen, he was six foot two and weighed under 150 pounds. He would gain eighty before he turned twenty-one. By then he would be powerful enough to be nicknamed "Diesel."

"One day and a getup," Troy said. "Forty hours. Short as a mosquito's dick."

The third member of the trio grinned, simultaneously raising a hand to his mouth to hide his discolored teeth. He was Gerald McCain, already nicknamed "Mad Dog" for insane behavior, the most notorious being the use of an aluminum baseball bat on a sleeping bully who had pushed McCain around. In the Hobbesian world of reform school, a maniac is given wide berth. Tough and mean is one thing; crazy is something strange, different and frightening.

The trio kept walking as the shadows lengthened. The background to their conversation was the crash of weights descending on the platform, the basketball dribbled on asphalt and rattling the metal

14

backboard and hoop, aided by exclamations of delight or curses of frustration. A few more steps and it was the special sound of a little black handball whacking into the wall. The tally was always called in *la lengua de Aztlan*, a street patois basically Spanish liberally laced with English. Handball was the game of the barrio, for it took but a wall and a ball. "Point! Cinco servin' three. *Dos juegos a nada.*"

The game over, the two losers left the court with each accusing the other of causing the loss. The Chicano who was keeping tally had the next game. He looked around for a partner and spotted Troy. "Hey, Troy . . . homeboy! Venga. Let's whip these farmers."

Troy looked at the competition, Chepe Reyes and Al Salas. Chepe was beckoning in a challenge.

"I'm wearing these shoes." He indicated the black dressouts, which would be scuffed badly on a concrete handball court.

"Go ahead," said Big Charley. "Use mine." He took off his low-cut athletic shoes.

Troy changed shoes, took off his shirt, and wrapped a bandanna around his palm. A handball glove was better, but in lieu of that, a bandanna would serve. He was ready. He bounced the ball off the wall a few times to loosen up. At fifteen a long warm-up was unnecessary. "Let's go. Throw for serve." He tossed the ball to his partner.

The game began, Troy playing front. They played hard, diving on the concrete for low balls. At one point, halfway through the game, Troy's partner ran forward to get a ball. Troy anticipated the opponent's shot—high and to the rear—and Troy was running before it was hit.

Looking back for the ball, he failed to see the three black youths with their backs turned until the last fraction of a second. He managed to half raise his hands before the crash sent two stumbling and knocked the other down.

"Oh, man . . . sorry about that," Troy said, extending a hand. He knew the black youth: Robert Lee Lincoln, called R. Lee. At fifteen he had the body of a twenty-two-year-old bodybuilder, an IQ of eighty-five and the emotional control of a two-year-old, plus he hated rich white people. Troy knew some of this; he had avoided R. Lee during the two months since the black arrived.

He wasn't surprised when R. Lee's response to apology was to put both hands on Troy's chest and shove. "Muthafucker . . . watch it. I don' be likin' you muthafuckers no way." The words dripped contempt and challenge. R. Lee's chin jutted, so he was peering down his nose with glittering eyes of racial hate. Inside Troy was the thought, This fuckin' nigger! The word was one that Troy used only in specific situations. It was applicable only to blacks who acted like niggers—loud, crude, stupid—just like redneck fit certain ignorant whites. But mixed with the first thought were two others. In a fistfight he would take an ass-kicking. He was tempted to sneak a punch right now without warning, while R. Lee was still posing. If the Sunday punch landed clean, he might be able to swarm and win before R. Lee got going. But if Troy did that, he would lose his parole. He could see The Man coming toward them. "Knock it off there," The Man said.

R. Lee turned away with the parting words: "We'll finish this shit later."

Troy turned back toward his waiting friends. A hollow sensation was spreading in waves from his gullet to the rest of his body. Fear was sucking his will away. He could never whip R. Lee in a fight; the nigger was too big, too strong, too fast, and could really fight. That was the smallest fear; Troy had planned ahead for such matters. He would unscrew a firehose nozzle and strike without warning. It would never be a fistfight. He would win a Pyrrhic victory, for his parole would go down the drain as soon as he struck.

"Damn," he muttered.

"That nigger's crazy," Big Charley said. "He's one of them hate whitey motherfuckers."

"Yeah." He managed a snorting half-laugh. "Right now I hate niggers."

What the fuck should he do? Maybe they wouldn't take his parole if it was just a fistfight, but that would mean getting an ass-kicking. Maybe he could get in a couple of punches. "I half-ass wish I didn't have this parole," he said.

"Oh yeah," Mad Dog said. "I forgot about your parole. That's a bitch."

16

Troy could go to The Man and seek protection for the last two days. They could lock him up for two days. He would lose nothing— except his good name in his world. He reviled himself for even letting it go through his mind. Anything like that was totally out of the question. If he did something like that, he would be marked in the underworld, where he intended to live, for his whole life. It would be a stigma he could never erase. It would forever invite aggression.

"Lemme take care of it," Mad Dog offered. "I'll steal him."

Troy shook his head. "No. I'll handle my own shit."

The blast of the police whistle, the signal to line up at the door into the building, cut the twilight.

As the youths filed inside, The Man stood in the doorway and counted them. Indoors, some hurried down the hall toward the TV room; they wanted the best seats. Those who had been playing handball or basketball or lifting weights made a left turn into the washroom. There were three communal washbasins, each with three faucets.

Troy watched R. Lee in line ahead of him. R. Lee turned left. Good. It would give Troy a chance to turn right into the dormitory. The firehose was just inside the door. The brass nozzle would bust a head like an eggshell if he swung it that hard. He had decided it was all he could do. He hated R. Lee more for his ignorance, for forcing this, for taking away imminent freedom.

R. Lee was no fool. He knew Troy was behind him. As R. Lee turned into the washroom, he watched the doorway behind him via the mirror. He stripped off his T-shirt and stepped up to the sink. Because he was watching the door, he missed Mad Dog in the stall toilet to the right.

Mad Dog flushed the toilet with his foot and turned. Down beside his leg was a toothbrush handle. It had been melted and, while soft, two pieces of razor blade had been fitted in. When it hardened the blades stuck out less than a quarter of an inch—small but very sharp. He came behind the youths at the washbasins. It took just two seconds to reach R. Lee.

Mad Dog put the blade on the brown back and sliced all the way

17

from shoulder to waist. The flesh lay open like lips for a moment; then the blood welled up and poured forth.

R. Lee screamed and whirled, simultaneously reaching back at the wound and looking for the attacker. Mad Dog was wide-eyed, a hyena looking for an opening to dart in and slash again.

Another black had seen the blow from across the room. He yelled, "Watch it!" and came pushing through.

Mad Dog cocked his arm back, a scorpion flashing its tail. The second black stopped out of range. "You fucked up, honky!"

"Fuck you, nigger!"

The Man saw the chaos and hit the panic alarm he carried.

In the dormitory door, Troy heard the yells and saw boys rushing toward the washroom. As he stepped into the hallway, R. Lee burst through the crowd in the opposite doorway and ran for the outer door. His whole back was covered with blood flowing profusely onto the back of his pants and the floor. He began kicking on the front door. "Lemme out! Lemme out! Lemme go to the hospital."

Troy saw a couple of blacks looking at him. He had the firehose nozzle wrapped in newspaper. If they made a move, he would bash a head.

The Man pushed through to the outer door. He unlocked it and R. Lee ran out.

Coming the other way were the freemen, carrying night-sticks, their keys jangling on their hips.

The cottage was put on lockdown, with extra personnel watching.

R. Lee needed two hundred and eleven stitches.

Mad Dog went to the hole.

On Monday morning. Troy was released on parole. He owed his release to Mad Dog. It was a debt he carried into the future.

1

Two nights alone in a room with a pair of one-ounce jars of pharmaceutical cocaine made Mad Dog McCain live up to his nickname. The cocaine was better than what was peddled on the street. It came from a doctor's bag he'd stolen from a car in a medical building parking lot. He'd originally planned to sell it after using a little bit, but when he approached the few people he knew in Portland, they either wanted credit or ridiculed cocaine as "powdered paranoia" or "twenty minutes to madness." They all wanted heroin, a drug that made them calm instead of insane.

A little bit made him feel great, so he used a little more, and the fangs of the serpent were in him. First he chopped the flakes with a razor blade, formed lines, and tooted them up the nose, and that was good. But he knew how to get a bigger bang. The doctor's bag had a package of disposable syringes with attached needles. All the pure cocaine took was a few drops of water and it dissolved. Drop in a matchhead-size piece of cotton to draw it through, and then tap the needle into the hard ridge of vein at the inner aspect of the elbow. It was hard to miss. Now his arm was black and blue and had scabs from earlier injections. His tank top was filthy and showed where he'd used the bottom to wipe away the blood from his arm. That didn't matter. Nothing mattered, except the flash. When the needle penetrated the vein, red blood jumped into the syringe. He squeezed a little; then let the blood back up into the syringe.

When the glow started to course through him, he squeezed off a little more. What a flash! If he . . . could . . . just . . . maintain . . .

the flash . . . Oh God! Ohhh . . . So good . . . so fucking good as it went through his body and his brain.

Stop. Let it back up into the syringe again. Squeeze off more.

Repeat, until the syringe was empty.

He closed his eyes, moaning softly as he savored the ecstasy. He was king of everything now.

From the nightstand ashtray, he took a cigarette butt. While he straightened it out to light, he saw Troy's letter from San Quentin on top of a pile of unopened mail. Good news. Troy had a parole date three months away. As soon as Troy raised, they would get rich together. Troy was the smartest criminal Mad Dog knew, and he'd known thousands. Troy knew how to plan things. What a great idea, heisting dope dealers and wannabe gangsters, assholes who couldn't yell copper. It would be great to have big money. He would buy Sheila the clothes she was always looking at in women's magazines and catalogs. He might even get her a Mustang convertible. She had it coming. She was a good broad. Halfass pretty, too, if she'd lose fifteen or twenty pounds. Then again he wasn't exactly Tom Cruise either. The thought made him laugh in the shallow way that cocaine allows. He had gaps in his dental work, a hole where a partial plate provided in prison had once been, until a Budweiser bottle in an Okie bar in Sacramento had wiped it out. Of course the evening hadn't ended there. When the Tulsa Club closed, he was waiting in the parking lot, a scuba diver's knife up his sleeve. When the bottle swinger unlocked his car, Mad Dog came out of the shadows bare-handed, as if it were a fistfight. When he was in close, his head on the guy's chest, Mad Dog let the knife slide down into his hand. He sank it into the guy's guts two or three times before the guy realized it and ran, trying to hold his entrails inside his body.

Remembering, Mad Dog grinned. That would teach a mother-fucker who to fuck with—if he lived. It was the reason Mad Dog had moved to Portland, where he had met Sheila.

He looked around the room. It was on the second floor and over-looked the flight of stairs to the street. Things were a dope fiend mess. Newspapers, socks, clothes, and bedding were strewn around. He'd torn the bedding off when a cigarette had fallen from his hand

and the mattress had started to smolder. He'd been watching the Trailblazers tear up the Lakers when he'd smelled smoke. Water from the goldfish bowl had failed to stop it. He'd had to tear the mattress open and dig out the smoldering cotton. The hole was now covered with a towel, but the odor still filled the room. What would Sheila say when she got home?

Who gives a fuck, he thought. Fuck her . . . fat bitch. Where was she? She was supposed to come back tonight with her chubby little daughter.

Mad Dog felt his armpit. Wet and slippery and smelling bad. The drug coming through his pores had a sour stench. He needed a shower. Shit, he needed a lot of things. But right now, he needed another shot of coke.

Thirty minutes and two fixes later, he had the light out and was peeking past the corner of the windowshade at the rainy night. When he'd started this cocaine binge, a fix would lift him to the heights for half an hour or more, and then let him down slow and easy. Now the cycle was quicker. Joy barely lasted until the needle was out. Within minutes the craving began and with it the seeds of dread and paranoia and self-loathing. The only remedy was another fix.

He peered down at the street from the old frame house that was built into a hillside near a railroad bridge. Because of the slope and the retaining wall, he couldn't see the sidewalk on his side of the street except where the stairs came up.

A car went by; then nothing but dark rain, the drops flashing momentarily in the glow of a street lamp. The craving for cocaine turned into a scream behind his eyes. He had delayed as long as possible, trying to make it last longer. It was nearly gone. Two ounces of pharmaceutical cocaine in forty hours. That was drug use of legendary scale. With heroin he would have folded into a drugged stupor long ago. Heroin had a limit, but cocaine was different: You *always* wanted more.

He found a vein and watched the blood rise. Instead of the usual practice of squeezing a little and stopping, and then doing a little more, he forgot and squeezed it all in.

It went through him like electricity. Instantly everything in his stomach flew from his mouth. Oh God! His heart! His heart! Had he killed himself? He spun and walked, careening off a chair, banging into a wall, then into the dresser. Oh shit! Oh God! Oh! Oh! Oh!

The flash dissipated, and with it his terror. He closed his eyes and savored the sensation. No more like that one, he swore.

Headlight beams flashed across the windowshade. Mad Dog went to the window. A car had made a U-turn and pulled up at the curb. The retaining wall blocked his view except for the bumper and headlights. Who the fuck could it be at this time of night?

He turned off the light and watched.

The car below pulled away. A taxi. Sheila and Melissa, her seven-year-old daughter named for a song, came into view at the bottom of the stairs. He could see Sheila's white face as she looked up. Mad Dog froze, certain she could see nothing except a black window. She would think he was gone because his car wasn't at the curb. It was in the service bay of the neighborhood Chevron station awaiting his payment for an alternator, but she didn't know about that. Good enough. It would give him time to shoot the last of the cocaine before he had to listen to her nagging bullshit. Forgotten was the surge of affection he'd felt earlier. Instead he thought of how she bitched at him about cocaine, and everything else, too.

Mad Dog heard them come in the front door and move around on the bottom floor. He could hear the child's quick feet, then the back door opening and closing. She was feeding the cat, no doubt. She was a worthless little brat most of the time. She disliked him and refused to do what he said until he promised to beat her butt if she didn't straighten up. When she complied, it was with a resolutely hangdog manner, pouting and dragging her feet. The only good thing about her was her love of the cat. She was always thoughtful and generous; she'd once used her last dollar for a can of cat food. Mad Dog had a grudging affection for such loyalty.

When he heard the canned laughter on the TV downstairs, he turned on the nightstand lamp; it threw a yellow pool of light on the ritual paraphernalia of the needle. He squirted a small syringe of water directly into the jar; then put on the lid and shook it. That way he would lose nothing. He sucked it through the needle into the syringe. He held it up and squeezed very gently, until a drop appeared at the tip of the point. That meant the air was out of the syringe. He took his time fixing it, savoring it as long as possible. If he could only hold this sensation forever; that would be heaven indeed.

Within minutes the joy was frayed at the edges by inchoate anguish, by self-pity. Why me, God? Why has life been so shitty from the very start? His earliest memory was from age four, when his mother had tried to drown him in the bathtub. His six-year-old sister, who later turned dyke and dope fiend whore, had saved his life by screaming and screaming until the neighbors came. They had stopped his mother and called the police, who had taken the children to juvenile hall, and the judge then sent his mother to Napa State Hospital for observation. Another time, the nurse at school had found the welts on his body where his mother had pinched him, digging in her thumb and forefinger and twisting his flesh. The pain had been awful, and afterward there was a bruise. Remembering it now, three decades later, gave him goose bumps.

She'd gone to Napa twice after that, once for eight months, before she died when he was eleven. He was away from her by then—in reform school. The chaplain called him in to tell him; then looked at his watch and told the boy he could have twenty minutes alone in the office to express his grief. The moment the door closed after the chaplain stepped out, Mad Dog was on his feet reaching for the drawers. He was looking for cigarettes, the most valuable commodity in the reform school economy.

Nothing in the drawers. He went to the closet. Bingo! In a jacket pocket he found a freshly opened pack of Lucky Strikes. L.S.M.F.T. No bullshit! He took them and felt good. He stuffed the pack into his sock and sat back down. That was where he was when the chaplain came back. He wanted to have a talk and he looked at the folder and frowned and said something about ". . . your father . . ."

Mad Dog stood up and shook his head. He didn't want to talk about it. Indeed, he had nothing to say. He knew nothing of his father, not even his name. It wasn't on his birth certificate. By now his sister, who did have a name on her birth certificate, was calling him "trick baby." When he looked in the mirror, he was ugly and resembled nobody in the family. Although they were a nondescript bunch, they tended to be tall and pale with stringy hair, whereas he was short and swarthy, with curls so tight they neared being kinky. A loudmouth older boy had once even asked if his mama had a nigger in the woodpile. Ha ha ha. The bully was too big and too mean to challenge, but when the dormitory lights were out and the bully was snoring. Mad Dog crawled along the floor and beat his head soft with a Louisville slugger. The victim survived, but he was never the same; his speech was forever impaired, as was his brain. It was then that Gerry McCain had gotten the nickname "Mad Dog." It was a nickname he had lived up to in the ensuing years.

The last fix was wearing off; the headache was pulsing behind his eyes. Aspirin. Naw. Aspirin wouldn't touch this one. Besides, the aspirin was downstairs and he wanted to avoid Sheila's nagging ass as long as possible. Her shrill voice worked on his brain like fingernails on a blackboard. If he had some dough he would pack up and leave and wait for Troy in California, maybe even Sacramento. Things had cooled off by now. He even had a couple of scores in mind, but he hated doing anything alone and the only possible crime partner around was Diesel Carson. Mad Dog had known Diesel ever since reform school. They'd even taken a score together. That was the reason he wouldn't do anything with Diesel until Troy resurrected.

His headache was awful, and he could suddenly smell the stink of his own body. Booze and cocaine smelled terrible when you sweat them out. Cocaine was the worst drug. Terrible shit. He hated it. Yet he also craved another fix to postpone the hours of hell fast approaching. What he really needed was a fix of heroin. That was the perfect remedy for the gray scream of depression in his brain. The crash was starting. If he could only sleep through it . . .

Then he remembered the Valiums. The big ones. Blues. The vial might have eight tablets left. That many would poleax him to sleep. He wouldn't care about the night sweats and the terrible dreams.

24

He went to the dresser and opened the drawer. Among ballpoint pens, empty butane cigarette lighters, Pepto-Bismol tablets, and other effluvia, he found the little brown vial. He pried off the cap and dumped the contents into his palm. Six! *Six!* The bitch had been in the bottle.

Anger worsened the headache. He swallowed the six blue tablets with the help of a cold cup of coffee. He threw the empty vial into the wastebasket and started to lie down.

That was when the door opened and the overhead light went on with one hundred watts of brightness. Sheila stood there, her eyes going saucer-wide at the sight of him. She let out a little cry of surprise and her fist went to her mouth.

"What are you doing here?" she asked.

"What the fuck does it look like? Get outta here and leave me alone." He looked at her and hated her moon face with the blemished skin. How could he have ever thought her pretty? It must have been because he was fresh from prison and a female crocodile would have looked good. "I told you never to come in here without knocking."

"I didn't know you were home," she said. "Your car's not downstairs and you didn't come down to say hello. Where is your car?"

"It's at the gas station getting fixed."

"Don't talk to me with that tone of voice. I don't like it."

"She doesn't like it," he mimicked with scorn. "Ain't that a bitch." He leaned forward, looming over her. "I don't give a rat's ass what you like or don't like—bitch!" The pounding blood in his brain made him dizzy. He might have backhanded her except for the child's voice calling out, "Mommy! Mommy!" The sound of the girl's footsteps preceded her appearance in the doorway. She went to her mother. When they both faced him they looked alike.

"Let's go downstairs, honey," Sheila said, arm around the girl's shoulder as she turned her and walked her out the door.

"Can I watch *Star Trek*? It just started."

"Sure. If you go to bed right afterward. Go on." She sent the child out and turned back to Mad Dog McCain. She had gotten herself under control. "You've got to leave. I don't want you here anymore."

25

"Great. As soon as I get my wheels out of the gas station, I'm gone."

"Don't even think about charging it on my card. In fact, gimme the card back." She extended her hand and snapped her fingers.

"Hey, if you want me to go . . . I gotta get the car out first."

"No. Give it here."

He saw she was unafraid. Why? Because she knew too much about the robbery of the merchant ship's payroll. She'd worked in the offices of a shipping company, and told him that merchant seaman were still paid in cash at the end of a voyage. She'd told him what ship, when and where. He and Diesel Carson had ripped off eighty-four grand. Sheila knew everything, and even though she was a conspirator, the authorities would certainly drop charges if she testified against Diesel Carson and Mad Dog McCain, a pair of lifelong criminals. Yeah, the bitch thought she had him by the balls. Why the fuck had he trusted her?

He took the Chevron card from his wallet and threw it at her. It fell on the floor. "Bastard," she said, picking it up and going out, slamming the door as she did so.

He blinked at the door while spinning down, down into the hell of a cocaine crash. Inside him was a silent scream of despair and a growing brute rage. Without the credit card he couldn't retrieve his car, and without his car he could never make any money. He was stranded. He could become homeless. He had a .357 Python and an AK-47 with a thirty-round clip, enough firepower to heist almost anything—but he couldn't run around on foot. He needed wheels, and not a carjacking. That was for young niggers who didn't know how to steal anything worthwhile. Still, he needed wheels more than anyone in their right mind could imagine. It bordered on obsession, and maybe paranoia.

Through the closed door, he heard Sheila and the child enter the next room. Melissa's bedtime. The thin wall allowed enough sound for him to visualize what was going on. The brat was saying her prayers. Jesusfuckingchrist—he hated religion. He hated God. He loved evil more than good and lying more than speaking the truth. He decided that he was going to get the credit card right now.

When he opened the bedroom door and peered out in the hall,

the bedroom door to his right was ajar. They were in there. The stairs were to the left. He was careful to make no noise as he went down. She usually left her purse in the entrance hall next to the front door, but not tonight.

The kitchen. He went that way and, sure enough, it was on the sink. He opened it and removed the billfold. Eight dollars. No Chevron card. He returned the billfold to the purse and looked around. Where had she put it when she came downstairs?

He spotted her cardigan across the back of a chair. She'd been wearing the sweater when she came into his room. He picked the sweater up and felt the pocket. Sure enough, there it was.

He was feeling for the pocket when Sheila came through the door. He pulled out the credit card. "Don't fuck with me, Sheila. I gotta get my car."

"Don't fuck with you. Don't fuck with *me!* Gimme that!"

Again she extended her hand and snapped her fingers. The action itself was a slap in the face, and he reacted with rage. He lunged forward. She opened her mouth to scream a moment before his left hand slammed against the side of her head, stunning her.

His right hand darted forward, his fingers closing on her throat.

She kicked him and twisted loose. He open-handed her again, hard enough to knock her against a table, which slid across the floor. A flower vase fell off and crashed on the floor.

She came at him, flailing with both hands, eyes closed. A bony fist crashed into his mouth and drove a tooth into his lip. He could taste his salty blood. He bent over to spit it out away from his body where it wouldn't get on his clothes.

Sheila used the respite to whirl and run for the front hall and the telephone. She was gagging. His crushing fingers had hurt her throat. Her indignation was gone and she was terrified.

In the kitchen, he jerked open a drawer and snatched a butcher knife. She heard the clatter as he dug through the drawer; then the sound of it slamming shut. The phone was a rotary. It took precious heartbeats for nine to spin back so that she then could dial one. She never got to the last digit.

"Hey, stool pigeon bitch," he said, standing in the doorway with the severed telephone cord. The big knife was hidden down by his leg.

She dropped the phone and turned to run. Two strides and her foot slipped on a throw rug across a hardwood floor. She did a split and fell on one hand.

He leaped on her back like a predatory cat. His fingers were claws entwined in her hair, twisting her head so her throat was exposed. He raised the butcher knife and drove it down where neck meets shoulder.

It was as if he'd stabbed a wine sack. When he pulled the blade free, a fat stream of blood followed it like a geyser, spewing onto the wrist and forearm of the hand holding her hair. He tried to shift his body position to avoid the blood. He might as well have turned on a hose; now it was spraying onto the front of his pants.

Still she struggled wildly, banging her elbow into his thigh, fighting for her life even as it poured out of her.

He struck again. This time she hit the blade with her forearm, which was sliced to the bone at the wrist. She managed to deflect it from her heart, but it cut through her right breast and opened the flesh over the ribs. When the blade hit bone, his grip slipped because the handle was covered with slippery gore. His hand slid down over the blade and his fingers were cut deep. He let go of the knife and stepped back.

Her strength gave out and she went limp and fell. She spasmed, and in another minute she expired. She was lying in a virtual lake of her own arterial blood.

When Mad Dog looked down, his bare feet were in the same puddle of blood. He raised a foot. The blood had suction. Like a fly, he thought. He took a step, then another, then sat down in the chair next to the telephone stand, looking at his footprints in blood. He would have to clean them up. They had to be like fingerprints, identifiable.

As he sat looking at the horror, a great wave of drowsiness rose through him. Terror surged. Something was wrong. Had she somehow poisoned him?

"Mommy! Mommy!" The noisy stairs gave off their squeak. She was coming down. "Mommy . . . are you all right?"

28

"Stay up there," he bellowed, jumping up.

Too late. He saw her legs; then her head as she bent over to look. He lunged at the stairs. He'd hoped that he could let Melissa sleep while he hid the body and cleaned up the mess. Then tomorrow he would put Sheila in a grave somewhere in the vast northwest forest. If questions were asked, he would brazen it out.

Now it was different. She had seen the truth. He bounded up the stairs and followed her into the bedroom. She was across the bed. "You killed my mother," she screamed.

As he moved forward, she tried to slide away. He was too quick, grabbing her wrist with one hand and reaching for a pillow with the other.

She screamed and he dragged her closer. The screams were muffled when he put the pillow over her face. Her limbs thrashed as he forced her head down. Then he got both hands on the pillow and raised up, as if doing a push-up, crushing the pillow down over her face. Her feet beat against his legs. They might as well have belonged to a butterfly. "Die! Please die!" he begged.

It seemed to take forever, but finally the struggle ceased. By then he was also reeling, fighting unconsciousness, thinking that he was also dying. Then he realized it was the Valium he'd taken, not poison. He was bombed, not dying. The realization made him quit the struggle. The Valium had pulled him down. He closed his eyes and fell asleep on the bed beside the child's body.

In the morning, when he awakened with a pounding headache, for a moment he thought it had all been a nightmare. Then he saw the little corpse, waxy white because the blood had all drained toward the bottom of the cadaver. The truth proved to be worse than the nightmare.

He sat up and saw his bloody footprints across the floor. He had a lot of cleanup to do. He had to hide them somewhere until he could drive into the mountains and bury them where they would never be found.

Money. He needed money, too. The credit cards. Sure. He knew the numbers on the MasterCard so he could draw fifteen hundred in cash. He could take orders too, half price of what they cost, from people on things he could buy with the card. Thank God he had a little money. It saved him from a desperate move, like a robbery. This way he could move to Sacramento and wait for Troy.

He stood up. When he moved the headache was worse. He went for aspirin; then went downstairs to look at Sheila. The pool of blood had coagulated. He couldn't believe a body held that much blood.

Was she starting to smell? He sniffed the air. He couldn't be sure—but he knew it would be soon. Bodies turned putrid real fast at room temperature.

2

Around the teamsters local, it was assumed that Charles "Diesel" Carson had gotten his nickname because he weighed two hundred and sixty pounds and was as relentless as a train in a brawl. Actually his name had been attained in reform school, when he played football once without a helmet and they began to call him Dieselhead. The name fit, so it stayed. It had been shortened a bit to "Diesel." His wife called him Charles.

Nineteen years after reform school, three years after parole from San Quentin, Diesel Carson was off parole. He had a wife, Gloria, a kid named Charles, Jr., and a three-bedroom tract house in a suburb of San Francisco. He belonged to the Teamsters, and he was a favorite of the local's officers. He did them favors such as punching out anyone who didn't agree with how things were done. He was loyal. Who else would give an ex-con a job, even a lousy job, much less a good job.

Diesel also took contracts (not murder contracts) from Jimmy the Face and others. He'd set something on fire, or break somebody's arm, but he refused to murder for money (punch a ticket was the operative term) because it was an automatic death penalty and he could never be sure the person who sent him could keep his mouth shut if the police had him alone in a back room somewhere, telling him he could go home if he just confirmed what the police knew already. No telling what someone would say. Murder played on some guys' minds. They wanted to confess. Bobby Butler had confessed a prison murder two years after the fact. They took him out and gave him a life sentence. He deserved it, the damn fool. The founders of the Aryan Brotherhood had also gone crazy. Three years after Jack Mahone, one of their members, left Folsom, he walked into a police station and told the cops, "I wanna tell you about this murder that me and Tank Noah committed eight years ago." Poor Tank went to death row over it. Diesel wasn't afraid of prison, but the gas chamber made him nervous. It was almost silly considering how few actually went to the gas chamber, although there were plenty waiting for appeals to run out. Diesel would kill someone, but he would never trust another human being to know about it—nobody but Troy, that is. He trusted Troy all the way.

Diesel got out of the shower and put on clean underwear and fresh linen slacks. Life was great now. He was getting over the values of the Catholic orphanage, juvenile hall, reform school, and prison. Anyone who stayed out of prison for three years was doing great even if they were penniless, but to have a new car and own a house made him a monumental success. He had Hickey-Freeman suits and Johnston and Murphy shoes on his feet—and ringside seats at the fights. Next week the general secretary was arranging to pay him for featherbedding. While the truck trailers loaded with new autos rode across country on flatbed railroad cars, he was being paid a teamster's wages, with overtime. Only the guys really favored by the union got things like that.

Jimmy the Face had provided the introduction. In return, he did favors for The Face. Tonight he was driving to Sacramento to burn up some trucks. Some fool was bidding against The Face for a trucking contract. After Diesel was through the fool would be out of business.

From a closet shelf, Diesel took out his attaché case and unlocked it. Inside were his pistols. The .45 was for serious shooting but was too heavy to carry. It made his clothes sag. The second pistol was a .22 Colt Woodsman with its muzzle threaded for the silencer resting in the niche beside it. With a hot load and a silencer, it was the perfect murder gun. It made almost no sound and the bullet stayed inside the skull instead of blowing bone and blood all over the wall. The last weapon was a snub-nose .38 Smith & Wesson five-shot revolver. Light and small enough to carry, it still had enough hitting power to do the job. It was the ideal personal protection weapon. He checked to make sure it was loaded, then clipped the holster to the inside of his waistband. It was unlikely that he would need it, but better to have it and not need it than to need it and not have it. No John Q. Square was going to bump into him committing a felony and make a citizen's arrest—not unless he thrived on lead in his stomach.

He returned the attaché case to the closet and took out a tan leather jacket and Bally loafers. He'd carry them along and maybe stop in the city afterward. Too bad that he'd miss the fight card, but afterward the sharp guys would be at Charlie's in the Mission.

He put on low-cut Reeboks and zipped up a windbreaker. In the mirror he could see no bulge. Everything was snug and he made sure nothing would fall out when he went over the fence. That had happened once and it had been embarrassing. He lingered an extra moment at the mirror. He looked pretty good, kind of handsome in a big, beefy way, the image of a big Irish cop. It made him smile. He raised his hands in a boxer's stance, added the rocking rhythm, and snapped off a couple of jabs. He boxed smooth for his size. In the gym they said he moved like a welterweight, but the gym was not the arena. When the crowd was loud and the bell rang, he forgot all he knew about boxing. He flailed like a wild man and got his ass kicked. That ended his dream of being the great white hope and making millions in the ring. He went back to driving a rig and stealing for a living.

Now it was time to go commit a crime.

He looked around the bedroom. He had forgotten nothing. The sharpened screwdriver, claw hammer, and Clorox bottle of kerosene were in the car trunk. His gloves were in the glove compartment.

When he opened the bedroom door, he was assaulted by the bump and grind of rap music. "Turn that nigger shit off," he yelled toward the kitchen. When there was no reply, he became furious and rushed down the hallway, muttering that it was too fuckin' loud to hear himself think.

The kitchen was empty. Through the back window he saw Gloria hanging shirts on the clothesline. Junior sat in a stroller.

33

Diesel went to the back door. "What's wrong with the fuckin' dryer?" he asked.

"'Fucking' dryer. Honestly, Charles. Your son—"

"Fuck all that. He don't know words yet."

"He'll learn quick."

"Yeah, okay. I'm goin' now. Say, how come you listen to that rap shit? I can't believe how stupid that shit is. It's got as much to do with music as a fart."

She gestured in a manner that was half dismissal and half good-bye, and returned to what she was doing. As she raised up on tiptoes, it accented her legs, and when she reached, her breasts pushed against her shirt. Whatever her other flaws, she had a great body. Did he have time for a quickie? Naw. "How come you don't use the dryer?"

"I starched your shirts the way you like them. The dryer pulls the starch out."

"That's reasonable. I'm outta here, baby."

"When'll you be back?"

"Tonight sometime.

"Be careful."

"I'm always careful, baby."

"Give me a call if you're later than midnight."

"That I'll do," he said, adding to himself: If I remember.

Walking down the driveway to his new red Mustang GT convertible, Diesel felt good. Since running away from the Sisters of Mercy Catholic Home for Boys at age ten—and going to juvenile hall for the first time when they caught him breaking into a mom and pop market—he had never gone six months without an arrest. Not all were felonies, and not all were convictions, but they were damn sure arrests where he went to jail. That was, until now. Had he outgrown jail? Now he knew men who lived entirely by crime; they made big money and never went to prison. Maybe he could do it, too, especially with Troy doing the planning and calling the shots. Diesel smiled, thinking about how Troy would appreciate how things were ready for him. In the garage were his tools for crime, oscillators that they would use on electronic burglar alarms, a scanner to follow police calls, and even a Navy surplus portable acetylene torch.

Diesel got into his car, started the engine, and put down the convertible top. He was backing out when the front door opened. Gloria stuck her head out. He braked. "Telephone," she called.

"Who is it?"

"McCain."

"Mad Dog?"

She nodded.

"What's he want?"

"He didn't say."

"Tell him you couldn't catch me."

Gloria shut the door and Diesel continued out. As he drove away he asked aloud, "Why'd that dingy motherfucker call me?" The last time he'd talked to Mad Dog was a year ago when they had heisted the merchant ship payroll. Because Mad Dog's girlfriend worked for the shipping company and she had fingered the score, when they were splitting up the money, Mad Dog wanted a share for her. He hadn't mentioned it before. "Sure," Diesel said, "and I'll take a cut for Gloria."

"Whaddya mean?"

"If Sheila gets a cut, why not Gloria?"

"That's bullshit, man."

They confronted each other across a kitchen table. The moment had been tense. Diesel half rose from his seat and leaned forward. He outweighed Mad Dog by over a hundred pounds. Mad Dog's pistol was holstered. He would never get it before Diesel broke his jaw. Mad Dog backed off from the confrontation, but Diesel knew a seed of hate had been planted in a mind already fertile with madness. He'd kept away from McCain ever since. Troy said he could manage the little maniac. Time would tell if Troy was right. Troy was up for parole in two months or so, and he had a plan for a three-man mob that would specialize in heisting pimps, drug dealers, and gangsters, all people who couldn't go to the police. Diesel had one good thought about Mad Dog: "At least he ain't no stool pigeon. But why is he calling me?"

Three hours later, Diesel stood in the shadows of an oak tree in a field of dry grass. Thirty yards away was the raised Southern Pacific right-of-way. Beyond that was a sloped embankment that ended at the fence of Star Cartage. As the moon moved in and out of clouds, he saw the silhouettes of the big trucks and the quonset hut offices. The windows were dark. Jimmy the Face had arranged for the watchman to call in sick. It seemed The Face was right again.

Beyond the trucking company was U.S. 99. Traffic was light, mainly trucks of farm produce rolling through the night. Several hundred yards down the highway was a liquor store with a neon sign. It looked easy.

Diesel rolled up the canvas bag with the tools and kerosene. It was easier to tuck it under his arm like a football than carry it dangling from his hand. Bending over to lessen his silhouette, he trotted across the field and over the railroad tracks. The gravel dislodged as he slid down the embankment to the fence.

He had wire cutters in the bag, but as he looked around it was obvious that he could climb the fence more easily than he could cut it. It was equally safe, too, for the buildings hid the fence from the highway. He pitched the canvas bag over and jumped up, hooking his fingers over the top.

The fence rattled down its entire length. No matter. Nobody was around to hear. He dropped to the ground and froze in a crouch, watching for any sign of arousal or alarm.

Nothing. Silence except for a truck shifting gears as it went by. Oh yeah, this was going to be easy. He'd taken three Dexamyl spansules and was glowing inside. He kept the buildings between himself and the highway as he moved toward the trucks.

Again he paused; again no alarm. He grabbed the big, sharpened screwdriver. It easily went through the fuel tanks. No need for the hammer. Diesel fuel ran out into dark wet circles on the ground. When it was pouring from all five trucks, he poured kerosene between them, so all the inflammable liquids were connected. He was a little winded. Too many goddamned Marlboros, he thought.

He brought out the wooden matches. Would it blow up?

If it blows, it blows. Fuck it. He snapped a match alight with a thumbnail and pitched it into the kerosene.

As the bluish flame crept across the ground, Diesel raced the other way.

No explosion, but the fire was swift. He saw it light as he went over the fence, and it was blazing high by the time he reached the oak tree.

He was on the highway, half a mile away, when the fire engines with screaming sirens and flashing lights came the other way. Dutifully he pulled over and watched them go by. "Good luck, fellas," he said with a grin.

On the interstate, he was exhilarated by what he'd done. The pressure was off. Jimmy the Face would appreciate what he'd done. Diesel liked torch jobs. They were easy. The problem was finding customers to trust. He couldn't advertise in the classifieds: ARSONIST FOR HIRE. Too bad. Such things were gifts. What would Troy say? "A bird's nest on the ground."

It was 3:30 A.M. Diesel had gotten home and was in the kitchen eating cornflakes and milk. The telephone rang. He looked at the clock. "Who the fuck . . . ?" He picked up the receiver. "Hello."

"It's me, Mad Dog."

"What's up, man?"

Gloria appeared at the kitchen door. "He called three times."

"I need help, bro," Mad Dog said. "I'm in big trouble, man. I'm busted up here. It's a chickenshit credit card beef, but if I don't make bail by Monday, the parole officer's gonna put a parole detainer on me. You know how it is."

Diesel understood. "What kinda bail?"

"Just fifteen hundred. A hundred and a half to the bondsman and security."

"What about Sheila?"

"She's in Colorado visitin' her folks. I don't have the number. I got fifteen bills at the pad."

"Send the bondsman. He's gonna make money. Throw him a little extra."

"Naw, man, I don't trust bail bondsmen. What if he stole it and said it wasn't there."

Diesel said nothing. He resented this imposition even though he knew he would go when the plea came. It came next:

"Look, man, I swear I got the dough at the pad. I wouldn't bullshit you about that. I'll kick back what you put up . . . and give you whatever you want."

"You already got it, right?"

"Yeah, homeboy, swear to God."

"*That* really makes me believe you. Ha, ha, ha . . ."

"Hey, man, don't put me on. Please, man, don't leave me in the slammer."

Diesel would have let Mad Dog McCain rot in jail—but what would Troy want? He would say to post the bail. "I need five hundred for my expenses."

"You got it, man. As soon as I raise."

"Don't fuck me around, Dog. If you're bullshittin', we're gonna have serious motherfuckin' trouble, y'know what I mean?"

"Yeah, D. We know each other. I wouldn't fuck you around."

"Okay. The cavalry is on the way. I'm rollin' right now. I should have you out sometime tomorrow."

"I'm countin' on you."

"Hey, if I say a pissant will pull a plow, hitch the harness to him."

3

The speedometer hovered between eighty-five and ninety as the Mustang tore north along Interstate 5. The lush vineyards and rolling landscape of the Napa Valley became rougher terrain as the interstate climbed the Sierras. The car's tires whined on the curves and it flew past the giant trucks that inched up the grades. Passing Lake Shasta, Diesel looked at rows of houseboats that waited at the docks. That would be fun. Maybe after Troy had a girlfriend they could rent one for a few days, explore the many miles of waterway. Gloria would like it for sure. Then again, it might not be ideal for Troy, who preferred bright lights and fast action.

He really loved his friend. "My main man," he muttered, thinking that he would follow his pal through the door into Hell if Troy said there was a score down there. Troy had been the leader from their first meeting in juvenile hall; they had escaped over the fence a few days later. Of all the criminals that Diesel knew, Troy was the only one whose ambition was to be an outlaw. "I'm no heir," he once said, "and I'm not going to be cipher in the horde." "What's a cipher?" Diesel asked, and Troy had laughed loudly and embraced his friend. Remembering it, Diesel felt a surge of affection. He would do most anything for Troy, and much of the reason for this trip was knowing it was what Troy wanted him to do.

The daily rain of the green Northwest began to fall as he neared Grants Pass, Oregon. The wet road slowed him so it was nighttime as he neared Portland. The Dexamyl spansules had worn off and he had started to doze at the wheel. He stopped and put the convertible top down. The cold air would keep him awake. As long as the car continued moving, the windshield kept the rain from wetting him.

In Portland, the traffic signs and stop lights made him put the top back up. What should he do now? Bail bondsmen stayed open twenty-four hours a day, but he was too tired to take care of business. Ahead of him appeared the green neon of a Travelodge. He turned into its driveway.

In his room, he sat on the bed and removed his shoes; then fell back and closed his eyes, intending a small nap before looking in the Yellow Pages for Bail Bonds. Sleep pulled him down, fully clothed. Within a minute his snores could be heard through the door.

When Diesel opened his eyes, coming instantly alert like a forest predator, he saw black sky through the window and thought it was night. Damn. Had he slept through the whole day?

His wristwatch said 6:50. It was running. He went to the window. The sky was solid with clouds and the city was wet, although no rain was falling at the moment.

He tore the listing for Bail Bonds out from the Yellow Pages and went to the telephone. The first listing, A.A.A. Bail Bonds, 24 hours a day, proved to be an answering service. They wanted a number to call back.

The next one was Byron's Bail Bonds, State, Federal, County, 24 hours a day, 365 days a year Byron will bail you.

Diesel dialed. It rang once. "Byron's Bail, Byron speaking. What can I do for you?"

"All right, man," said Diesel. "I wanna bail out a buddy of mine. He's busted here in Portland."

"What's the charge?"

"I'm not sure, something with credit cards."

"Could be a misdemeanor or a felony."

"I'd guess it's a felony."

"Have you got money?"

"I've got a gold Citibank Visa card."

"That's money. What's your buddy's name?"

"Uhhh, McCain."

"First name?"

"I . . . uh . . . don't know it."

"He's a buddy and you don't know his first name?"

"I just know a nickname," Diesel said, adding to himself, I'm not going to tell you it's "Mad Dog."

"McCain's enough, I guess. It's not that common. Do you know what jail he's in?"

"Nope."

"I can find that out. When was he arrested?"

"I'm pretty sure it was Friday."

"You're coming down here with the money?"

"Sure. Except I don't know how to get there. I don't know shit about Portland."

"Where are you?"

"I'm at a Travelodge you can see from I-Five."

"Good. Get back on I-Five and cross the bridge going north. Get off at the first off ramp . . ." Byron continued with directions; it was easy. One turn after the off ramp.

He checked out of the motel and started driving. It was Sunday and traffic was light in the dismal weather. As he turned onto the street of two-story brick buildings, the rain started coming down. His headlights illuminated an XJS Jaguar parked ahead of him. Through rain-blurred windshield and storefront window, he saw the small neon sign: Byron's Bail Bonds.

As he hurried toward the door, he noted the Jag's license plate said BAIL BND. The expensive car gleamed under the street lamp in the rain. The bail bond business was a money-maker, no bullshit—if you could bring yourself to bust people and take them to jail. Himself, he could kill a chump, but taking him to jail, that was snitching. It wasn't snitching if a cop did it, or even a square. That was part of the game. But a bail bondsman was kind of in between, half square, half thug.

Inside, at a scarred desk five feet behind a bare countertop, Byron was on the telephone while writing on a yellow legal tablet. The desk had baskets of papers and documents.

Diesel leaned on the counter. He could smell cigars, and sure enough a couple of stubs were in an ashtray on the desk.

Byron said good-bye and hung the phone up. "You're . . ."

"I called about McCain."

"Right . . . right. I didn't get your name."

"Charles Carson." Diesel took out his wallet and extracted the gold piece of plastic. It was five grand in hand. Money said all that was necessary.

"Okay, Mr. Carson. I did some checking. Your buddy is in the Multnomah County Jail on suspicion of violation of Oregon Business and Profession Code, Section One-eight-five-three, subsection A—whatever that is. Credit card something. There's no bail right now, but the recommended bail is fifteen hundred. I can get the writ signed in half an hour. I already found the judge on call. He's at home and I talked to his law clerk."

"Very good. You're on your job. What's the tab for all this?"

"Three fifty to run the writ, ten percent of the bond as premium, and the security, which you get back when he shows up in court."

"Here you go, champ." Diesel pushed the card forward, then stopped. "One thing, when it gets exonerated, the money comes back to me. Not him. Got it?"

"No problem." He took the credit card and went to the phone to call and make sure it was good. "Have a seat," he said.

Diesel sat down and picked up a *Sports Illustrated* with an article on Mike Tyson's trial for rape. Dumb fuckin' nigger, Diesel thought, with more feelings of compassion than contempt. Diesel was certain that the "victim" had played the hard-dicked buck like a fish on a line. She'd known exactly what he would do, and what she would do afterward. It made Diesel feel smart. He was ignorant about many things, but he was smart about the games that people play.

Byron put the phone down and got up. He was a little guy. He made an O signal with thumb and forefinger, and winked again. "Good as gold," he said, reaching for a raincoat hung on the back of a chair. "I'll get the writ signed right now. You've got a car, right?"

"Yep."

"You'll pick him up?"

Diesel nodded. He sure was. He had money to retrieve from Mad

Dog. The little maniac wouldn't have a weapon when he came out of jail, and Diesel would make sure that he couldn't obtain one until the money was paid. If he doesn't have it . . . Diesel stopped his thought right there, not wanting to commit himself to anything even in his own mind.

Byron checked his watch. "I can get the bond signed and drop in at the jail in about an hour. But they won't let him out until after they finish booking in the daily catch. Get it? The catch of fish . . ."

Diesel grunted and half grinned. It was all the laughter the joke deserved. "So . . ."

"So why don't you be at the jail around ten, or ten-fifteen. That's when they start the bail releases."

"That sounds good. Where is it?"

Byron winked again, making Diesel want to ask if he had a nervous tick. He brought out a mimeographed street map with a series of arrows showing how to go from "Byron's Office" to "County Jail."

Byron then turned on his answering machine and ushered Diesel to the door.

Diesel ate at a Denny's, and vowed never to do so again. A few minutes after ten o'clock, Diesel drove past the Multnomah County Jail. It was a nineteenth-century fortress of granite blocks, reminding him of Folsom. It had bars and frosted-glass windows, behind which he could see moving shadows.

He drove around in the rain for another fifteen minutes and came back. He cruised slowly past. No parking places at the curb.

About fifty yards from the entrance, he found a space at a fire hydrant. That was okay. He wasn't leaving the car. He would move if a fire truck appeared. He could see the jail door.

He turned on the radio and ran through the dial, seeking an oldies but goodies station but stopping when he heard a sporting event. Basketball . . . It sounded like the Trailblazers. He turned the dial again. Natalie Cole. He'd go for that. He drew the station in clear and sat back to look out at the rain.

The jail seemed a crackerbox. Maybe it was super-maximum security from inside, but from out here it looked weak. No doubt it had some hard lockups somewhere down in its bowels. Even minimum-security institutions had a maximum-custody lockup somewhere, but for the average sucker, the security here looked light. Any jail where you could get at an outside window was asking for it. Anything could come in, anything go out. Cut a bar and a body would go through.

Headlights struck the Mustang from the rear. The glare filled the car and a bus went by and turned in, a jail bus with wired windows and faint splashes of white as faces stared out. "Poor suckers," Diesel muttered, and then added, "better you than me."

Soon a Jaguar pulled up and double-parked outside the lighted entrance. Quickly the driver got out and ran through the rain toward the entrance. Diesel exited the Mustang and hurried along the sidewalk. "Byron! Hey, Byron!"

The entrance gate buzzed and Byron entered. Diesel continued up the walkway and stopped next to the door. Should he wait here? The overhang kept away most of the rain. Then he saw the closed circuit camera. As soon as he looked at it, a voice came from a speaker, someone obviously watching on a monitor. "State your business, sir."

"I'm waiting for a bail bondsman. He just went in."

"Sorry, sir. You'll have to wait on the sidewalk. Nobody is allowed to loiter where you are."

"Okay, you got it." Diesel grinned his biggest Irish grin and touched his forehead in a loose salute. He went back to his car and lowered the window to better see the entrance.

A minute later, a couple of deputies came out and got into a car parked closer to the walkway. Diesel pulled up to their space. When Byron came out, Diesel flashed his headlights, then got out and went over. "There you are," Byron said. "Your buddy's coming out in a little while. I talked to him and told him you'd be waiting."

"You did great," Diesel said. "Thanks."

"I told him, but I'll tell you, too. The court appearance is on Thursday, Division Two. Remind him . . . if you want the money back."

"I'll remind him," Diesel said.

44

"Gotta get outta this rain," Byron said. "Good luck."

"You, too."

They shook hands and Byron hurried toward his car. The Jaguar engine had a powerful, humming roar as it pulled away, taillights blazing as it braked for the stop sign on the corner. Then it turned and disappeared.

Half an hour later, men started coming out of the jail every couple of minutes. To Diesel it was obvious, as the first two walked by, that they were being released—one of them wore a tank-top undershirt in the rain.

Half a dozen more came out before Diesel recognized Mad Dog McCain. It was too dark and distant to see the face, but Diesel knew the body language of the walk. He flicked on the headlights and opened the door. "Hey, punk!" he yelled. "Here's your man waiting for you." He hoped the jailhouse banter would soothe residual hostility from their last meeting. As the bony little figure came over and got in, Diesel tried to read the face for attitude. He wanted a toothy grin. Instead he got a tight smile. "Let's blow quick before they change their minds," Mad Dog said. "How ya doin'?"

"Kickin' ass and takin' names."

When the car was underway, Mad Dog said, "Thanks for saving my ass, man."

"Where to?" Diesel asked.

"I gotta pick up my car at the impound. You got any dough on you?"

"No, man. I gave the bondsman all my money," Diesel lied. "I gotta get money off you. I can't get gas to go home without it."

"Yeah, okay. You know how to get to the house?"

"Uh-uh. Not from here, anyway."

"Turn right at the second light."

During the drive, Mad Dog said he'd been arrested at the gas station when he went to pick up his car and tried to pay with Sheila's Chevron card. "She reported the fucker lost."

"She can straighten that out, can't she?"

"Yeah . . . sure . . . whenever she gets back."

Diesel was uninterested in what Mad Dog said. He disliked Mad

Dog and, although he would have sneered if someone accused him of fear, the truth was that Mad Dog made him uneasy. The guy was too paranoid and unpredictable. In San Quentin, he and another maniac had stabbed a guy about a dozen times because he thought the guy was staring at him. The prison surgeons were able to save the guy's life, but his plumbing would never be the same. Diesel knew many killers who didn't give a rat's ass if it clouded up and rained dogshit, but they were predictable. Maniacs like Mad Dog were liable to go off for any reason—or no reason. Except for Troy, who said he could handle Mad Dog, Diesel would never have had anything to do with him. Troy's final argument, which carried great weight, was, "At least you never have to worry about him ratting you off."

"Turn here," Mad Dog said.

Diesel turned. Now he recognized the street. The old frame houses were on a slope, high above the street with the garages dug into the hillside beneath them. He parked below the house.

"You wanna wait down here or come upstairs?"

Diesel envisioned Mad Dog going out the back door and over a fence while a big fool sat waiting in the car. "That's okay. I'll go up with you."

"Suit yourself."

Mad Dog got out and Diesel followed him up the stairs. Mad Dog led the way around the side of the house to the back porch, where he took a key from under the steps and let them in. They walked past a refrigerator and freezer on the old porch and entered the kitchen. Mad Dog turned on the lights. The kitchen was immaculate and reminded Diesel that Mad Dog was a "clean freak," a name used by convicts for compulsive cleanliness. It was a common trait among those laden with guilt.

They went through the kitchen and entry hall to the living room. "Wait here," Mad Dog said.

Diesel started to say he was going along, but that was both disrespectful and a sign of weakness. It would look as though he was scared of being ripped off. "Go ahead," he said, and sat down on the decrepit sofa. He heard the front stairs squeak as Mad Dog went up to the second floor.

While waiting, Diesel felt the need to urinate. He remembered the half bath next to the kitchen. As he entered the bathroom, he heard Mad Dog coming down the narrow rear stairs to the kitchen. Motherfucker's getting slick, he thought, listening intently. If he heard the back door open, he would charge out and beat the shit out of the little turkey. He inched forward to the kitchen door. He could see Mad Dog on the back porch, lifting the lid of the freezer. Getting the money, Diesel thought, pulling back out of sight.

He went back to the living room. A minute later, Mad Dog appeared, holding out a wad of money. "Two grand," he said. "Wanna count it?"

"I trust you."

"You're gonna drive me to the impound so I can get my car?"

"Sure. Let's roll."

They went out the front and down the steep stairs to the car. Mad Dog gave directions to the impound garage. When they got there he had to fill out a form and wait in line.

"I'm rollin', Dog," said Diesel. "You don't need me anymore."

"No. I've got it covered from here. Thanks, brother." He extended his hand and smiled. As Diesel shook hands, he looked into Mad Dog's eyes. They were flat and somehow empty. If you could see the soul through the eyes, Mad Dog had none.

"See you when Troy raises," Mad Dog said.

"Yeah—and then we'll all get rich."

As Diesel pulled away, he saw Mad Dog McCain smoking a cigarette outside the impound office door. Should I do it? he thought. What's the downside? Lose his friendship? That was no loss at all. Maybe have to kill him? Doubtful.

Ahead was the intersection where he had to decide. Left to Interstate 5 southbound, straight ahead to the old house and the money in the freezer.

The light was green and he went straight ahead.

He drove past the house, went around the corner and parked. Better to walk an extra half block than risk Mad Dog coming back and seeing the car. From the glove compartment he took the .38 and a flashlight. He got out and walked back.

Diesel went up the stairs with surprising speed and agility for someone his bulk. If it was big money, he could wait and waste Mad Dog when he came back.

Around the rear of the house, no hesitation. The key. Up the steps to the back porch. It was dark and he didn't want to turn on a light. A neighbor's window threw off enough light to outline shapes. He went straight to where Mad Dog had looked, the freezer. He lifted the lid with one hand and held the flashlight with the other, training the beam down inside.

The flashlight illuminated Sheila's face and open eyes, frozen solid and covered with a layer of frost.

The hair on the back of his neck stood up, something he'd never previously experienced. He yelped and jumped back, letting the lid crash down. His heart pounded and he shook. Good God. No wonder the motherfucker wanted out of jail so bad—before somebody else looked in the freezer.

What about the kid?

Diesel saw a dish towel hanging over the refrigerator door handle. He grabbed it and used it to lift the freezer lid again. This time he knew what to expect. Sure enough, the child was under the woman, part of her arm sticking out. "Dirty, stinkin' motherfucker," he muttered. He could accept that an adult deserved to die for something, but a little kid . . . It knotted his stomach in pain and disgust. For a moment he thought of something he had never once considered in his entire life: putting a coin in a pay phone and snitching. He erased the idea instantly.

He had to get out of here. What about the money? Fuck the money. He had no idea where it was. Mad Dog had checked on bodies, not the money stash.

Diesel wiped the freezer lid with the dish towel. He had left fingerprints elsewhere in the house, but there was no way to get rid of them. All that really mattered was the freezer, and that was okay.

He went out, locking the door, and headed for his car. During the long drive back to the Bay Area, he repeatedly saw Sheila's face covered with frost. He didn't want to see it. He wanted to forget it.

When he got home, the memory of the horror weighed so heavily that Gloria asked him if anything was wrong. He almost blurted it out, but then he shook his head. "Everything is cool."

A few weeks later, Mad Dog McCain called Diesel to say that he had moved back to Sacramento. He left his phone number and said that he had already written Troy with the address. "He raises pretty soon; right?"

"Four or five weeks."

"Man, I'm jack ready. We're gonna be a crime wave all by ourselves."

When Diesel hung up, he was shaking. What would Troy say about the murders? Maybe he could explain how somebody could kill a little kid. It was beyond Diesel's understanding. "Junior, come here," he called, catching his son and swinging him up into his arms.

4

Unlike most of San Quentin's inmates, Troy Augustus Cameron was born solidly to the upper middle class. His father was a wealthy Beverly Hills urologist, his mother the U.S.C. Homecoming Queen. For the first twelve years of his life, Troy lived in a two-story house in Benedict Canyon and attended an exclusive private school, where his grades were perfect and tests indicated his IQ was 136. Contrary to outward appearance, his life was less than idyllic. His father was a periodic binge drunk and wife beater. Once or twice a year, a binge ended in a psychotic episode. He drank until he became an animal, blind and brutal, invariably knocking his wife around while accusing her of infidelity.

At age twelve, with pubic hair and testosterone, a boy thinks he is a man and should protect his mother, even from his father. Troy got between them and was backhanded across the room. He took a .22 from an upstairs closet, loaded it, and put three bullets in his father's back.

His father survived, which was probably worse for Troy, because his mother denied what Troy described. That raised a question of sanity; however, the psychiatrists said he was legally sane and extremely intelligent and very rational—but also extremely sociopathic. His values, his beliefs, what he saw as the right and wrong of things, were atypical. They also talked psychological jargon about unresolved Oedipal complex. Notwithstanding all of that, he might not have been served to the Beast except that he had seriously injured a black youth who had stolen Troy's shoes. The black kid was two years older and thirty pounds heavier. When they were in the mess hall, Troy picked up a mop wringer from a bucket and slammed it into the back of the extortionist's head. He lay there, toes pointed upward, in the expensive athletic shoes. Troy grinned; he thought of the Wicked Witch of the East . . . The officials found his grin especially damning. It got him sent to the Fred C. Nelles School for Boys.

Reform school was harder for him than most, at least initially. An only child from the upper middle class, he stood out among the generally underclass youths of all races. He talked with perfect grammar in the land of the vulgar and inarticulate. He was educated; most of them were illiterate. Within a few months, however, he had assumed the coloration of the world surrounding him, the argot, the swagger, and the codes of what was virtuous and what was not. His dreams, however, were born in the world of books, to which he escaped as much as possible, to Zane Grey, Jack London, Rudyard Kipling. Troy had a dearth of civilizing influences and was alien to the position in the world that Fate had decreed for him. He was incapable of the 11th Commandment, Thou shalt adjust.

Even then he might have blended back into his former world, except that he found himself ostracized. The girls he'd known as a child were now forbidden to see him. He was as marked as Cain by what he'd done at age twelve. The Christian myth of forgiveness and redemption embodied in the Prodigal Son was bullshit. In a way he was glad it was bullshit; hypocrisy provided him self-justification—and self-justification is all anyone needs to do anything.

If the bourgeoisie cast him out, the underworld gathered him in. By the time he was sixteen, he had robbed several supermarkets, invested the money in Humboldt County's premium-grade pot, and was the Grass King of West Hollywood. His next bust came when a full-fledged transvestite turned out to be a state narco agent. In the precinct, Troy looked at the agent in eyeliner, lipstick, and heels, six foot three and deceiving nobody, and just shook his head. Who the fuck woulda thought it? A drag queen narc bull? That got him sent back to the Youth Authority until he turned twenty-one. By then he was a hardened criminal, as devoted to crime as a novitiate is to Rome.

It took them five years to get him again. During those years he finished his apprenticeship and became a journeyman thief. He burned open safes with acetylene torches and planned armed robberies for Diesel Carson and Bobby Dillinger. The robberies included hijacking cigarette and whiskey trucks, supermarket safes (before they went to drop safes and double keys) and ticket brokers. When he first found Carson and Dillinger, they were sticking up 7–11 stores. It was risky and petty. He fronted them living expenses, went out and found them places to rob, spent time studying how to do it, where the money was, when it was there, and who had control over it. He took them and walked them through every step, rehearsed them, and they were happy to go do it. They got seventy-five percent of a whole lot more than the few hundred dollars they'd previously made. It was a lot safer, too, because the scores were planned, not hully-gully where you might run into any kind of a surprise. Indeed, Diesel was sent to San Quentin after he tried to rob a Sacramento poker room on his own. When he came out, the parking area turned as bright as a Yankee Stadium night game. "Freeze!" He froze. "Five years to life," the judge said. He joined Mad Dog and others in San Quentin.

Two years after Diesel went to prison, a Hollywood Division narco officer planted Troy with twenty-eight grams of cocaine. It was an ounce, a small amount, but it was in gram bindles, "packaged for sale" in legal argot, making it a felony with a mandatory term.

Troy made bail with the deed to his mother's house as surety. A few weeks before the trial, she had a mastectomy; she would die while he was imprisoned. On the day he was to surrender, he came to court with a 9mm Browning in his boot. He waited until all the words were said, the sentence passed, and the judge declared that "bail is exonerated." The moment his mother's house was no longer in jeopardy, he pulled the pistol and backed out of the courtroom. In the corridor, he ran past an off-duty policeman in civilian clothes. The policeman followed him to the stairwell, leaned over, and shot downward. One bullet shattered Troy's ankle and he fell to the next landing and lay helpless.

They charged him with an attempted violent escape, but then plea-bargained it down to a simple escape, six months to five years instead of five years to twenty years. They had him for ten years on the drug case, another five made fifteen. That seemed eternity.

The Parole Commission determined the actual term within the statutes. With Troy, they could set the term anywhere between one year and fifteen years. He expected to serve five or six because the average for such offenses was about thirty months—and he knew what he'd done was twice as serious as the average escape. He used the first several years to educate and rehabilitate himself. He expected parole. His plans and dreams began to collect dust and atrophy when birthdays picked up speed after number thirty. The Parole Commission apparently thought his escape was many times more serious than the average escape; they kept denying him parole, year after year. After five years of a perfect record, his mother lost her fight with cancer; he wasn't allowed to attend the funeral. Buried with her was his last connection with law-abiding society. He never again considered being other than a thief.

At ten years, they set his term at twelve years within the walls and three more on parole. He smiled and said "thank you," but deep inside his heart was stone. He was irrevocably committed to being the criminal outsider. He had nothing vested in society. It had turned him out and expected him to be satisfied as a menial worker as the price for staying out of prison. Real freedom has choices attached; without money there is none. After eleven and a half years in San Quentin, he was no longer a novitiate. Long since ordained, he was at least a monsignor of the American underworld. He loved crime. There was no moment when he felt more alive than when he was cutting a hole in the roof of a business to crack open its safe. He was the predatory leopard and they were domestic house cats—mostly declawed, too.

Six months to get ready. He'd always exercised moderately, now he increased the tempo. He ran laps on the Lower Yard, circling the outfield at a jog that became a sprint down the left-field line to home plate. The days fell away.

At lunch, when most convicts waited in lines in the Big Yard, he stayed in the gym, pushing iron to harden already firm muscles. While he did sit-ups, he remembered an English thief explaining to him it was how they got ready for a caper. In London, nobody carried guns, not the professional thieves, not the cops on the street—

so if you could outrun them, or outfight whoever caught you, there was a good chance to get away. Being in good shape was a top requisite for a London thief. It helped in America, too, although Smith & Wesson was at least equally useful. All things being equal, he preferred to run to escape than shoot his way out.

Troy Augustus Cameron felt perfectly justified in being a thief. At the very bottom of his justification was a belief that he needed none. Dostoevsky, through the voice of Ivan Karamazov, had put it succinctly: If there is no God, then all things are permissible. Troy's parents had never attended church, nor had he. As a child he had believed in God and Jesus because everyone else seemed to and nobody said anything to the contrary. Later on, he fervently wished there was a God, but he could find no evidence thereof. It seemed absurd that God created the universe a few billion years ago; then waited 99.9 percent of its existence to put creatures "in his own image" on a minuscule planet in the tail end of a minor galaxy. It would be as if someone went to a beach, picked up a single grain of sand, and said, "Voilà, I will put my image on this." God was arguable when mankind thought earth was ten thousand years old and the center of the universe. Francis Bacon began the revolution against God, and Darwin put the final dagger in God's heart. Only the ignorant and the frightened (who made the leap of faith notwithstanding the facts) now believed in God.

Troy had spent many nights wanting to believe—but he was more committed to truth than to inner peace. His was the only position that fit the facts. To Troy, there was no more God in a crucifix than in a totem pole or a Star of David. Man was free to make God—and he did.

He marked the last six months off the calendar, day by day. Twenty-two days remained when the Pass Window called his job assignment in the gym and said he had a visit.

A visit! He'd had no visit since his mother got too sick. It was a joke that if he was killed and buried under the Big Yard, nobody in the world would ever inquire about his fate. He borrowed a clean shirt, combed his hair, and decided to forgo a shave. He hurried up the worn concrete stairs to the Big Yard and headed down the road toward the Captain's Office. Convicts were coming and going. With the few he knew, he exchanged a nod or another gesture of greeting—convicts were sensitive about minor signs of disrespect. The guard in the Yard Office waved him through. He circled around the Garden Beautiful. It was early summer, and the incongruous formal garden, complete with a pattern of walkways the convicts weren't allowed to use, was in full, riotous bloom.

At the Pass Window the sergeant gave him a visitor's slip. It had his name and number. "Visit" was typed in; and behind that was a dash and "atty." A lawyer. What lawyer? Was somebody suing him? Not bloody likely. That sure would amount to kicking a dead horse.

He headed toward the Between Gates sally port. As he neared the gate, the guard inside looked him over and let him in. After he was given a quick pat-down frisk, another door was opened and he stepped into the visiting room. It was a weekday and so visitors were few. Convicts sat on one side of the long tables behind chin-high partitions, visitors sat on the other. His gaze swept the room but he recognized nobody. Then a man with gray hair stood up and beckoned. Troy went toward him, frowning. The visitor was grinning. When Troy was across from him, recognition came. It was Alexander Aris, nicknamed "The Greek" or "El Greco." The last time Troy had seen him, the Greek's hair had been black. Now it was prematurely white. What a difference a decade can make.

Greco grinned. "Hey, ol' thing . . . you surprised?"

"Does a bear shit in the woods? What the fuck are you doin' here? How'd you get in?"

"All a chump needs is the right ID. I got one that says I'm admitted to practice in the courts of California."

"I'm gonna need some ID."

"That's easy. I've got a Mexican in Tijuana. Complete set, driver's license, credit cards, everything . . . five hundred."

"Damn, when I came here it was only a hundred and a half."

"Inflation, brother, inflation. You look great."

"You, too, except for the hair."

"Hey, fool, that's the distinguished look. I'll say this, the heat don't roust gray-haired old men."

"I heard you were in power out there. Then you disappeared."

55

"I got back in the weeds. I got some crazy Mexicans that front it."

"Dealin'?"

Greco nodded. "You know."

"Big?"

Greco shrugged. "I dunno. I don't move tons . . ."

"You hear about Big Joe?"

"No."

"They moved him to Pelican Bay. He's got cancer and they won't parole him for medical treatment."

"Damn, I visited him in jail last year when he was down on the subpoena. He looked great. You know, he might be the toughest guy I ever met. In the mind, I mean."

"Shit, man, that's where it counts."

Greco leaned closer and lowered his voice. "What're you gonna do when you raise?"

"I'm gonna try to make some money, whaddya think?"

"Got anything going?"

Troy shook his head and grinned. "After a decade, what can I have goin'? What I wanna do is make some dough and get outta this country before it turns all the way fascist without knowing it."

"Hey, bro', you didn't turn into a prison revolutionary on me, did you?"

"Hell, no. I'm capitalist to the core. But in ten years the prison population went from thirty thousand to almost a hundred thousand. It's gonna get worse, man. Fear, man, fear."

"It's the niggers got 'em scared."

"Yeah, but they can't write laws that say for niggers only, can they? Besides, I'm an old white nigger to 'em. Anybody with a record automatically becomes a nigger."

"Hey, bro', you sound . . . kinda weird."

Troy grinned and nodded. "What the fuck can you expect after twelve years in the garbage can? But I'm not completely crazy. All anybody's gotta do is know a little history and look the facts right in the eye . . . But fuck that . . . I know you didn't come four hundred miles and con your way into San Quentin to get my view on the state of the nation. What's up?"

"I'm gonna put you in business so you can make a pile of money."

"I'm no drug dealer. That's too much like . . . business."

"Nothing like that. I've got a lawyer who specializes in representing big-time drug cases. He'll set 'em up to get robbed."

"Shit, tell me more, big man."

"You'll need a crime partner."

"I've got two waitin' for me now."

"Do I know 'em?"

"I don't think so. Diesel Carson and Mad Dog McCain."

Greco shook his head.

"They're from up north, San Francisco and Sacramento. They're okay. One of 'em is crazy, but what the fuck's wrong with that?"

"Nothing. Here's the deal with the lip. He wants twenty-five percent."

"Twenty-five percent! Bullshit! If I gave up twenty-five, I'd have to rob him afterward or feel like a damn fool. He'd be in bed with his old lady while I'm risking my ass."

Greco gestured for Troy to calm down as he raved. When Troy finished, he said, "We get first count . . . and he has no idea *what* we took. We give him twenty-five percent of what we say. We might get—five times that much."

"You didn't say that."

"You didn't let me, motherfucker."

"You know I really don't like deceitful games. I like to come off the top of the deck with no hidden agenda."

"I know you don't. That's why I'm seeing you. I know other people who are already here ripping and tearing . . . I don't have to wait for 'em to get outta San Quentin. The problem is . . ."

"You're scared to trust them with so much. The kind that might kill somebody instead of paying off."

"Lotsa money on the table." Greco smiled, his eyes twinkled. "But I trust you one hundred percent."

"You know my track record."

"So how many days you got?"

"Twenty-one and a getup."

Greco filed it mentally and nodded. "You parole to L.A.?"

"No. To 'Frisco."

"You're from L.A. Born and raised among the rich and famous. I remember what you scratched on the wall in juvenile hall—Troy de Beverly Hills."

The memory made them laugh so loud that the guard across the room frowned at them.

"You gotta go back to the county you came from. I got popped in 'Frisco." Troy said. "That bull is still burning us."

"I better go before they roust me for having too much fun in San Quentin. I'll give you a number where you can leave messages."

"I can remember it for right now—but I gotta write it down as soon as I leave the visiting room."

"I better mail it to you." Greco stood up. "I'll leave off the area code."

"They won't pay any attention. Write down it's Aunt Maude's number, or something." Troy stood up across from Greco. Troy looked to the other guard, who nodded okay for them to shake hands. "Glad you came, bro," he said.

"I'm glad I came, too. I think I'm gonna make some dough from the trip."

Greco went to the exit and looked back and waved as the guard turned the key and pushed it open for him. Troy gave a little salute and thought about the Greek being amidst the North Beach neon when night came to San Francisco. "Damn," he said, and headed back to the Big Yard.

5

When Troy Augustus Cameron got out of bed on the morning of his release, his cell was already bare. The few things he was taking with him had already been checked into Receiving and Release. He would get them in a brown paper package with a wax seal—to make sure nothing was added after it was searched and packed. What he was leaving behind, he had already given away: his *Webster's Collegiate Dictionary*, thesaurus, and a *Columbia Encyclopedia* that some private citizen had donated to the prison—and the library clerk peddled out the back door.

He'd shaved the night before. Now, as he brushed his teeth, he could hear the cellhouse coming awake. Flushing toilets, someone calling down the tier for a partner to bring the Chronicle at the unlock, and the idiot next door, who happened to be black, already had his TV turned on. Troy had given his own away a week earlier, as was standard practice. Convicts could buy thirteen-inch Sonys, and were required to donate them when paroled. The purchaser could donate it to a specific inmate, but when the recipient departed, he had to donate it to the prison, whereupon it was issued to someone without resources. Over the decade that TVs had been allowed, enough had come in so that now everyone had one, at least everyone who wanted one.

The tier tender came by, lugging the heavy water can with the long spout; it was used to pour hot water through the bars. The cell sinks ran only cold. The toilets used water from the bay, and occasionally someone found a small dead fish in the john.

"It's all over, huh?" said the tier tender. He was a skinny white man in a T-shirt, his pale arms covered with blue jailhouse tattoos. He was in his early forties, which made him ancient by prison standards, serving a third term for trivial offenses.

"Yeah, I'll be in Baghdad by the Bay this afternoon."

"Good luck." He reached through the bars to shake hands and continued down the tier, pouring water.

The morning unlock began, top tier down, with a crashing volley as eighty cells were slammed shut. Trash rained down as the convicts trudged toward the stairs, kicking over what they had swept from their cells.

Troy picked up the shoebox with toothbrush, toothpaste, and a few letters and waited for the security bar to raise.

Instead of going to breakfast, he stepped out of line in the Big Yard and waited while the mess halls emptied. Soon his few close friends arrived for a last embrace and handshake and wish of good luck.

At 8:00 A.M., the work whistle blew, seagulls flew from their rooftop perches, and the yard gate opened. Convicts spilled forth, heading to their jobs. Troy walked down the road toward Between Gates. Receiving and Release was across from the visiting room.

A skinny old sergeant with stooped shoulders and rheumy eyes, nicknamed Andy Gump by the convicts, took Troy's ID card, found his papers in a short pile, and handed them to one of the convict clerks. The convict brought the hanger with his dress-out clothes. The two other men being released were already changing. Everyone got the same issue, khaki pants, black Navy-style shoes, and a short-sleeved white shirt. The one difference was in the color of the windbreaker.

The other two men were black. While they got ready, one of them touched glances with Troy and gave a slight nod that Troy returned with a smile. After that there was no communication between Troy and his companions, although they talked to each other, and one of them muttered about how the clothes made them look like clowns. The man was nervous, fidgeting with his belt buckle and sleeve buttons; his focus was on his clothes, but his real worry was about going from one world to another. The fear upon release after years

60

in prison is similar to the fear upon entering prison in the first place. Troy recognized the symptoms and it made him smile.

At the administration building they were given "gate money," parole papers, and bus tickets. From there a guard walked them to a prison van and drove them to the Greyhound bus depot in San Rafael. The guard watched them enter before driving off. That was the moment they were free. The two black men spotted the liquor store next door and went to get a couple of short dogs.

Troy stood looking out the window. It was weird. Twelve years was such a long, long time. Confronting it made it seem like life, but now, the moment it was over, it was the past and of small importance. No, that was a partial truth. Twelve years of monasticism in San Quentin prison was more than that. It was where he had learned such words as monasticism from years of nights roaming the universes of the written word, and days studying human nature stripped of façades in a world of thieves and killers, madmen and cowards. Still, it was now behind him and he would not look back except to guide his path forward.

Should he step out on the sidewalk and wait for Diesel there? What about the bar across the street? No, he might miss the big guy that way. Where is that fool, he thought rhetorically.

A flashy blue convertible with the top down pulled up to the curb. Diesel was behind the wheel. Before he could get out, Troy exited the terminal door. "Hey, boy!"

Diesel broke a grin and leaned over to open the passenger door. Troy came over, eyed the pale blue car with the white leather upholstery, and stepped back for an appreciative appraisal. "What is this, homeboy?"

"Brand new motherfuckin' Mustang GT. Five fuckin' liters of engine. It kicks ass and takes names. Get in."

Troy slid into the passenger seat, noting that Diesel's short-sleeved golf shirt exposed myriad blue tattoos down his arms and on the backs of his hands. Such self-defacement was virtually a rite of passage in reform school. Troy had avoided using his body for graffiti. Now he could remember why. Later on he would tell Diesel to wear long-sleeved shirts. Every cop in California knew that blue

61

india ink tattoos came from jail. They were a sign that announced, "I am a thug."

"Throw those things in the backseat," Diesel said, indicating the brown paper package and shoebox with the string around it. Troy did so. He turned back and fastened the seat belt.

"Here we go," Diesel said. "Check this ride." He punched the gas and popped the clutch. The five liters of V8 power threw them back against the seat and the car burned rubber as it catapulted into the traffic. "Heigh-ho, Silver!" Diesel said, "the masked men ride again." He pointed toward the glove compartment. "Open it. It's your coming home present."

Troy did so. Inside was a blue steel automatic in a belt-clip holster. Troy pulled the pistol free and looked it over. Browning .380. Nine quick shots—ten if you jacked one into the chamber and added another to the clip. It was an expensive weapon.

"It's clean, too," Diesel said. "Won't trace to nobody. The ammo's in the glove compartment, too."

Troy took out two flat, hard, transparent packages. Hot loads with a coating of an alloy that would penetrate bulletproof vests.

"Thanks," Troy said, fitting the weapon inside his waistband with the holster clip attached to his belt. It gave him a sense of power.

"Where you takin' me?" he asked.

"I thought we'd go into the city and get you some clothes."

"Whatsamatter? You ashamed of me?"

"No . . . but I remember how you always dressed real sharp. You ain't changed, have you?"

"Nope."

"So that's what we'll do. Then we'll get a steak and have some drinks and make some plans. I've got a lotta things to tell you."

"Sounds good. But somewhere today I gotta call the Greek in L.A."

"We can do that right now." From between the white leather bucket seats, Diesel retrieved a flip-open phone. "Cellular," Diesel said, pushing the on button. "Just dial. I got it hooked up yesterday."

"I'll wait," Troy said. "Let's go do some shopping. What's your schedule? Anything you gotta do?"

"Uh-uh. I'm at your disposal."

"How's the old lady and the kid?"

"He's great . . . she's a standard naggy bitch. 'Where you goin'? What are you going to do? Stay away from that guy. He'll get you in trouble.'"

Troy laughed at Diesel's squeaky mime of his wife's voice. Diesel looked over and grinned. "Man, I'm so glad you're out."

"Me, too."

"The Greek came to see you."

"Yeah. He had lawyer ID. Walked right in."

"I asked Tony Citrino—"

"What's he doing?"

"He tends bar in the Mission District in the city. We'll go by there if you want."

"I'd like to see Tony. He's a good dude."

"He hung up the gloves. Said he couldn't do the time anymore. What I started to tell you was that the Greek's supposed to be rich handlin' that go-fast shit. I think he's got a lab and makes it."

"Lotta money in methamphetamine, especially if you make it. Goddamn, it smells bad when you manufacture it. You can smell it for a mile."

"I never got to know the Greek very well. Everybody says he's a stand-up dude."

"Yeah, he is. Solid as a rock. And he's got some drug dealers lined up for us to rip off. How's that for a game plan?"

"I like that . . . motherfuckers who can't yell copper. All they wanna do is kill a sucker—and that sure ain't nothin' new. They been tryin' to kill me all my life. I hope they're niggers."

"No, no, bro'. This is equal opportunity."

"Yeah. Equal opportunity. I like that."

Ahead, through an opening in the rolling hills, the huge orange pillars of the Golden Gate flashed momentarily in the noonday sun. Within minutes they were on the grade leading to the bridge.

In the city, Diesel parked in a garage near Union Square and they walked to the London Men's Shop, one of San Francisco's better stores, featuring Brioni, Cornelini, Raffalo, and Hickey-Freeman suits. The shoes were Bally, Cole-Haan and Ferragamo. Men's style had changed in Troy's lost decade. From trim single-breasted suits and slim slacks without pleats, fashion had returned to pleated and draped pants and double-breasted suits with wide lapels and solid backs. It could have been 1950.

"When did you start getting sharp?" Troy asked. "You were a jeans and tank top man."

"Hey, brother, it wasn't that bad."

"It wasn't? I've got pictures." Troy laughed at Diesel's blush and gave his arm an affectionate squeeze. "How'd you find this place?"

"Those union guys. They love to be sharp. They try to outdress each other."

Troy looked through the rack of size 43 jackets. The prices had risen considerably during his absence. It was going to cost far more than he had expected to dress the way he wanted. After trying on several jackets, he selected a dark blue Italian cut (no back vent), a single-breasted cashmere blazer, and pearl gray flannel slacks. He would have them cuffed. For dress shoes he took a pair of cordovan slip-ons with tassels from Cole-Haan. He added a wool turtleneck in burgundy, plus an ecru pinpoint oxford with spread collar and a necktie that the salesman recommended. The single outfit cost sixteen hundred dollars. In the mirror, he was a handsome personification of a Princeton lithograph. Nobody would ever look at him and think he was a hoodlum. He tried his boyish smile. He'd often wondered why those outside the law often assumed a style that marked them. Even now the young thugs wore baggy pants and floppy shirts, turned cap bills backward, and left their shoelaces untied. Children of the bourgeoisie copied the fashion, but its origins came from reform school where clothes were oversized, and to the police it aroused the same hostile suspicion that zoot suits and ducktail hairdos had two generations earlier. Troy preferred to look as if he belonged in Newport, Palm Beach, or the Upper East Side of Manhattan. Anyone he wanted to know that he was a criminal knew him personally; all others he wanted to think he was a born-again Christian Republican. Or at least rich. That was what he saw in the mirror.

When measurements for alterations were taken (he could cuff the slacks himself), Diesel pulled out a fat roll of one-hundred-dollar bills and counted out cash. The manager took the money, but he also eyed the tattoos, and Troy was sure he thought they were drug dealers. Nobody else paid that much cash. Check or credit card was how the squares did it. Troy would have to get the big green American Express card and either Visa or MasterCard. You had to have those to fulfill the façade.

When they walked back onto the sunny street, he carried the clothes in a bag on a hanger. He would be dapper enough for anywhere they went—dressed for success, he thought with a smile. If he had nowhere else to dress so expensively, he would certainly wear the outfit on capers. A talisman? Not quite. When he was in reform school and already half-committed to crime, he saw a photograph of his idol, Legs Diamond, when the gangster was killed. Face and head were blown away, but the elegance of the three-piece Glen Plaid was plain—and the shoes were high-topped kangaroo skin. Very comfortable, very expensive. That was when Troy decided to get as sharp as possible before going on a caper. If he got busted, he wouldn't arrive in jail looking like a bum. Very particularly he wouldn't return wearing the "hot dog" dress-out shoes issued on release. Men who returned wearing dress-outs were ridiculed and laughed at.

At a Macy's, he picked up everyday clothes, twill pants and chambray shirts, sweaters and Rockport walking shoes. As they headed toward the Mission District, they pulled over and gave a homeless begger the bundle of prison issue.

"You hungry, brother?" Diesel asked.

"Yeah."

"Remember Paul Gallagher?"

"Was doin' time for illegal abortions?"

"That's him. He owns a steakhouse not far away."

"Sounds good."

"He won't let us pay either."

"Sounds even better."

The beef tenderloin parted under light pressure from the steak knife, reminding him of the once-a-year rib steaks served in prison. Tough to start with, they were cooked to a texture approaching leather, but still, they were in demand. Extra guards were put in the mess hall to keep convicts from doubling back for seconds—and when the serving lines ran out before everyone had eaten, it was a tense moment. If they disliked the ham steaks in replacement, stainless-steel trays could sail across the mess hall like a cloud of Frisbees. As Troy savored another bite, he remembered a preference for pork chops when he was young—before he knew better.

"Great steak, huh?" Diesel said.

"Very good."

"Lemme tell you what bein' state-raised does. I used to think that you had to cook a steak well done. I didn't know any better until I was out about a year."

"Who pulled your coat?"

"Jimmy the Face."

"How're you and the old mafioso getting along?"

"We're ace deuce. I beat the shit out of who he says, and he gives me money for it." Diesel glanced around to make sure nobody else could hear; then he tilted his head closer. "About a year ago, he gave me a contract. I think some of those guys back east—Brooklyn or Jersey—sent it to him. The guy was on bail on one of those RICO laws and they were scared the feds would roll him over into a Valachi. In a way it was easy because I locked my mind and didn't fuckin' think about it. Afterward it fucked with me for a couple weeks. The old lady even noticed.how fuckin' jumpy I was." Diesel paused. Troy watched the big, beefy face and sensed that Diesel had never mentioned a word of his worries to anyone else. To whom else might he confide? "I've fucked up a lot of dudes," he continued. "I hurt that one guy pretty bad, that nigger that tried to stick me in the joint. He still walks like a drunk. But this one I'm tellin' you about, that's the first I ever knocked out of the box.

"They set him up. Sent for him. I was waitin' in the parking lot with a twenty-two and a silencer. He went and knocked on the door. They weren't there. When he went back to his car, I stepped up behind him and put one right in his head. He dropped. Boom."

Diesel snapped his fingers to illustrate how quick. "Then I put a Baggie around his head so he wouldn't leak in my trunk. He's up there in the mountains under the dirt with a sack of lime. Ain't much left now except maybe his teeth.

"Afterward I started thinking about going to hell . . . all that crazy ass shit that those fuckin' nuns and priests stuck on me. I know it's bullshit . . . but it's hard to get away from 'em."

Over Diesel's shoulder, Troy saw Paul Gallagher approaching and was glad for the interruption. It was poor underworld protocol to talk about one's crimes if unsolved, and this was especially true of murder, which had no statute of limitations. If you knew nothing, nobody could wonder if you might snitch. Troy preferred to know nothing unless it involved him, and Diesel's contract for Jimmy Fasenella failed the criterion. He indicated with his eyes that someone was near. Diesel stopped talking as Paul Gallagher arrived with a grin. "You don't get steaks like that in the penitentiary. How ya doin', big T?"

"Doin' great today, my man. You've got a nice joint here."

"Yeah . . . but people don't eat red meat like they used to."

"You look like you're doing okay. All the tables are full."

"It's the first time in weeks. We only did twenty dinners last night."

"Like I told you," Diesel said, "if things get too bad, we can always repaint the place."

"What's a paint job gonna do for business?" Troy asked, making both men grin. "Okay, hit me with it," he said.

"Tell him," Gallagher said.

"You buy the paint and thinner and you start painting—and there's an accident that starts a little fire. You open the doors to get the smoke out. A tarp falls on a hot stove top, a can of thinner gets kicked over. All of a sudden it's too big to handle. No way they can say it was deliberate. Cool, huh?"

Nodding, Troy asked, "You thought of it?"

"Hell, no! The mob does that shit all the time back east . . . so why not out here?"

"Sounds like a winner to me," Troy said—and it did. Without a confession there was no way to disprove an accident. It was much better than setting a fire in the night. The police could prove that in five minutes.

Gallagher insisted on their having dessert and coffee. Troy thought it was the best coffee he'd ever tasted.

"Man," said Diesel, "I remember you knocking down that instant coffee. What were you, a Nestlé's man or a Maxwell House?"

"Maxwell House. But after this, I don't know if I could drink it again."

"Hell," Gallagher said, "they sell coffee now they didn't even have back then."

"I know. This has a great taste."

"Hawaiian Hazelnut."

Diesel glanced at his watch and let out a sound.

"What's up, bro'?" Troy asked.

"Oh shit. The old lady expected me to call two hours ago."

"Go call her. Blame me."

"I don't have to do that. She'll blame you all by herself. Are you sure you don't wanna come home with me? Wait'll you see my kid. He's fuckin' big, man. Tough, too, and mean . . ." Diesel spoke with pride; being tough and mean were virtues in his view of the world. It was what he had been taught throughout his life.

"I'll see him," Troy said, "but not tonight. I kinda wanna be loose. Walk around the city. You know Gigolo Perry?"

"Uh-uh. I know who he is by reputation, but he left the joint a long time before I got there. He owns a club on the other side of Market, doesn't he?"

"Yeah. I've never seen it, but I've got the address."

"Want me to drop you there?"

"No. I was thinking about that Holiday Inn in Chinatown. I can walk to North Beach."

"Hey, bro', North Beach ain't what it used to be."

"Nothing's like it used to be. What time can you come for me tomorrow?"

"Whenever you say."

"We gotta drive to Sacramento and hook up with Mad Dog."

"We *gotta* do that, huh?"

The voice inflection was not lost on Troy. He looked at the hard set of Diesel's face and started to ask questions, but Gallagher arrived. The meal was on the house, but they should tip the waiter. He walked them to the door and gave Troy a hug of affection by way of good-bye.

The long summer twilight was still on the city. A clock in a jeweler's window said seven-thirty. In San Quentin the evening meal was over. Shower unlock was in progress, and in the cells the convicts were watching the Giants-Dodgers game on the little TVs that prison officials used for mental pacifiers. Some left it on throughout the test patterns in the night and the predawn morning citrus report. Troy had once smashed a cell partner's TV. The fool never shut it off; he was fixated on "Jeopardy" and "Wheel of Fortune" and other audience participation programs, so much so that he had to answer the questions aloud, and was usually wrong. It distracted Troy. Subtle comments were unavailing, so finally Troy waited for unlock, carried the TV out of the cell, and threw it over the tier. "If you don't have a cell move tomorrow morning, you go with the TV." "Hey, man, I didn't know you took it personal." The cell partner moved, but Troy carried a shiv and magazines for body armor for a few days, just in case it wasn't over. He wished he hadn't lost his temper. He watched movies and sporting events, football, basketball and boxing, and public service programs. When he tallied the hours, he thought they were mostly a waste, junk food for the mind. How many more books could he have read? Not that the printed word was panacea; most popular novels were pablum, too. During his decade in prison, his taste had changed immeasurably.

Looking from the car window out at San Francisco, probably America's loveliest city, Troy was surprised at the number of homeless. It was something new to him. In his childhood the few bedraggled creatures wandering about with dirty hands held out were invariably older white men, brains in a permanent fog from alcohol or insanity. Now every corner had someone with a sign or a spray bottle to wash windshields, and most were young black men.

A billboard had a dog pulling a blanket from a man in bed. It reminded him again: "We gotta go see Mad Dog tomorrow or the next day."

"I gotta tell you something," Diesel said. "Something I've never mentioned to anyone. I wanted to, 'cause it fucked with my head."

"Give it to me."

"Two months ago, Mad Dog called my pad. He called two or three times and got Gloria. It was a Friday and I was doin' a favor for Jimmy the Face. When I finally talked to him, he's busted in Portland on some chickenshit credit card beef. But if he don't make bail by Monday morning, the parole officer would see his name on the booking list and slam him with a parole detainer. He wanted me to come bail him out."

Diesel continued with the story, at one point inserting the scene of the dispute after the ship payroll robbery. As he told it, he relieved it in his mind. He ended with the opening of the freezer: ". . . my hair stood up. I swear it did. I got my ass out of there. I kept lookin' to see if their bodies turned up somewhere, but I don't think they did. If you wanna do a little work, it's easy to put a body where nobody will find it—except maybe some fool-ass archeologist five hundred years from now."

"He doesn't know you know?" Troy asked.

"No way. I was outta there so fast—"

"Right."

"I haven't talked to him since then."

Troy saw it plainly, the dead bodies of mother and child frozen solid. It made him shudder inside. He had never killed anyone, partly because he understood the gravity of taking life, and partly because circumstances had never come together, but he knew how common it had been since Cain and Abel, and he knew a lot of killers. He had friends who'd killed, many in anger from a dispute or for revenge, a few who had killed a cop or a store owner in a shootout, a few for money in a contract killing—but maniac killers were outside his sphere of experience. He knew about Mad Dog's paranoid nature. Was he too dangerous to have around? Would it be too dangerous to cut him loose? Would that stimulate all his paranoid ideas?

On the other hand, Troy knew that Mad Dog respected him more than anyone in the world. He remembered the reform school night of years ago.

"You know what," Troy said, "I can handle him."

"He scares me a little. You never know what's in his mind. You remember what him and Roach did to that guy in the East Block. What was his name, Carrigan or something. They were all tight buddies. Remember? They stabbed him about twenty times, didn't they?"

"Yeah, but he threatened Roach, talked bad. He should have known they weren't friends anymore."

"Any way you say, Troy. I'm with you. But I wanted you to know what was happening with the guy."

"I'm glad you told me. I know he's crazy. We'll watch his ass. If he acts too crazy—" Troy shrugged, a gesture that said nothing and yet said everything. "You ready to go to L.A.?"

"Whenever you say."

"Just a couple days. I'm not even going to check in with the parole officer. They don't look for you for jumping parole. They wait until you get picked up—"

"Or somebody fingers you."

"That, too—but nobody's gonna finger me. If they just stop me, I've good ID, don't I?"

"Oh, yeah. It'll stand up against everything but a fingerprint check."

Diesel wheeled the car through the narrow, twisty streets of Chinatown and turned up under the porte cochere of the big Holiday Inn.

A doorman was instantly at hand.

"What time you gonna be here?" Troy asked.

"Ten . . . eleven . . . whenever you say."

"Call me when you leave the house."

"Will do."

They clasped hands and Troy got out.

Diesel pulled away.

6

Alone in his room on the eleventh floor of the Holiday Inn, Troy took off his shoes and socks. It was the first time since his arrest that he'd walked barefoot on carpet—or barefoot on anything except cold concrete. He doused the lights, sat on the bed, and dug his toes into the thick, soft carpet, meanwhile looking through an open window, the cool night in his face, out across San Francisco's hills and the dark bay dotted with lights from ships and buoys. How did he feel being free after so long in the cage among the numbered men? In a way he felt less different than he had anticipated. Men had told him of weird fears, bolts of confusion and panic. He felt none of that, but he did feel a sense of the unreal. He would look at the world and see distortions that reminded him of abstract art, Dali or Picasso.

The room TV had closed-circuit movies. He ordered one from the Playboy channel. No cable stations came into San Quentin, so he had never seen anything like this. These were not trashy sluts with pimples on their butts. These Playboy women were lovely enough to be movie stars, long-legged, high-breasted, with silky hair and velvet skin and asses full and round. He wanted one so intensely that it made him dizzy. Going without sex for years was easier than the average person would imagine—and there was always the release of masturbation. His fantasies had been about women like these. One thing was sure, he knew he could buy some pussy. He had money and he knew where to go.

He dressed in his new clothes, and he liked what he saw in the mirror. It was a loose, draped look that reminded him of movies when Robert Mitchum, Burt Lancaster, and Kirk Douglas were young

72

men. His first awareness of men's fashion was stovepipe pants that made feet stick out like flippers and jackets with narrow shoulders and lapels. He liked this better, the pleated drape of the pants and the loose jacket with shoulder pads (it was easier to hide a pistol).

Should he take it with him? Yeah, why not. If you're going to be a criminal, be one twenty-four hours a day. The Greco had told him that—and Greco lived up to it. "Gotta call him later," Troy muttered to himself as he slipped the pistol with the tiny clip holster inside his waistband at the small of his back. It would be hidden even with the jacket unbuttoned and flapping open.

Going out, he stopped in the doorway. Had he forgotten anything? His key? No, he had that. As he pulled the door closed, he realized it was the first door he'd locked for himself in many years.

He pushed through the front door to the porte cochere, and the Chinese doorman beckoned him a taxicab.

"You know where the Fish and Shrimp is?" he asked.

"No."

"It's the other side of Market downtown. Maybe on Folsom."

The cab took off, blasting its horn as it cut in front of a car and accelerated. It was too fast. Time was money for the cabbie, while time was cheap for Troy.

"Hey," Troy said, "slow down."

The driver looked around, furrowing his brow. He was dark and smelled of curry. Troy figured him as coming from India.

"Take it easy," Troy said, "and I'll double what's on the meter for your tip."

"Yes, sir."

The cab slowed markedly. Before they found the Fish & Shrimp they wandered around many dark streets. Again Troy stared out. California had always seemed bright and new to him; now it was frayed and seedy. He'd read of recession, national debt, the fraying of the welfare net. It had seemed the usual cry wolf bullshit on the printed page, but outside the window was a new reality. Every other traffic light, it seemed, had a black man ready to wipe off the windshield. As the cabbie waved one off, he said, "Why not they get a job," in fractured English. Troy wanted to answer that maybe the immigrants took them, but instead he chose a diplomatic comment: "Maybe they don't know how to do anything."

"Ach. Most are lazy. Their women do the work. They did the work in Africa: they do the work here. Over there they sat around and told war stories with their balls hanging out and feathers on their heads. I saw it in *National Geographic.*"

Troy chuckled despite himself. Even a fool could be funny.

"Here we are," the cabbie said, pulling over.

Troy looked out. No wonder they had missed it. The narrow façade was ebony tile, and beside the door was a small blue neon logo of a fish and a shrimp, with the name in thin script: Fish & Shrimp. Not bad for an old thief and rounder, Troy thought. The name was rhyming slang from the eighteenth-century London under-world, now known to a very few thieves and con men. It was quaint for Gigolo to use it.

The meter was thirty-one dollars. Troy gave the driver a fifty-dollar bill. It was less than he'd promised, but he suspected that the man had wandered on purpose. The cabbie looked at it and frowned. "That's all I've got," Troy said, wondering what the racist cocksucker would do if he got beat about the head with a gun butt. The cabbie nodded and Troy said nothing more. It was said that if one was going to be a sucker, it was best to be a quiet one.

A three-hundred-pound doorman looked him over. He passed the examination, for the doorman opened the door for him.

Inside, cut-glass mirrors reflected soft light. The bar ran straight ahead on the right. On the bar stools were several pairs of long legs encased in silky stockings. He could see flashes of thigh, and he could almost smell more. Short skirts had returned, thank God.

The bartender was at the far end. Troy walked along the bar. In the mirrored wall behind it, eyes looked at his reflection. He would leave here with a woman, no doubt of it. He had the price.

The bartender saw him approach and turned from a young woman to see what he wanted.

"I called about half an hour ago . . . for George Perry."

The bartender pointed toward the rear booth across the room. Troy turned. Gigolo had already seen him and was getting to his feet. He came forward with a grin and spread arms. He was in his late seventies but looked twenty years younger. How could it be when he had dissipated in every way known to man until about fifteen years earlier? The only change Troy noticed was that his hair and goatee had turned from gray to pure white. He was dressed sharp, in camel-hair jacket and flannel slacks. He encircled the younger man in a bear hug. "Damn, I didn't think you were ever gonna raise."

"Me neither."

"When was it?"

"Today."

"You ain't had no pussy yet."

"Nope."

"Look over my shoulder and see what I got for you in the booth."

Troy looked. Two women sat in the booth. One was fifty or more. Trim and stylish, she was still too old. The first thing he noticed about the other was the luxuriant mane of red hair.

"She's no slut streetwalker that sucks a dick for a toot on a crack pipe. This one's a courtesan . . . y'know what I mean?"

Troy nodded, still looking. She had bright blue eyes and a faint sprinkle of freckles around her nose. He couldn't see her body, but her face was certainly pretty. She noticed him looking and smiled. It had been so long since he'd even talked to a pretty woman that he instantly grew hot with shy embarrassment and felt himself a fool. It was ludicrous, ex-con, tough guy, afraid of almost nothing that walked the earth—and he was totally nonplussed by a smile. He started to tell Gigolo to forget it, but that would have been more embarrassing. Gigolo would rib him with the accusation that prison had turned him to young boys.

"Before I introduce you," Gigolo said, "remember one thing."

"What's that?"

"Don't fall in love."

"Don't what?"

"Fall . . . in . . . love."

"That sounds crazy, man. You finally got old enough so you're simpleminded?"

George Gigolo Perry shook his head. "You know it's true when

75

you think about it. Guys come out of the joint, or even the army, where they haven't been around a woman in years, and the first one that gives 'em some pussy and kisses 'em on the ear, bang, they fall in love. The broad may have five rug rats and be fat as Roseanne, it don't matter. They get pussy-whipped. This one here is as fine as they come. Wait'll you see her body. If I was fifty, I'd try to catch her. Anyway, I told you."

"Don't sweat it, brother. I can handle it."

"I know you can. You got control of your dick. C'mon."

They turned to the booth and George made the introductions. She was Dominique Winters, and Troy wondered if that was a name taken to hustle. Her face had the open freshness of a cheer-leader.

George sat next to the older woman, whose name was Pearl, and Troy sat next to Dominique. Her perfume was light, but because it had been so long since he'd smelled anything sweet, its effect was unusually powerful.

George raised a hand toward a passing waitress. She veered over immediately; he was the owner. "One more round. What do you want?" he asked Troy.

"Vodka tonic is okay."

George nodded to the waitress and she went away. While they waited for the drinks, George asked about mutual friends in the California prison system. "How's Big Joe?"

"Morgan?" Troy asked.

"Yeah. Is he ever gonna get out again?"

Troy shook his head. "He's in Pelican Bay. Oh, lemme tell you a story he told me. He came down to Quentin for some medical reason. They put a bull on his door in the hospital, but the bull let me visit him.

"Check this," Troy continued. "Somebody subpoenaed him to L.A. last year. They make a production number—two cars, six bulls, automatic weapons, all that shit. They don't tell him he's goin'. They don't want him to know. They just snatch him up, strip him down, take the wooden leg, put him in the white jumpsuit, and dump him in the backseat.

"Off they go down the highway, two cars, six cops—and Joe with one leg. Somewhere along Ninety-nine, he tells 'em that they didn't tell him ahead of time and he's gotta take a piss. They tell him to hold it, and he tells the cop that if they don't stop, he's gonna piss on the car seat. It's the agent's private car.

"So they radio from car to car and finally pull into a Mobil station. They form a perimeter, weapons ready, like they expected a hundred of the Mexican mafia to jump out and rescue Joe. They check the toilet to make sure there's no pistol under the sink, and they finally let him go.

"While he's in the shitter, this brother in an old pickup pulls into the gas station and gets out to fill up. He doesn't see what's happening until he's pumping gas. Then he sees these white men in business suits with Uzis and dark glasses with this perimeter behind the cars outside the bathroom door. You can imagine what's going through his head. Who the fuck is this?

"The door opens, out comes Joe, hippety-hoppin' along on one leg, draped in a ton of chains. The guy forgot he was pumping gas. It ran out on the ground. He said, 'Man, you gotta be the baddest motherfucker that e'er walked the face of the earth.'"

Laughter explodes from George. "That's funny, man."

"Joe was cracking up when he told me. What about Paul Allen? How's he doing? He's been out for three years. That's hard to believe."

"Paul died, man. They found him in a hotel room in Hollywood about a month ago."

"Paul! Damn, that's a bummer. I've known him nearly twenty years and never saw him outside of jail."

"At least he died outside."

"That's true."

"Willy Hart told me."

"Willy. What's he doin'? How's he doin'?"

"He's doing good, except instead of being the lean and mean handball player, he's got a pot gut from too much beer. I think he sells aluminum awnings."

"A tin man."

"Yeah, he's pretty good, too."

"God knows he runs at the mouth enough."

The mutual recollection made them both laugh.

"Who else?" George asked. "Where's T.D.?"

"He's buried in Leavenworth or Marion."

"Probably Marion. Didn't he pick up a murder beef in the joint?"

"Yeah. Some fool riled him up and didn't know what he was fuckin' with."

"I hear Marion is fucked up."

"Like Pelican Bay—right out of Kafka."

"It can't be any worse than when I went to the joint. Bulls had canes with lead at the end. When you lined up for lockup, they'd walk along beside the lines. If your foot was one inch on the line, they'd bust your instep with the lead tip of the cane. Lousy mother-fuckers. Some of 'em couldn't even read back then."

"They're not much smarter now, but they sure get paid better. It's the biggest employees' union in the state. They've got it all down. They shoot a laser in the cell, then run in and hit you with a couple hundred milligrams of Thorazine . . . then kick your ass. And after they do all that, they write a report that they used the minimum amount of necessary force after you assaulted them."

"Then they wonder what makes a sucker antisocial."

"It's a wonder more guys don't take it out on old ladies."

"I remember when I went to the joint in thirty-five. The public didn't hate thieves like they do now. Shit, man, down in Oklahoma, they liked Pretty Boy Floyd. I haven't been arrested in twenty-eight years. If I wrote a bad check, they'd give me life under that three-strikes-you're-out bullshit. You know why I think it is?"

"Tell me."

"Two reasons. One is niggers. There didn't used to be so many doin' shit, and those that were thieves, they know how to play con, or boost. They had some game. Young niggers today, they don't know nuthin' about nuthin', and they don't give a shit. They think killin' somebody makes 'em a man, some kinda way. Where there used to be fifteen, twenty percent in the joint, now it's sixty percent."

"What's the other thing?"

"It's the violence. Look here," George said, "when I was a thief, I never carried a piece except on a heist. I'd steal with a gun if the score was right. But if anybody got hurt, it was a failure. The idea was to be smooth. Now I'm an old man and I'm scared to go lots of places at night unless I'm packin' a pistol for self-protection. The world has changed in twenty years."

All of it was true, Troy thought. Not that it mattered to him very much. He might go to the morgue, but he wasn't going to jail. Never again, never more. Unlike most denizens of the underworld, his childhood had let him see what a difference money made in life, in what one experienced, in what freedom one could have if one could afford it. He had no aspiration for riches: The wealth of moguls constrained them. What he needed was enough to find a sunny town on a seacoast where he could live in a small house on a hillside, with a woman to cook and clean. A few hundred thousand would be enough, thank you, and he had nothing to invest but his life.

Dominique leaned close and whispered, "Want to go?"

"Sure."

"I'll be right back. Excuse me."

She slid from the booth and strolled between the tables toward a side hall with a restroom sign. They had to watch, her body and the way she walked made it impossible to do otherwise.

"Damn, you look serious," George said, leaning over the table to give him a playful slap. "Smile, sucker. Look at her ass. Goddamn, I wish I was sixty again."

Troy had to grin. He wished he had George's view of life.

"So how long are you going to be here?" George asked.

"A day . . . maybe two."

"What about the parole?"

"There's no way I can do a parole. I'm not even going to report."

"I did a parole. I don't know how I did it. I never intended to. I sort of staggered into straightening up. One day led to another. I even took off a couple scores way back—and got away. I feel like I quit ahead of the game."

"Sure you did," Pearl said, "if you don't think about the sixteen years you spent in prison."

"Not when it's over," George said. "Right?" he asked Troy.

Troy nodded, but not wholeheartedly. The memory was too close.

Pearl gathered her purse. "Time for me to go home. Are you coming?" she asked George.

"What else can I do? We're in your car."

"Let's go."

George grinned. "Look here, man," he said to Troy, "I'm supposed to be an exploiter of women—Gigolo Perry. Man, I'm a rest home for a whore."

"Quit running your jaws and let's go," Pearl said.

"See, man, see," George said.

Dominique appeared. Everyone got up and gathered their things.

"Need any dough?" George asked.

"Uh-uh. I'm okay."

"We're parked out back," George said.

The two men shook hands. Troy promised to call when he got to L.A. He would pass on George's regards to Greco.

Troy was lightheaded as he followed Dominique toward the door. Watching her body move under her clothes, he could imagine her naked, opening her legs—and he got an erection.

On the sidewalk, Dominique stopped. "Are we getting a room or what?"

"I've got one at the Holiday Inn in Chinatown."

"No car?"

He shook his head.

"I left mine at home."

A taxi was going by the other way. She put two fingers to her lips and let forth a blast of a whistle.

Troy looked at her. "Damn, baby."

"I lived a couple years in New York City."

The cabbie looked and made a fast U-turn. "Where to?"

"Chinatown Holiday Inn."

During the ride, the sway of turning corners and changing lanes jostled their bodies together. Each time it happened, Troy felt a surge of arousal and imagination. He glanced at her profile and confirmed her delicate beauty. Because she was quiet and her smile was soft, his imagination gave her attributes of character that he found desirable, adding an affectionate tenderness to desire. Although he liked whores, most of whom had been through hard times and had a fatalistic view of life, with this one he only felt pity. She was too pretty and nice to be a whore. He wondered why; then laughed to himself. It was the standard question of the trick.

They crossed the lobby and took the elevator. As he unlocked the door and she walked past, he asked if she wanted a drink. She smiled softly and shook her head. She looked around, opened the bathroom door a few inches and turned on the light therein, then she turned off the room lights. Enough came from the bathroom to softly light the room. Through the window from far below came the distant muffled sounds of the city.

Dominique knew how to stir a man's fire and she began to strip and taunt. Watching him with eyes that glittered, she slowly unbuttoned her blouse while doing a slight shimmy with her shoulders. Her smile was full of tease. She pulled the blouse open, flashed her breasts, which were small but erect; then pulled it shut and turned away, finally rolling her shoulders so the garment fluttered to the floor.

She wiggled from the tight skirt in a provocatively graceful way. When it dropped to the carpet, she stepped out and stood in bikini panties, high heels, shiny white stockings, and garter belt. He thought she had the prettiest ass he'd ever seen, round and smooth. Her body was shapely and firm—she was either a dancer or worked out, and although men would say she epitomized the sexually attractive body, she would be insufficiently thin for the fashion of the era. She put a foot on a chair and reached to unsnap her garter belt.

"Don't," he said.

"Oh, you like that," she said, arching an eyebrow.

"Yes," he said, "with legs . . . like yours." It made him grin; passion had made him momentarily lightheaded. Was he going to faint over pussy before he got it? He was like a horny schoolboy in the clutches of a horny housewife. He wanted to laugh at himself, but he wanted to put his hands on Dominique even more.

"Do you fuck with your clothes on?" she asked.

"Uhhh. No, no, no . . ." He kicked his shoes off and nearly tore the shirt buttons loose while unfastening them.

The pistol! He remembered it as he started to slip from the shirt. Too many women were weird about firearms. As he took the shirt off, he turned and shielded the pistol as he pulled it and the clip-on holster from his waistband and put it under his jacket on the chair. She was pulling down the bedspread and missed it. Good. Even a whore might get antsy if she saw a piece.

When he took off his socks, he remembered that wearing them now would be the most unromantic thing in the world.

Dominique removed the bedspread and fluffed the pillows. Her breasts danced with the motion.

She took something small from the nightstand and turned toward him. As she crossed the room, naked save for garter belt, stockings, and high heels, he was hypnotized by radiant warmth from her body; he felt it five feet away. He had no wish to say anything. He was too seduced, blind as Samson from desire.

On reaching him, she grabbed him between the legs with such perfect pressure that he trembled—and then with the dexterity of a farmer preparing a stallion for a mare, she slipped the latex condom down over his penis. He didn't care what she did, as long as she spread her legs and he could slip it into her. Never in life had he wanted to fuck a woman the way he wanted this one.

She took his hand and led him to the bed. Whores had taught him how to give a woman pleasure. It was no esoteric secret from the Kama Sutra; it was simply patient and prolonged touching and stroking, with gentle hands and the tip of the tongue. A woman's body took much longer to get ready to fuck, a truth that horny youth found difficult to appreciate.

Troy had the same difficulty this time. His fingers touched the warm silky skin inside her thighs and then he got dizzy as she spread them like the wings of a resting butterfly.

"Want a little head?" he asked.

"That's nice . . . I love it . . . but this one's for you. I'm gonna fuck your brains out. Come on . . ." She pulled his hand and moved to open her legs for him. She clipped the dark mound of hair so it was a neat V. Its bottom tip marked the spot.

She guided him inside. She was a little tight, but she could take it, and she quickly relaxed her body. She dug her heels into his butt and pressed her pelvis upward so he was totally inside her. "Let's fuck," she said.

He kept his arms extended as he fucked her, so he was up above her, looking down at her face looking up from the pillow. He was blind except for the sight of her face and the feel of her pussy and thighs cradling him.

She fitted her rhythm to his and began to coach him, "Cum for me, baby . . . cum for me, sweet man. Ohhh, fuck me good."

It goaded him and he reached for the orgasm. Up . . . up . . . strain the brain . . . and when he reached the top, he fell down through it in a series of convulsions. His arms ached and he was dripping sweat.

Dominique smiled in the manner of the Cheshire Cat. George had paid her well, but this was more than business. It wasn't love, but it was a pleasurable roll in the hay. She enjoyed the obvious ecstasy she'd provided. Some women had the power to lead men by their dicks; Dominique was among them, and she enjoyed her power. She had exercised so she could control the muscles of her vagina. She could knead a man's penis with her pussy as surely as her fingers could milk a cow. It took but a few minutes to arouse him again.

It took longer for the second orgasm, and afterward he flopped, dishrag weak and soaked with sweat, beside her on the bed.

Dominique ran a finger down his sweaty chest. "Mind if I smoke?" she asked.

"Smoke away."

"Do you want one?"

"Nope."

As she fired the match, lighting the cigarette and making a momentary glow around her face, he felt warm affection, protective and tender. Did she have an old man? He'd have to ask Gigolo Perry. Then he realized what he was thinking, and remembered what George had warned about falling in love. He began laughing. Sweet Jesus, he could see what George was talking about.

83

7

Diesel tossed socks and underwear into the overnight bag. Gloria stood in the bedroom door, arms folded as she glared at him and tapped her foot. Her short fuse was burning down; she was ready to explode any moment. Diesel knew it and kept his eyes averted. Maybe he could get away before she got all the way worked up.

He zipped the bag shut, grabbed the suitcase from beside the bed, and started for the door.

"I see you took your arsenal," she said.

"So?"

"I want to know where you're going." As she spoke, she stood away from the doorframe and blocked the doorway just as he arrived at it. He had to stop or drive over her. He wasn't ready for that—not yet. He raised his eyes to the heavens, a charade of seeking patience from God. Then he backed away from her.

"Please lemme go, baby. I don't wanna fight." It was as true as anything he'd ever said. He would brawl while choking on his own blood. He would fight anybody who walked the earth—but he was gun-shy of Gloria. He loomed over her, and he could flatten her with one punch. He outweighed her more than two to one. He would rather do anything than hit her; yet she would goad him until it was either submit or physically throw her aside. He'd done that once—and when he got out the door, she came behind him and jumped on his back. What a scene, him spinning around as he tried to dislodge her. Curtains stirred in neighbors' windows. That musta caused a lotta gossip. He wanted anonymity.

"Either you tell me . . . or it's a fight. Look, Carl, you've got a son. You can't run around whenever you feel like it anymore. Grow up, man."

He looked down at her face, her jaw muscles flexing hard ridges. He decided to tell her. Troy would disapprove, but Troy would never know. "We're going to Sacramento to pick up Mad Dog."

"Mad Dog! You said he's crazy."

"Yeah . . . Well, a lotta people are crazy. I'm crazy, too."

"You don't even like the guy."

"Troy okayed him."

"Oh, that's all it takes . . . Troy's okay. If he's so fuckin' smart, how come he spent so much time in the penitentiary?"

"You wanted to know, I told you. Don't push it . . . don't try to tell me what to do . . ." He stopped, leaning back, looking down his nose, his blue eyes flecked red and glassy. She bit her lip and stilled her tongue. He kept talking to mollify her. "When we get done in Sacramento, we're probably going to L.A."

"What's in L.A.?"

"A lawyer Troy needs to see."

"How long before you get back?"

"Maybe five days . . . at the outside." It was a lie. It would be ten days minimum.

"If you get busted and go back to prison, don't expect me or Junior to be around when you get out. This body isn't going to shrivel up waiting for a fool."

"Yeah, you've said that fifty times already."

"And you don't seem to give a shit."

Her scornful tone got under his skin. In reflex, he dropped his bag and started forward to grab her blouse. He stopped himself, but she knew it was time to step aside. She did so. He retrieved the bag and walked out, pushing the screen door open with his shoulder and letting it slam afterward.

Gloria watched him reach the convertible, where Troy waited behind the wheel. Diesel threw his bags in the backseat and got in. He didn't look back as Troy took off.

"Troy's driving the whole show now," she muttered, while inside she felt the hollowness of fear. Her husband was lost. "No," she said, shaking her head; she didn't want to think something that might jinx him or worsen his odds.

She closed the front door and went into the kitchen. Whatever happened, life went on—and she had to fix dinner for her son. Maybe the child would make something of his life. She hoped so. As she opened the refrigerator and looked at its meager contents, she thought: "Why wasn't I born rich?" Then she grinned at her momentary self-pity. As she took out the bottle to warm, she hoped Carl would call regularly. He'd been better about that lately. Maybe there'd be a miracle and he would straighten up. Yeah . . . and they might hit Lotto, too.

Eighty miles an hour was fast enough even for flat empty stretches. More than that might attract the Highway Patrol. Seventy was better if there was any traffic whatsoever. Stay in the fast lane and keep a distance. Seventy split the difference just right—faster got a ticket, slower was wasting time. He remembered reading that long ago. Was it true now? He would see.

"How'm I driving?" he asked Diesel.

"Cool, man, considering."

"It's like fuckin': Once you've learned it, you never forget."

"Man, who was that chick I ran into?"

"Some chick Gigolo Perry cut me into."

"I'd buy some pussy off her."

Troy was surprised to feel a flash of possessiveness, and of consequent anger at Diesel's casual remark. It was a meaningless nothing in their world. It wasn't about a wife or lover, and it wasn't even uncomplimentary by street thief standards. After all, she sold pussy for a living. If it wasn't for George's astute observation on life, Troy might have wondered if he was half in love. God knew that being with her was pleasurable, and he might look her up when they came back from L.A. She was lovely enough to have on his arm while dining in all the right places.

They crossed the Golden Gate at twilight. Westward an orange half disk sank below the horizon, making a fiery path across the sea and turning the pillars of the bridge into flaming monuments for a moment. The highway followed canyons whose bottoms were already dark. When they came out of the hills, the sun was gone and the light was inky. All the cars had their lights on, an opposing double river, white and ruby red.

A Highway Patrol cruiser passed them on the right.

"Will my driver's license stand a check?" Troy asked.

"If they call in? Yeah, it's cool."

"Al Leon Klein. Born twelve fifteen fifty-nine. Denver, Colorado." Troy made sure he had his pedigree ready. He remembered Boonie going down because he couldn't spell the name on the driver's license he was using for an alias. To give the devil his due, it was a Polish name. Still, he should have been able to spell the name he was using. "Who was this guy?" he asked. "Do you know?"

"Yeah. It's his ID. We just changed the picture. He was a fruiter. He died in the Gay Men's Hospice. He had that bad shit."

"Cancer?"

"Cancer, my ass. AIDS!"

"Yeah, I know," Troy said. "You don't even like to say it, do you?"

"Scares me, man. It kills motherfuckers all kindsa ways. Some of 'em die horrible deaths. Shit growing in their throat, eating at their brain. How many dudes got it in the joint?"

"I dunno. I guess a few hundred are infected without bein' sick—"

"They will be somewhere down the line."

"So will all of us."

"Yeah, you're right."

"Anybody that comes up HIV positive, they get put in a segregated unit."

"Dudes are scared of 'em, I bet."

"You got it," Troy said. "Some of 'em are scared shitless. You know how stupid they are. And you'd be surprised at some of the dudes that got it. The ones that are already sick are mostly faggots, but those that are infected are mostly dope fiends. I knew a lot of 'em since reform school. Jimmy Villa, Don Wilcox, Wedo Karate. And guys I don't know their names."

"Al Leon Klein," Diesel said.

"Yeah, now you make me a dead fruiter."

"Better'n being a live fugitive."

"Better quit fuckin' with me. I'll hurt your big ass."

"You will?"

"Yeah." Troy reached down with his right hand and grabbed a fat piece of inner thigh between four fingers and the heel of his hand. The pain was so great that it froze Diesel.

"Oh, God! I'm sorry! I quit," Diesel pleaded. "Leggo, brother. Please!"

"Call me Daddy."

"Yes, Daddy. Please, Daddy."

Troy released his grip. Diesel raised a clenched fist in a parody of Jackie Gleason. "One of these days . . . one of these days."

"If you ever *dream* of jumping on me, you'd better wake up and get your mind right."

"Oh, yeah?"

"Yeah. Pssst." He gestured for Diesel to look down.

Diesel looked. In Troy's left hand was a pistol.

"How 'bout that?" Troy asked.

"I quit," Diesel said. "Put that away."

Troy slipped the pistol back under his thigh where he could retrieve it instantly. It was unlikely that he would need it out here on the highway. And if he did need it, the chances are it would be useless. The only need would be if the Highway Patrol, or some local cop, pulled them over, and for a decade or more, virtually all policemen wore bulletproof vests under their uniforms, or as part of their uniforms. Head and arms and legs were still open, but those were harder shots and, except for the head, unlikely to instantly incapacitate. The instinct in the extreme moment was to shoot at the biggest target, the body. He would need to practice. Once upon a time he'd been extremely good with various small arms, especially the pistol. It had been a long time; at the least, his skill must have deteriorated by half.

Diesel was playing with the car radio. The preset stations were for the San Francisco Peninsula, not the East Bay. He had to find what he wanted by searching. He was looking for golden oldies, but when a voice was reading the news, Troy told him to hold up a minute.

Congress was rushing through an urban aid bill . . . a plane from Mather Field was missing in the Sierras . . . Sacramento police had raided a topless bar . . . a car had been hijacked in Oakland, two of the four bandits had been caught after a shootout in Berkeley . . . Palestinians were causing the Israelis trouble on the West Bank . . . The INS was increasing its presence along the border . . . the Court of Appeal had upheld the "three strikes" law.

"Turn on some music," Troy said. "That shit's too depressing."

"Are you eligible for three strikes?" Diesel asked.

"It depends if they can use my juvenile case. I don't think an appellate court will uphold that part of it. A juvenile case doesn't have the constitutional protections—no lawyer, no trial by jury, no presumption of innocence, no confrontation with witnesses, none of that shit. So it can't be constitutionally viable to enhance a subsequent case."

"If you say so."

"What about you?"

"Dead and stinking. Even a chickenshit beef like havin' a gun gives me life. Fuck all that. I'm holding court on the spot."

"Yeah, they've made all crimes into capital offenses."

"How they gonna do it, Troy? I mean, damn, where they gonna put all them fools? How they gonna take 'em all to trial? It seems insane to me."

"It is insane. But they're scared."

"I do understand that. I get scared, too, and I'm a two-hundred-and-fifty-pound grizzly bear, armed to the teeth. Them young niggers, they're on some kind of outer space trip. I read yesterday where they went to rob some sucker. He showed 'em his empty wallet, so they shot him six times. What kinda shit is that? What're they thinkin' about?"

"Who knows?"

"Just ignorant-ass niggers," was Diesel's judgment. "All they know how to do is sell dope and hurt people. Somebody said they learn that shit from movies and TV."

"They learn it somewhere. Everybody learns everything somewhere.

Maybe it is TV. Nobody else teaches them anything—at least nobody teaches a lot of 'em. A lot of 'em grow up with nothin' to civilize 'em in the ghetto."

"Kinda like that movie, *Lord of the Flies*."

"Not a bad analogy . . . except it started as a book."

"I didn't read it, but I saw the flick. Whaddya think about niggers? You hate 'em?"

"Uh-uh," Troy said. "Not unless they hate me."

"That's how I feel . . . if they be fulla hate, fuck 'em in their ass. If they respect me, I respect them. If they bad-vibe me, I give 'em redneck vibes right back. I ain' done nuthin' to the motherfuckers. What the fuck, I been fucked over bad as them. You, too. What about all that hate in gangsta rap? They call that shit music."

"Duke Ellington must turn over in his grave."

"No bullshit about that."

Lights and buildings and traffic increased as they entered the outskirts of Sacramento. It was dark now. In a gas station, Diesel filled the tank while Troy went to a pay telephone. The number was to a communal pay phone in the hallway of a rooming house. A girl answered: "Hello."

"Hi. Say, can you knock on Larry Jones's door and see if he's there?"

"Is this Troy or Diesel?"

"Uhhh . . . I'm calling for them."

"Larry told me to tell them that he's in the Onyx Club playing poker."

"What's your name?"

"Jinx. I'm Larry's old lady."

"Where'd you get a name like Jinx?"

"Larry gave it to me. I walked up when he had a full house—and he lost. He said I jinxed him. He didn't really mean it."

"Where's the Onyx?"

"Do you know downtown Sacramento?"

"Nope."

"Okay. I'll give you directions. You're coming from the Bay Area, right?"

"Yep."

She gave him directions, where to exit the freeway, which way to go, where to turn. It was simple enough and he mentally filed it. Diesel had pulled the car away from the pumps and was waiting behind the wheel. As they returned to the traffic flow, Troy started to explain. Diesel knew the whereabouts of the Onyx Club. A moment later, the big man slammed the heel of his hand on the steering wheel. "He's got another girlfriend. I hope to fuck she doesn't have a kid."

"She sounds like a baby herself."

What they knew stifled conversation during the rest of the drive.

When they spotted the Onyx and looked for a place to park, Troy said, "Be cool when you see him. Don't bad-vibe him."

"I'll be cool. I don't want to stir up paranoia toward me. That would make me paranoid. And two of us paranoid . . ."

The Onyx had a long bar and, ten feet away, a brass pipe rail separated the gaming area, half a dozen tables featuring various kinds of poker games: Seven-Card Stud, Lowball, Texas Hold 'Em, Pai Gow. Only two were in action, both against the far wall.

The bar area was dim, but the lights were bright over the poker tables. The light flashed on the shiny backs of the playing cards as they slid across the green velvet. The game had six players, Mad Dog among them. A mediocre card player, like most poor gamblers he thought he was great—and when he lost, he thought luck was against him. For the moment the cards confirmed his delusion. He was having a rush of luck. The game was Seven-Card Stud, and he could do no wrong. Three times he and another player had a flush, and each time his was the best flush. Twice he had two pair against a straight, and twice he made the full house on the last card. He'd been too hot to quit even to meet Troy and Diesel, so he had phoned Jinx and left the message.

He had won another small pot and was stacking his chips when he looked up and saw Troy watching him. Mad Dog grinned and saluted. Troy nodded, face impassive. It was enough to trigger anxiety in Mad Dog. He began picking up his chips. "That's it for me, boys."

When they were underway in the car, Troy asked: "How come you told that chick my name?"

"You mean Jinx. Did I give her your name?"

"She asked if I was Troy or Diesel."

"Oh, shit," Diesel said.

"How long would it take to identify us if she told the cops 'Diesel' and 'Troy'? They'd be showing her our mug shots in about an hour."

Mad Dog's instinct was to deny and defend, but this time he knew better, so he apologized. "I'm sorry, brother. I wasn't thinking."

"Yeah . . . okay. Just remember this. Nobody should even want to know anything they don't have to know. I know I don't."

"I know what you mean," Diesel said. "I was on fish row in Vacaville when I went to the joint. There was four or five dudes that knew each other—Gary Jackson, Danny Trejo, Bulldog, and Red Howard. Red was cuttin' the bars to his cell. He told us, just these four or five dudes. Somebody ratted him off and they busted him. I felt fuckin' terrible, and Gary Jackson told me the same thing. We wished we didn't know, so it couldn't even cross Red's mind that it might've been one of us."

"Did you find out who it was?" Mad Dog asked.

"Yeah, it was the dude that got him the hacksaw blade. But after that, when somebody started to tell me something, if it didn't concern me, I don't wanna hear it. So if anything goes wrong, there's no question about my good name."

"I know how it goes," Troy said.

"I'll watch myself," Mad Dog said.

"I know you will. Are you ready to roll?"

"I'm packed . . . but my fuckin' car's in the garage. It won't be ready until tomorrow."

"Is that the same car you had in Portland?" Diesel asked.

"Yeah, the old GTO. It's a classic, man."

"It would be better if it was a classic that would run."

"It'll run," Mad Dog said in a flat tone of challenge—and Troy felt the tension between his confederates.

"We're gonna make enough dough so you can buy a Jaguar if you want it."

92

"Hell, no," Diesel said. "They're in the garage more'n that old GTO."

"You get the car back tomorrow?" Troy asked.

"So they told me."

"What's wrong with it?"

"A radiator hose."

"Oh, yeah, that'll be done tomorrow," Diesel said.

"We could check into a motel and wait," Troy said. "Or we can drive tonight and you come when you get the car. That way I can see Greco tomorrow. How's that sound?"

Mad Dog nodded.

"Sounds like the best move to me," Diesel concurred.

"How'll I find you down there?" Mad Dog said. "Make it easy, 'cause I get fuckin' lost in L.A."

"We'll be in the Roosevelt Hotel on Hollywood Boulevard," Troy said. "Under the name Al Leon Klein."

"Al Leon Klein. I'll just think of Jimmy Klein. Whatever happened to that dude?"

"He snitched on too many people," Diesel said. "The Mexican mafia's got a contract out on his ass."

"Is that right?" Mad Dog asked. "He turned snitch."

"Yeah," Troy said. "He's a con man down to his core. The kind of dude that thinks everybody's a sucker or a mark. It's easy to rationalize and say, 'Let that mooch go to jail.' That's what he did."

"Jimmy Klein . . . a rat . . . Damn . . . They guy had a helluva personality," Mad Dog said.

"That he does . . . but he's still a rat," Diesel said. "You wanna go back to the Onyx or what?"

"Uh-uh. Take me to the pad. I'll tell you the way."

Ten minutes later they pulled up outside a decaying two-story apartment building. When Mad Dog was getting out, the front door opened and Jinx came out. She had the face of a child and the body of a woman. It was impossible to avoid an introduction: "Carl, Troy, meet Jinx, my old lady."

"Hi, guys. I've heard a lot about you."

Diesel was behind the wheel. "I'd like to hear about it some time," he said, "but we are running late and gotta hurry."

He gave the girl a quick smile and Mad Dog a half salute and pulled into traffic. Ten minutes later, the Mustang GT convertible turned southbound on U.S. 99, heading toward L.A., four hundred miles away. Once upon a time, U.S. 99 had been the main inland route north and south through the San Joaquin Valley, and although its number-one position had been taken over by Interstate 5, it still carried lots of traffic. They passed through small farm towns and truck stops. Sometimes for miles the world was black beyond the strip of highway, but the smell of growing things conveyed the richness of the earth.

Headlights illuminated signs. Bakersfield, 100 miles, Los Angeles, 220. Troy looked out at the night and Diesel watched the endless line of broken white unfold before the lights.

"Radio?" Diesel asked.

"Sure."

In the Central Valley, all the radio would pick up was a country station and another with twenty-four-hour news. "Which one?" Diesel asked.

"Let's listen to the news," Troy said. Although he had read voraciously in San Quentin, the day-to-day news held little interest for him. What does a convict in the belly of the Beast care for a flood in Tennessee, or a hurricane in New Orleans, or how the dollar fluctuates in currency exchanges? It might be of academic interest, like Pompeii in 79 A.D., but true concerns were more primal: If the race war breaks out again, I gotta walk between those honkies on the tier to get to my cell. For many in prison the world's horizons stopped at the prison wall. The only thing they wanted to hear from out there were baseball scores, horse race results, and what the Vegas point spreads were for the weekend games.

Troy was less indifferent than that extreme, but time had added to the natural insulation, so he had paid little attention—until they said he was going free, whereupon his mind suddenly hungered for knowledge of all that was happening in the world that he would enter once more.

". . . for NAFTA creates strange bedfellows. The spokesmen for extreme right and extreme left both decry free trade with Mexico,

94

and billionaire dilettante Ross Perot says the sucking sound we hear is jobs going south of the border . . ."

"You pay attention to that political bullshit?" Diesel asked.

"Yeah, sometimes."

"Most of the time I don't know who the fuck to root for. They all say all kinds of shit. They lie! Goddamn, they lie!"

"Yeah," Troy agreed. "Sometimes they lie when the truth would be as good."

"You know what, man, I think I'd rather be a thief than a politician. That way at least I know what I am. Some of them got identity problems."

"No bullshit about that," Troy agreed, and to himself he added that so many men are hypocrites without even realizing what they are. He put hypocrisy among the most contemptible of vices.

"I'm gettin' tired," Diesel said when they reached the outskirts of Bakersfield. Downtown L.A. was less than two hours away, and L.A.'s northern boundaries in the desert were half that far. You could drive through L.A. and take all day if you stayed off the freeway.

"Sure, man, lemme push this sucker."

"Watch out for the highway patrol on the Ridge Route. They stay up there a lot."

On the side of the highway, Diesel stretched out on the back seat and Troy took the wheel. The night was warm and they left the top down. As the car began to climb the grade through the mountains with the San Fernando Valley on the other side, Troy looked up at the canopy of night filled with stars, his body full up with the glow of amphetamine high, and he felt wonderful. His thoughts followed the joy of his body. He thought about his plan to specialize in ripping off pimps, bookies, wannabe gangsters, and drug connections. The victims would be enraged. They would want to kill him— but how would they know who he was, or how to find him if they did learn his name. Besides, all of them could bleed, too, and he certainly wasn't afraid of them. He might be afraid of the police and of going back to prison, but he didn't give a shit about an illiterate Compton dope king or all the crippled niggers in the world. They were predatory, sure enough, but he was the predator they had never imagined, coming suddenly from nowhere. Afterward, they would never imagine the truth . . . It made him laugh as he thought about it. If Compton aroused no fear, he was almost licking his chops as he thought about the soft white boys pushing keys on the Westside or with the Pacific sloshing in the background. He would outthink the baaadass niggers, and outtough the white boys. The danger was that one might have a corrupt cop as an ally, which might become risky. Ah well, nothing worthwhile in life was without risk. What had Helen Keller said? "Life was a dangerous adventure—or nothing . . . ?"

Robbing drug dealers had other advantages, not the least of which was the amount of the possible score. It was very possible that they could take off a million-dollar drug score. It was most unlikely that they could steal a million dollars in cash from a bank, or even an armored car. Even if that were to happen, there would be legions of FBI agents assigned to the case. The other ways to rip off big scores, diamonds and computer chips, had their own problems. Both were easy to sell, but the knockdown on the price was itself robbery. He'd taken a jewelry store and the papers proclaimed 1.3 million was the estimated loss. That was 1.3 retail. Wholesale was half of that, six hundred and fifty grand. The standard price for stolen goods is one third wholesale, two hundred grand and some change. Split three ways, his end came to near seventy thousand dollars. Not bad for ten minutes in a jeweler's, but terrible if he went to prison for ten years. Ten, shit, twenty-five. He was prime third strike. He had a better idea for crime than fancy jewelers or armored cars. He also had an alliance with one of L.A.'s best drug lawyers, and the lawyer would send word about the who, what, and where of big drug dealers. Unlike diamonds, heroin and cocaine depreciated very little when they were stolen property.

When he piled it all on the scales of decision, he preferred to risk death than go back to prison. Maybe he would win the game, take the big score, and spend the rest of his life on a sunny beach in a faraway place, play Gauguin or Rimbaud. He realized that at thirty-eight he was worn in many ways. He had burned the candle as if it were a blowtorch. He had been distorted by his experiences, so although he spoke the common language, he lacked some common traits. One of them was fear; his threshold for fear was many times higher than average. Around him, all he felt was fear—fear of violence, fear of censure, fear of rejection, of disapproval, of poverty, of everything. But he who survives a decade in San Quentin can attain a stoicism beyond fear. He'd taken blows that drive men to madness, suicide, or Jesus Christ. It had made him hard. He did fear death, or at least the dying part. Afterward was easy. Indeed, at some point, death was sure escape from pain. But if he could salvage a few years of peaceful solitude, maybe even find a sweet-natured brown-skinned girl to warm his feet, it was worth sitting down in the game of crime for the last time. "Deal the cards," he muttered to God. He would play whatever came off the deck. It was two decades too late to quit the game now.

It was the darkness before the dawn when the Mustang came off the Ridge Route onto the L.A. freeway system. Diesel sat slack-jawed and bleary-eyed beside him. The usual torrent of vehicles was a trickle, a handful of automobiles and a greater number of giant trucks timing themselves to arrive early in the morning. When he had gone to prison, L.A.'s vast sprawl ended at the north end of the San Fernando Valley. A few outposts of civilization, Magic Mountain among them, were in the desert beyond the rim around the valley. Now that was the Santa Clarita Valley, and it covered the desert with tract homes, Arco gas stations, and Denny's coffee shops. The sight astounded him.

As they whizzed along the fast lane, the terrain became more familiar. Troy felt excitement in his gut. He was coming home. Off to the left he could see the cross atop the mausoleum in Forest Lawn where movie star cadavers were entombed. Griffith Park bordered the freeway. It was ten times the size of Manhattan's Central Park. As a boy, Troy had rented saddle horses to ride the myriad bridle trails of Griffith Park. As a man, the body of a friend had been found with a bullet in his head on a park road. The murder remained unsolved. A sign read GENE AUTRY'S WESTERN HERITAGE MUSEUM, RIGHT LANE. That was something new. Then another sign stirred the emotions of memory: DODGER STADIUM, 1 MILE.

Interstate 5 angled left, cutting through East L.A. Troy held to the right, up a slope onto the inbound Pasadena Freeway. It sliced through the hills of Elysian Park, home of the Police Academy, and when it came out of the hills it looked at the downtown L.A. skyline two miles away. What Troy saw was totally different from his memory. All his life the twenty-five-story City Hall had risen high above the low L.A. skyline. Now it was nearly hidden amid a forest of tall skyscrapers, nearly all built while he was gone. Had his city changed as much as the skyline?

At 4th Street, they got off the freeway. The Westin Bonaventure was near the bottom of the ramp. Despite the hour, the Mexican doorman and bellhops pounced on their meager luggage and were grateful for the tip.

When they were in the elevator, Diesel closed his eyes and leaned against the wall, and as soon as the room door was open, he fell out on the bed and started to snore. It reminded Troy of a little boy. He, too, wanted to sleep, but he had things to do first. He had no direct phone number for Greco, but he knew where to leave messages. He called the number Greco had given him. After two rings, "Sherry's lounge," a voice answered. "Alex the Greek told me to call here." "He did, did he?" "Yeah. Let me leave a number where he can reach me." "Sure. I don't know when I'll see him, but when I do . . ." "That's all I can ask. I'm at the Bonaventure, room eight-seventeen."

After the phone call, Troy went to sleep. Two hours later the phone rang. He rolled over and picked it up. "If this is a goddamned Greek fascist—"

"Hey . . . a *liberal* Greek fascist . . . When'd you raise, fool?"

"When yo' mama lemme out, sucker."

"Your mama's my mama. Wanna talk about her?"

They both laughed. "Hey, man, good to hear your voice," Greco said. "I was wonderin' if you were ever gettin' out."

"How're you doin'?" Troy asked.

"Chicken today, feathers tomorrow. Fuckin' lawyers get all the money."

"I heard they busted you."

98

"It won't stick. The search was so bad they can't even lie out of it. Of course, they overrated me again—two hundred grand bail. Plus the fuckin' lawyer already got a chunk. The lawyer and the bondsmen are pimping me. Ha, ha, ha . . . You're at the Bonaventure, huh?"

"Me and Big Diesel."

"You got that crazy motherfucker with you, huh? He's a big old tough guy."

"Where are you? When're we gonna get together?"

"I got some business 'til maybe noon. You gonna be there?"

"I'll be in and out—but I won't be gone more'n half an hour at a time."

"Do you need a little dough?"

"If the lawyer left you anything."

"I always got a little money for my ace. I got a good one for you."

"Oh, yeah."

"Uh-huh. I'll run it by you when I see you. You'll be around."

"Yeah." To himself, Troy added that he wouldn't hold his breath waiting for Alex Aris, aka Greco. Alex was notorious for being late. Once the police had a motel staked out, waiting for Alex to arrive. He was so late the cops gave up and closed the trap on those who waited. Alex drove up as the bust was going down. Instead of turning in, he kept going. The event had not added to his punctuality.

Troy and Diesel slept till noon, ordered breakfast from room service, and showered and shaved, all the while waiting for Alex Aris to call. Troy wanted to go out. "I gotta look at my city," he said. "I haven't seen it in a long time."

"What about the call?"

"He'll be here when he gets here. I don't wait for him."

"He's not gonna be hot if you're gone?"

"Hell, no! How the fuck can he be indignant?" Troy called the hotel switchboard. "Tell anyone who calls that we'll be back about six-thirty."

Troy and Diesel rode the elevator in the glass tube outside the building from the sunlight down to the shadowed canyons below. Figueroa's sidewalks teemed with business-suited men and tailored women. It was a different street than he remembered. It seemed that every building had risen during his absence—thirty, forty, fifty floors high, and as beautiful as any skyscrapers he'd ever seen, even if many of their names were Japanese. He'd read that half the downtown office buildings were owned by Japanese companies. That didn't bother him; nobody was going to move the buildings across the Pacific.

"Which way we goin'?" Diesel asked.

"Turn left. We'll go over to Broadway."

Broadway was several long blocks to the east. When Troy was a child, it had been L.A.'s main street. Back then, yellow streetcars ran down the middle. Sometimes several yellow streetcars backed up at the intersections, loading and unloading. The red streetcars of Pacific Electric ran to the outlying areas. Troy had read that General Motors, Firestone, and others got control of the streetcar companies to deliberately liquidate them so they could sell tires and buses to the public. What was more immoral, that or robbing drug dealers?

"You know something, Big D, a dude can justify just about anything to himself . . . and that's all that really matters, isn't it? I don't think anybody does evil in their own mind."

"Don't ask me, brother. I don't think about shit like that. I think about makin' some money. I mean, there's things I won't do, but they get fewer and fewer when the money gets bigger and bigger."

Troy laughed and clapped his buddy on the back. It made Diesel feel good. What Troy thought of him was more important than what anybody else thought.

As they crossed 7th and Olive, Troy remembered the furrier who had once been on the corner. One rainy night when he was a teenager, he'd tossed a cinder block through the display window. Amidst howling alarms he had reached inside with a broomhandle and pulled a mink coat through the window. The furrier was long gone, and any business that had merchandise of value now had steel shutters and folding steel gates.

Each block they walked had fewer business suits and more signs in Spanish. Every corner had a panhandler, mostly unkempt black men extending Styrofoam cups, with an occasional white guy mixed in for leavening. It was something new to Troy. When he had gone away it hadn't been like this. A mile to the east were the rescue missions for homeless men. At that time those who availed themselves of their services seldom ventured very far, and certainly not toward the office buildings to the west. A bleary-eyed black man sat in a doorway with a dog at his feet. Troy felt his pockets and turned to Diesel. "Gimme some ones."

"I only got a five."

"Gimme that."

As they went by, Troy handed the five to the black man with the dog. "God bless you, man," was his reward.

"The way I figure it," Troy told Diesel, "if a homeless fool can look after a dog, I gotta do something for him. Besides that," he grinned as he thought of it, "it might give me some good karma." He didn't really believe it—that fate made covenants—but why make the odds worse?

Ahead of them, Troy saw the signs: DIAMONDS AND GOLD, BOUGHT AND SOLD. It was the West Coast diamond mart, jewelry stores one after another, each one glittering with precious jewels and gold. Many had armed security guards lounging in the doorways. That was new, but at least it wasn't as bad as New York City, where shops along Fifth and Madison Avenues kept their doors locked and let people in only after looking them over. They'd been that way on his last visit fifteen years ago. From what he read in *Newsweek*, things had not improved.

"You got one of these, didn't you?" Diesel said.

"Not down here. On Wilshire Boulevard. It's gone now."

"You got a bundle, didn't you?"

"Not when it got counted down."

They reached Broadway and turned north toward the civic center half a dozen blocks away. Troy had walked this street since he was a child. Between 3rd and 9th Streets, Broadway once had a dozen movie theaters, not to mention the Paramount on 6th and the Warner's Downtown at 7th and Hill. Some weekends he would come here, walk along until a movie poster caught his fancy. Now Troy looked at the theaters, or where they had been, and remembered what movie he had seen in this one or that one. Only three still showed movies; others were flea marts or churches. Christian preaching in Spanish had spared the Million Dollar, one of L.A.'s first great movie palaces. Gone, too, was the original Broadway Department Store at 4th Street, but its offspring formed a chain throughout California. Likewise into history had gone the original May Company and Eastern-Columbia. What a pretty green Deco building had housed it.

The great shopping street was as busy as ever, but large spaces had been converted into flea marts, and smaller places into open-fronted stalls hawking cut-rate merchandise. Mexicans had always been part of any L.A. mosaic. All of the signs were in Spanish, as was the music coming from the open doors. "Damn, homeboy," said Diesel, "is this L.A. or T.J.?" He meant Tijuana. "It don't look like Beach Boys country to me."

Troy laughed at his cynicism. Southern California had once been close to paradise; now it seemed to be an outpost of the Third World—not because of skin color, but through its illiteracy, poverty, and class division. The ability to assimilate into the middle class had been overrun. At 4th and Broadway, they stopped to look west. A block away was a low hill. Once upon a time, L.A.'s famous Angel's Flight, a funicular railway, ran from Hill Street to what had once been Victorian mansions on top, although by his youth they were rooming houses. Now Angel's Flight was gone, as were the rooming houses, replaced by salmon and silver glass and aluminum shining in the hot sun of Southern California, somehow reminding Troy of the Emerald City in *The Wizard of Oz*. The buildings were even more imposing because they rose from atop a hillside; that made them reach even higher into the sky. The towers were symbols of greater wealth than ever before.

In contrast, beside them was the boarded-up bottom floor of the original Broadway Department Store, empty and gutted and life-less except for fat rats and an occasional derelict. In his youth the rich had a Cadillac and the poor drove a Ford. Now the rich were in limousines and the poor pushed market carts piled with recyclable Coca-Cola cans. "Fuck it," he muttered.

"What's up?" Diesel asked.

"Just muttering in my beer, bro." He draped an affectionate arm around Diesel. "Hey, man, do you know how fucked up the world is?"

"I like it that way. When it's all fucked up, that's when we fit in."

"No bullshit about that."

They walked toward the Civic Center, where suits and neckties were more common; then turned east on 2nd Street, and soon were again among the homeless poor; they overflowed the rescue missions and made condominiums from cardboard crates that they lined up on the sidewalk, usually outside parking lot fences or in an alley where nobody would bother them. Outside the rescue mission doors were long lines of black men. Troy saw nobody else in the line.

They passed a man selling loose cigarettes from atop an apple box covered with a towel, and on the next corner a Hispanic woman with dark Indian features sold cups of mangoes or cantaloupe slices for a dollar apiece.

"Check the alley," Diesel said as they passed the mouth of one. Troy looked. Three young black men were passing a crack pipe, which gives off a powerful odor, but it was hidden by one of the foulest stenches in the world—that of human beings. The city had no latrines open to the general public, and those in public buildings and Pershing Square were closed to the homeless, so the ragged men in ragged clothes pissed in alleys, creating a stink that made Troy turn away.

"Those suckers are sure bold," Diesel said, referring to the crack-smoking trio.

"I dunno. Would you go down there to bust them?"

Diesel laughed. "I dunno. Maybe not. I'd probably faint if I had to smell that shit."

"How come a dog's piss don't stink? And human piss stinks worse'n a cat's piss?"

"How the fuck am I supposed to know that? You're the one that reads the books."

"I don't know either . . . But it's something to think about."

"Let's think about making some money. Maybe we oughta get back to the hotel. What if the Greek shows up?"

They walked along Los Angeles, where, for several blocks, the shops specialized in men's wear. Store after store had suits and shirts and neckties.

"A dude could buy some nice rag around here."

"Yeah, if you know what you're doin'. It all looks nice in the window. It's after a couple cleanings that class shows."

"Kinda like life," Diesel said.

"Damn, bro', you got a streak of the philosopher."

"Hangin' around you does that to a fool." He laughed.

"Better turn here to get back to the hotel."

They turned the corner. Ahead of them was a wild-eyed young man in a sweatshirt cut off at one shoulder. His forearms were both tanned and grimy, while his upper arm was pale white. It was covered, as was his neck and cheek, with round sores that reminded Troy of ringworm. He held out a white Styrofoam cup, while from around his neck hung a sign: AIDS. The sores were cancer lesions.

Most of the passersby veered to pass at a distance, but a heavyset black woman stopped and unsnapped her purse. As Troy and Diesel went by, they could see she was handing him a dollar and a small Christian tract. ". . . Praise Jesus," was all they heard.

"You believe in God, man?" Troy asked Diesel.

"I don't wanna, but I do. You know, them nuns got my ass right from the start until I was about eight. They planted it so deep, I can't get it out no matter what."

"You're going to Hell, huh?"

"Yeah, I am."

"You believe that?"

"Of course I do. I know better, but believin' is deeper than knowin', right?"

"If you believe, you believe."

"I just hope Hell is way down the the line from now."

*   *   *

Back in the hotel room, the message light glowed on the phone. The switchboard said it was from "Larry." He was in town and would call them in the morning.

Troy would have gone out again, but Diesel's legs ached from their walk, so they decided to stay in the room and order *Dracula* on the hotel's cable service.

The vile creature was being driven from England when the room phone rang. It was Alex Aris. The Greco was coming up the Harbor Freeway. "You wanna eat?" he asked.

"I sure wanna talk," Troy said. "See what we got going."

"It's sweet, man. Where do you wanna meet?"

"What about the Pacific Dining Car? That's not far from the hotel. We could walk there."

"I wouldn't walk around there at night, not anymore."

"I've been walkin' around here all my life."

"Things change . . . and that area has really changed."

"What happened to all those old pensioners?"

"They're gone. Lemme tell you, that's the most violent area in L.A. All Central Americans . . . not Chicanos like we know. Say some fool is from Nicaragua. Every morning they walk outside the village and there's three or four bodies with their thumbs tied together and flies around the hole in their skull. When they see shit like that at five or six years old, an L.A. drive-by ain't shit to them. I know you can take care of yourself—but I wouldn't walk around there at night."

"Okay, you convinced me. How long 'fore you get there?"

"I'm passing Florence Avenue. Say twenty minutes."

"Okay, I'm getting ready now."

The Pacific Dining Car, on 6th Street a few blocks west of the Harbor Freeway, was an ancient landmark by L.A. standards, having begun in 1921 in a sidetracked railroad diner. Over the years it had grown and changed into one of L.A.'s great steakhouses. It was close enough to City Hall and downtown so that many stacked-cut deals were made in one of its several rooms. It thrived even as the surrounding neighborhood became a *colonia* of immigrant Central Americans with the highest crime rate in the city. The Pacific Dining

105

Car was an outpost of affluence amidst poverty. All of its customers arrived by automobile. The parking lot was fenced and secure, with parking attendants in red vests.

Troy gave over the car and took the stub. While getting out he did a quick mental inventory and decided there was nothing a parking lot attendant would see. Diesel had a nine on a clip under the dash, but the guy wasn't going to run his hand under there even if he did look in the glove compartment. Piz the Whiz had been working a parking lot in Vegas, and used the keys to open a trunk while the customer was gone. The trunk had three hundred and ten thousand in three cardboard boxes. Piz was going off duty in twenty minutes. He took the boxes with him when he went home— and never heard a word about it. He never asked, "What about the blue Cadillac? Did the guy just drive away?" Nobody ever complained, or asked a question, or acted as if it had happened. Somebody just swallowed the loss of three hundred grand without a sound of complaint. It was weird.

Troy remembered the story as he entered, where a maître d' waited by a reservations stand. "Aris," said Troy.

"Come this way."

The maître d' led him through several rooms to a rear room with two booths and two tables. Alex was in one booth that had been set up for two. When he saw Troy, he got up with a wide grin and the two men embraced. Their friendship went back two decades, and although there had been arguments, each knew the other was a friend to the core, something seldom experienced by men of the bourgeoisie. There were no façades between them, nor any need, for neither judged the other for anything; they were friends as only thieves can be.

"Hey, man, glad to see you, brother," Alex said. "They sure didn't coddle your ass, did they?"

"I'm not mad at 'em," Troy said. "It wasn't justice, but they knew what they were doin', 'cause I'm gonna rip somebody off."

"Siddown, man. Want a drink?"

Troy sat and looked around. The waiter was at hand instantly. "Gimme a coffee with some brandy," Troy said. The waiter was gone.

106

They eyed each other. Troy now saw changes that had gone unnoticed when Greco visited him. The changes had taken place in the four years since the California Supreme Court had reversed his conviction. They had ruled unanimously that the police could not break down his door to arrest him simply because he was on parole and therefore without civil rights. They still had to knock and announce their purpose under Section 844 of the Penal Code. The warrantless search was manifestly a violation of the Fourth Amendment. The judge knew it, but he also knew that if he ruled that way, he would have to exclude from evidence the six kilos of cocaine they had seized. With the cocaine excluded, the State had no case. The judge ruled against Greco while knowing it was contrary to law, but it was right on target with public opinion. If he'd excluded the evidence and dismissed the charges, he might well be voted off the bench in the next election. The case had some notoriety. He would send Alexander Aris to prison where he deserved to be. If it was done unlawfully, let a higher court reverse the conviction and cut him loose.

Troy was in prison when Greco arrived, and he was still there four years later when California's highest court said the search was illegal and remanded the case back to the trial court. Troy remembered what great shape the Greco had been in as he got on the L.A. County Sheriff's bus to go back to court.

Greco had aged since then. Troy hadn't seen him until the visit, but he had got word on the underworld grapevine that Greco was having a hard time getting over. He'd lost a sixty-kilo consignment when his runner got busted. A prison buddy had given up the stash to get out of jail on a drunk driving charge. It was just luck that Greco hadn't been on hand when the raid came. Close calls and disappointments had turned his hair prematurely gray. He'd once been classically handsome; he still looked distinguished, but life's hard miles were written in seams and creases on his tanned face.

Greco looked at Troy. "You're lookin' pretty good."

"Prison preserves a sucker. No booze, no drugs."

"Hey, this is me."

"Well, yeah, a little homebrew. Once in a while some drugs. But you can't maintain a habit in the penitentiary."

"Except for Vito. Remember?"

"Sure I remember that crazy, green-eyed motherfucker."

"He managed to get hooked in the joint. He had a run going before they locked him up."

"Man, that's a hard hustle if there ever was one."

"What do you hear about that Pelican Bay?"

"It's unbelievable. They inoculate 'em with hate. They're makin' monsters up there."

"That's what these fools want."

"They think they can stop crime by getting tough."

"I know. I can't believe the way they're building prisons. Then they fill 'em up with damn fools on nickel-and-dime drug cases. They make maniacs of 'em up there, and then turn 'em loose on the public. It's like they were growin' maniacs in hothouses."

"In a way you can't blame the squarejohns. They're scared of crime.

"Hey, man, me too," Alex said. "You know me, I don't commit no crimes with guns. No robberies or—"

"It's a bummer, too," Troy inserted," 'cause I'd sure rather have you with me than Mad Dog McCain."

"You got that guy with you?"

Troy nodded. "Yeah."

"Oh shit! Anyway, what I started to tell you. Much as I dislike guns, I pack a snub-nose thirty-eight sometimes when I'm gonna go into a bad area. I wouldn't do it then if the motherfuckers would just take the money. Them young niggers nowadays, they shoot anyway. It gives 'em prestige if they waste somebody. It don't matter who it is, even if it's an old lady; they still get respect for it. But fuck all that, how do you feel, brother? You ready to make a move?"

"I'm fine," Troy said. "I'll feel real good when I have some money."

"That's what I'm here for. Take this." From his inside breast pocket, Alex produced a narrow envelope swollen with $100 bills. "Five grand," he said. "I'll take it off the top when we cut up a score."

"That's a deal," Troy said, folding the envelope and putting it in a hip pocket. "What about these hijacks? Do I meet the lawyer settin' it up?"

"He don't wanna meet nobody. You can understand that."

108

"I'd do the same thing in his place. Run him down to me."

"He's the man in drug cases. They all get him. He knows more about search and seizure than anybody. He used to be a Deputy U.S. Attorney prosecutin' drug cases—but he was getting chump change and the defense lawyers were gettin' rich. He changed sides.

"He started making big money, so he bought a big house for his wife and kids. Then he got himself a hussy on the side, a little piece of young pastry he keeps in a condo in Century City. She's got him pussy-whipped, and she likes expensive stuff. He needs money that his wife won't know about . . . so he's ready to set up some clients for ripoffs."

"Do you think that's covered in his canon of ethics?"

"What?" Then Greco saw it was humorous and chuckled. "I dunno. It doesn't have to do with what he does in court."

"That's true."

"What he's got is all the shit he gets from the government on discovery motions . . . so he knows all that, plus he is in pretty tight, so some of 'em let things slip. There's some nigger down in Compton they call Moon Man. They used to call him Balloon Head, but now he's got too much dope, so they call him God. He's proud of bein' dumb. He tells the lawyer, "If you're so smart and I'm so dumb, Mr. Peckerwood, how come I got twenty, thirty million and you work for me?"

"Here's something else," Alex said, reaching under himself for a file folder. It had a Xerox of the complete DEA file on Tyrone Williams. "My man got it on a discovery motion."

Troy opened the folder. On the back of the cover was a mug photo of a round-faced young black man, head tilted, chin jutted out in angry challenge. He had bulbous eyes, a condition with a name that Troy knew but was unable to recall. It was also obvious why he was nicknamed Moon Man.

Flipping through the file, Troy got an impression rather than a clear picture—and what the impression conveyed was precisely what Troy anticipated. Prisons overflowed with young black men who had the same history, ghetto-born of a teenage mother, raised in the projects on welfare and food stamps, total failure at school, first arrest at nine, and often thereafter. He'd gone to reform school for throwing lighter fluid on a dog and setting it afire, a piece of information that made Troy loathe him more than if it had been a human being. He'd been released at eighteen, and in the four years since then had been arrested twice for murder without being prosecuted, and had been charged with possession of drugs for the purpose of distribution. The search warrant was flawed, the evidence was suppressed under the exclusionary rules, and the case was consequently dismissed.

"You need this file back?" he asked.

"No . . . but you flush the fucker when you get done lookin' it over. Here's some addresses. He's renovating an old mansion in the Lafayette Square area. You know where that's at?"

"Hey, man, nobody in the world knows L.A. like I do."

"He's got four cars and he has some three-hundred-pound fool he uses as a driver and bodyguard. He likes to use a new Fleetwood Brougham, but not when he's goin' into the ghetto. He doesn't keep anything at the Lafayette place. He probably keeps it at one of those other addresses. You're gonna have to find out which one."

Troy nodded. "Can you get us some police uniforms?"

"Yeah. I got a guy that works in a warehouse that rents costumes to the movies. I saw a whole rack of police uniforms."

"I'm gonna need three."

"Who else you got—besides that fuckin' maniac? I don't mind a guy bein' a little weird. What the fuck, that's why he's a criminal, because he's fucked up. But them paranoid dudes, they make me nervous. Keep him away from me."

"I can handle Mad Dog. He loves me."

"Yeah . . . well, didn't somebody real smart say that each man kills the thing he loves?"

"Don't worry . . . that guy's not gonna kill me . . . or even dream of it. But he'd sure kill anybody I told him to."

"I think he's unpredictable, like nitroglycerine."

"Big Diesel Carson from 'Frisco. You know him, don't you?"

"Not personally. I saw him fight some nigger in the joint. It was funny."

110

"I remember that . . . In the lower yard."

"Yeah. He lost his cool and started swinging like a madman. He ran out of gas and the nigger stopped him. Everybody fell out laughing."

"He don't talk about that. The guy he fought was a sissy, too, loved to suck dick."

"Oh yeah, that's right. They ribbed the shit out of Diesel over that."

"He wanted to stab the guy afterward. But he's got more sense now. He's been out of the joint for about three years, got an old lady and a baby."

"Man, that's one guy I wouldn't think would stay out three months. He never did before, did he?"

"No, he's state-raised. He got lucky this time, got in the Teamsters, and Jimmy the Face looked after him. He even got off parole."

"That's great. He's okay." Then Alex changed the subject: "You need any artillery? I know a guy with some full automatic M16s."

"Uh-uh. We're armed to the teeth. I like pump shotguns better anyway. One thing I could use is handcuffs."

"No problem. How many you want?"

"Half a dozen pair. I mean . . . if we're gonna be arrestin' drug dealers, we need handcuffs."

"You got 'em. Hey, you wouldn't want some credit cards, would you? Visa?"

"Uh-uh. I pass."

"They're good, man. No heat at all."

"I know. But I got priors, and these fools made credit cards the same as murder if you got a record. I might as well rip and tear as use finesse."

"You're gonna hold court in the street, huh?"

"I might as well, right? It's too late to quit, not unless I'm willing to be a cipher—and I can't do that."

"Look here," Alex said, "when you go down into the ghetto, watch yourself."

"I always watch myself."

"It's more dangerous than it used to be. Fuckin' punk kids are carrying nine-millimeter pistols. A nine is all they want."

111

"Where do they get the money? Good nines cost five, six hundred dollars. That's a whole welfare check."

Alex laughed. "Welfare! You sure are cold, bro'. They're not all on welfare."

"I know it. Still, where the fuck do kids get dough like that?"

"Crack and dust . . . angel dust. It's what makes 'em crazy, too. They don't have any sense of reality. Killin' somebody is what gets them respect . . . so they think."

Troy nodded acceptance of the warning. Alex Aris had walked the Big Yard at San Quentin. If he said the city's streets were more dangerous than before, Troy had to respect the admonition.

Alex looked at his watch. "I gotta hit it. Long ride down to Laguna."

Troy walked Greco to the parking lot. The attendant brought a new Jaguar convertible. Troy whistled. Alex winked. "The wages of sin," he said as he got in.

8

After studying the folder's contents and making some cryptic notes that nobody but himself would understand, Troy burned the folder, put the ashes in a shoebox, and dumped them on the Hollywood Freeway. A primary rule for successful criminality is to keep no records. Failure to follow that rule destroyed the Presidency of Richard M. Nixon. What the hell could he have been thinking when he recorded the conspiracy? Why didn't he destroy the tapes when the shit hit the fan?

Troy began his investigation of Tyrone Williams, aka Moon Man, formerly Balloon Head. Troy's scorn was partly envy. Moon Man Williams was twenty-two years old and had a gross income of an estimated one million dollars a month. Probably hyperbole, Troy decided; the police (and everyone else) inflated everything to either enrich themselves or add to their importance. Still, Moon Man had come up with $800,000 to successfully defend his last case. He'd delivered $500,000 cash in one day. It appeared that Moon Man was copping fifty kilos of cocaine at a time, and about forty of them were turned into rock. Apparently he had about twenty O.G.s and wannabes in his crew. Some sat on the dope, some made crack from coke, some made deals, and others delivered. It was hard to tell who was who from following. It was hard to loiter and watch in the ghetto. After dark, the only white faces belonged to the police.

Troy sat on various addresses at different times of day, trying to get a sense of what was happening. He also tailed Moon Man, falling in a block from his house and following him into the decaying

113

ghetto of South Central L.A. On the third day, Moon Man was going south on Vermont and suddenly turned into an alley. Troy started to turn into the same alley, but at the last moment straightened the wheel and kept going. He looked down the alley as he went by. Sure enough, the alley was long and straight. The other car, an old Pontiac, was stopped halfway as Moon Man looked to see if anyone was following.

The next time Troy followed the old Pontiac and watched it turn into the alley, he punched the gas to the next corner and went around the block. Sure enough, Moon Man and his bodyguard came out a minute later. After that it was easy. Moon Man led him to a neighborhood not in the files. Off the Santa Monica Freeway at Crenshaw, down to Adams, east to Budlong, and south again. Mean streets where dogs and boys ran wild. Graffiti defaced every flat surface and windows wore bars as often as glass. Every block had a liquor store with a group standing around outside the door. Homeless men with supermarket carts were abundant.

Moon Man's car turned into a driveway between a double row of court bungalows.

Troy drove past and looked in. Poverty. Poor black children running and yelling as they played kickball. At the rear was the Pontiac. The two men were getting out. Troy sensed that this was a stash pad. He punched the gas and took the next corner with a squeal of tires. Maybe he could sneak around and see something.

Ahead was an empty parking space at the curb. He pulled in and looked around before getting out. The neighborhood was seedy, with vacant lots, a corrugated metal building, a decrepit apartment building. The only person he saw was an old man with a dog on a rope. He never even glanced at Troy. As he got out, Troy was reassured by the pistol in the clip holster inside his waistband under his jacket. He had the badge, too. Once upon a time the combination of badge and pistol would control any situation. Still potent, they were no longer an absolute talisman. Greco had told the truth when he said the streets of L.A. had changed. Americans likened their country to those of Europe, but portions of L.A. were more like a Rio slum than anything across the Atlantic.

Troy went around the corner to the street parallel to where Moon Man had turned in. He looked at the roofs to the right; he wanted to get behind the court bungalows. He passed in front of tiny homes that had sold for $2,500, no down payment, when they were built long ago when L.A. housing was among the cheapest in the country.

He came to an unpaved alley with ruts from truck wheels. It ran beside the corrugated metal building behind the bungalow court. He turned in. Half-pulverized glass crunched underfoot. The stench of human piss assailed him, so he breathed through his mouth. Night was coming on and it was dark in the alley. He tripped over something that moved.

"Hey, mu'fucker," said a voice. "Watch where you be walkin'."

"Sorry, man," Troy said. He should have brought a flashlight. He was keyed up but calm. Afterward he reacted, but while things were in progress he was icy calm.

The alley turned and ran behind the corrugated building. A sagging board fence was on the other side. He could see the roofs of the court bungalows above it.

A dog barked, loud and angry, but it was a couple of yards away. Nobody would pay any attention unless it continued. How could he get through the fence? It looked as if it would crash if he tried to climb it.

Then he saw the missing boards. The ground said it was the way others had gotten past the fence. He squeezed through. The space between the fence and a bungalow wall had a little light from a neighbor's rear window. Voices . . . the sound of a TV.

At the corner of the bungalow, he kneeled and looked around with his face near the ground where he was less likely to be seen. He could see part of the car and children flashed across his line of vision. A curtain puffed from a broken window. From inside came the sound of James Brown, ". . . black and I'm proud . . . Unnh!"

"Glad for you, bro' James," Troy whispered. He could hear the excited voices of the playing children. "You're it! You're it!" one of them called. A game of hide-and-seek. What if one of them hid back here? If he was spotted, a prowling white man, Moon Man would think it was police and would never come here again. Troy was certain one of the bungalows was the stash pad—but which one?

Troy moved across the passage between the bungalows and went to the corner. A narrow space ran between its wall and an old wire fence half-covered with ivy. Troy moved along the wall. Trash was knee-high, sinking down as he stepped on it. He scraped the wall. The old paint would mark his clothes. Fuck it. He came to a barred window. It was dark. Ahead was another window with light coming through a drawn curtain and a windowshade. He ducked under the first window and moved to the next. He could not see inside, but he heard snatches of conversation, "motherfucker . . . niggah . . . and sixteen keys . . ." This was the stash pad, no doubt of it.

Time to leave. He squeezed back along the wall. He was less careful and his foot kicked a bottle and bounced it off the wall.

The house went silent.

Troy cursed silently and moved faster, trampling a cardboard box. Instead of going to the hole in the fence, he climbed it in the corner. It weaved and tottered without collapsing. He jumped down and made his way toward the street. A voice called, "You fuckin' kids stay outta here!" Troy laughed without sound, and kept going as the nearby dog barked in the background.

As he started the car, he began to bounce and rhythmically pop his fingers. "Awright awready. We gonna nail this nigger. Whee, baby, they gonna be mad. Well, they can scratch their ass and get glad." And he laughed at the anticipation.

9

Diesel studied himself in the mirror. He was wearing the uniform of the Los Angeles County Sheriff's Department, complete with sergeant's stripes. It was a big uniform, but Diesel's two hundred and fifty pounds bulged at the waist of the trim-cut shirt. He turned to Troy. "Whaddya think, brother?"

"You don't belong in *Gentlemen's Quarterly*, but they won't see anything but cop, believe me."

Diesel nodded. He felt weird in a police uniform, but if Troy thought it was cool, that was good enough for him.

Mad Dog came out of the bathroom. He, too, wore a deputy's uniform. "What about me?" he asked as he fastened the clip-on neck tie.

"Looks great," Troy affirmed.

"Yeah. I'm gonna enjoy arrestin' a nigger," Mad Dog said, punctuating the statement with a laugh.

Spread on the bed were handcuffs, surgical gloves, two cellular telephones, and the hand-held spotlight with the red cover fastened over it. A regular flasher for the car roof was what Troy wanted, but Alex was unable to get one right away, and such a bright light might summon one of the police helicopters that perpetually cruised over L.A.'s South Central ghetto. The pulsing blue light would be visible for miles from the sky.

Troy picked up one of the cellular phones. "Okay, I'm outta here. You guys move in about half an hour."

"Cool," Mad Dog said.

When Troy was gone, Diesel turned on "Monday Night Football," trying to relax. The first half was almost over and Dallas was on a drive. He became engrossed and paid no attention as Mad Dog brought a glass of water from the bathroom; then produced a dirty handkerchief wrapped around a disposable syringe and needle and a bent spoon with a burned bottom. He was unfolding the bindle of cocaine when Diesel looked over. Diesel stood up to look over Mad Dog's shoulder and make sure. "What the fuck are you doin'?" he asked.

"What the fuck does it look like? I'm slammin' some coke."

"Jesus Christ! What the fuck! Coke'll make you crazy, man. That's the last shit you wanna take on a caper."

"Hey, man, you do it your way, I'll do it my way. This shit makes me king of everything."

"You just think it does."

"That's good enough. Whatever it does, it's my motherfuckin' business, y'know what I mean, man?"

Diesel stifled the urge to backhand Mad Dog across the room. He knew he would have to kill the man if he did that—or else Mad Dog would kill him the moment his back was turned. "Do whatever you want, man—but don't fuck this caper up."

"I'll pull my end. You worry about yours."

Diesel nodded. He would have to talk to Troy about this maniac. Mad Dog returned to readying his fix.

Diesel looked back at the TV. Dallas had scored a touchdown that he had missed. It was halftime. He kept staring at the TV without seeing it. If he turned and looked at Mad Dog, he might lose his temper.

They didn't speak when they went out to the rented white Chevy. It looked like a police car. The license plate, taped over the real license plate, had been stolen from the long-term parking lot at LAX. Even with windbreakers over the police uniforms, they looked too much like cops to tail Moon Man. He would surely spot them before they were ready to move. Following him was Troy's job. They would wait watching a drive-in movie far down Vermont, ten minutes from where they expected to pull Moon Man to the curb. When Troy called on the cellular phone, they would move out and close in. He would tell them where to go. They already knew what to do when they got there.

Troy knew several locations where Moon Man might be. Because it was early evening when he set forth, he first cruised past the split-level ranch style in Baldwin Hills, one of the nicest black neighborhoods in all of America. The lights were on and the wife's Mark VII was in the driveway—but no Cadillac. The next stop was a pool-hall on Crenshaw where Moon Man sometimes went. As the Mustang went through the rear parking lot, a pair of young black men followed him with burning eyes. Whitey was unwelcome in this neighborhood. Troy grinned and waved as if he knew them; then watched in the mirror as they looked at each other and asked who he was.

Up Crenshaw, east on Florence, into the land of the California drive-by. The ubiquitous automobile made it feasible to carry an assault rifle out of sight on the floorboards. Any gathering of young men in enemy turf was fair game.

At Western Avenue, Troy turned south. Moon Man had once visited a storefront church with a red neon cross on the roof. He decided to check it because it was on the way to the cocaine house.

A block from the neon cross was a corner liquor store with a brightly lighted parking lot. He glanced over as he went by. The Cadillac was there, shining in the light, and Moon Man's bodyguard was approaching it with a bag cradled in his arm.

Was Moon Man in the car? He had to think so. He kept going, but he slowed considerably and kept his eyes on the rearview mirror. Headlights appeared, turned onto Western going the other way. He had to make a U-turn. Fuck the double line.

He hit the brakes and made the turn, grateful that Western was a wide street. At first he couldn't tell which taillights belonged to the Cadillac. He punched the gas and swerved between cars. A driver honked a protest that he ignored. Usually he was a cautious driver because he committed no small crimes—and why risk being pulled over for a traffic violation? Tonight he punched the gas and five liters of Ford V8 threw him back into the seat and hurtled the car forward.

He closed enough to pick out the quarry as its turn lights began to pulse and its brake lights flashed. Another five seconds and he would have missed it. He reached for the cellular phone. Time to get the "deputies" moving. He would guide them to a meeting point. It looked like it was going to work. Shit and Jesus and hurray for the white boys.

In the Cadillac, Moon Man had no sense of impending danger whatsoever. The car was clean except for the "nine" his driver carried—and he was paid to take the case if he was busted with it. It was only a misdemeanor in any case. Moon Man's worries were not about cops or ripoffs; they were about his jive-ass wife wantin' a divorce and money, too much goddamn money for anything she ever did to earn it. Bitch didn't do nothin' but lay around the scatter eatin' fuckin' sweets and givin' him a hard time: "Where ya goin', when're ya gonna be back?" She suspected he was messin' with that fly bitch Tylene . . . Oh, man, she was fine. His dick got hard as Chinese arithmetic as soon as he thought about her. She was a dumb bitch, but she sho' had nice trim . . . "Hmmm, mmm, mmmm," he muttered in wordless appreciation. Actually, a dude like him, with his game tight as he could be, he should change bitches as soon as they got a little worn.

Ahead the traffic light turned from green to yellow. The Caddy slowed to stop. Moon Man rode up front with the driver. He reached over to turn on the radio. What issued first was gangsta rap. He made a face and began to scan for something more mellow.

The car flooded with red light. Oh, shit! Heat!

He leaned forward and looked. A deputy sheriff was waving a flashlight at them. "Pull over," the deputy said, waving the flashlight to indicate.

The driver looked to Moon Man. It was a Caddy with a Northstar engine. It would fly. Should he hit the gas when the light turned green?

"It ain't nuthin," Moon Man said. "Just some redneck pigs wantin' to roust a nigger in a hog. We're clean, right?"

"Oh, yeah . . . just the piece."

"Pull over. Keep your hands in sight. They be scared, but they

120

be dangerous. Never give 'em a chance to waste a nigger. They got huntin' licenses for us." Moon Man had absolute belief in the truth of his words. It fit the facts he saw through the prism of his experiences.

The driver pulled across the intersection and angled to the curb on the other side. The white Chevy pulled in behind and turned off the red spotlight. Moon Man used the mirror to watch the deputies get out. One of them reminded him of a TV version of the fat-assed Irish cop. The other was smaller. They came up along each side of the Cadillac. Moon Man's heart raced, but he was confident it was a routine roust. White cops always wanted to know why a nigger was pushing a Cad, or a Jag, or any other expensive set of wheels. If it was a real bust, if they knew who he was, there would be DEA agents swarming over them.

The driver lowered the window. Diesel arrived, leaned down so he could look them over.

"What's the problem, boss?" Moon Man asked; he could play the game as well as any other chump. Niggers got themselves in trouble by huffin' and puffin' whenever the police pulled them over for a traffic ticket.

Diesel ignored the question. "Sir, do you have your driver's license?" he asked the driver.

The driver nodded and reached up to take the California operator's license from where it was clipped to the sun visor. He kept it there for precisely this situation.

Diesel looked the license over and handed it back. He looked at Moon Man. "You, sir, do you have identification?"

"Me. I don't need ID. Man, that's what the Supreme Court said last year. Said you didn't have to carry ID."

"Sir!" Diesel cut him off. "Can I see some ID?"

"I mean . . . what're you . . . Oh, shit," he finished in exasperation, angrily reaching for his wallet in his hip pocket. His hands were shaking as he fumbled through the wallet and took out the driver's license.

Mad Dog was on the sidewalk, watching the cars zoom back and forth. A few blacks were gathering to watch, like filings to a magnet.

Across the street and down the block, the Mustang was in shadows as Troy watched the scene. It was going great. All that could go wrong was for a police car to happen by. The whole world would blow up if that happened.

Diesel handed the driver's license to Mad Dog. "Check this through R and I," Diesel said. He'd been through it enough times in life to make it seem realistic.

Mad Dog took the card and went back to the white Chevy. As he stood by the open driver's door and feigned making a call, he was looking over the top of the car at the half score of African-Americans on the sidewalk. Most of them were young males, teenage to early twenties. A few were young females. All watched with silent hostility at the two white cops rousting the brothers in the nice ride. Mad Dog felt fear. Blacks always aroused more fear than whites or Mexicans— not fear that they could exploit, rather fear that made him dangerous as a cobra with flared hood. He eyed the spectators. Somebody called out, "Let the brother go!" But someone else said something else. Mad Dog didn't hear the words, but they must have had ghetto wit, for the crowd broke into laughter at whatever was said.

Mad Dog walked back to the car. It had all been planned. He motioned Diesel away from the car, as if to consult. "You see Troy across the street?" Diesel asked. "Yeah. Let's take him," Mad Dog said. "I'll cover the driver."

Diesel walked to the front passenger door and opened it. "Would you get out of the car, sir?"

"What? What for?"

"Would you step out, please?" His voice was harder.

Mad Dog was at the driver's window, standing so he was looking down over the driver's shoulder. In his hand, down by his leg, was a razor-sharp skin diver's knife. If the big man blinked wrong, Mad Dog would drive the knife into his neck.

Moon Man, anger and fear mixed into a tangle inside him, got out of the car. He knew he was going to jail, although he had no idea why.

"Face the car and put your hands behind your neck," Diesel said. Moon Man did so, and felt a sinking sensation as a hand bent

122

his arm down behind his back and fastened a hand-cuff; then the other hand. "Hey, man, can you tell me what this is?"

"The computer says you got outstanding traffic warrants."

"Ahh, man, that's bullshit, man."

"That's what the computer says."

Moon Man called to his driver. "Call my old lady and get down to the slam with some scratch and get my ass out."

The driver, all three hundred pounds, still sat with hands on the steering wheel. The illegal nine-millimeter under his arm felt big as a football. He nodded at the instruction, glad that he had not been pulled out and searched.

Diesel took Moon Man's arm at the elbow, as police had done to him a score or more times, and guided the drug kingpin to the Chevy, where Mad Dog waited with the rear door open.

"Hey, ol' rich nigger!" called one of the spectators, "you shoulda done paid them tickets." The others laughed.

Diesel guided Moon Man's head down enough to clear the roof. Diesel was glad the crowd was led by a comedian rather than an agitator.

Moon Man was in the car. Diesel slammed the door. Mad Dog was already behind the wheel. Diesel got in and nodded.

The white Chevy started moving. Diesel and Mad Dog forgot their mutual antipathy, at least for now. Act one was over. They had the sucker in hand. Now to break him down and rip him off.

Looking out the back window, Moon Man frowned. "Hey, man, where we goin'? This ain' no way to the substation."

"Shaddup," Mad Dog said.

"What the fuck, man. I can ask where I'm goin', can't I?"

"No."

"Damn!"

"Shaddup."

Moon Man, leaning to the side as required by the handcuffs behind his back, began nodding his head in a gesture of anger. What kinda shit was this?

The Chevy followed the Mustang. Troy made sure he kept them

close. Once he had to pass through a traffic light where they were stopped for the red. He waited on the other side. A black-and-white went by the other way. Would they notice the Sheriff's Department uniforms?

The light changed. The white Chevy and the black-and-white passed each other. The Chevy went by Troy. He was watching the other car. It kept going. A little luck was always good. Troy took off and passed the white car.

When the cars began turning onto side streets, Moon Man sensed that this was more than a roust for traffic warrants. Not for a second did he doubt that they were deputy sheriffs. His imagination ran toward police hit squads. The idea of a hardcore white robbery crew never crossed his mind. He might have wondered about two niggers in uniforms, but not a pair of honkies.

Troy parked in a factory lot. It had a dozen cars in enough spaces for fifty. It was near enough to the Harbor Freeway so that the traffic's hum drowned out sound. The few nearby buildings were small shops and factories. Troy got out of the Mustang and walked back to the Chevy. He opened the back door. "Move over," he said to Moon Man, raising the pistol and extending his arm so the muzzle was a few inches from Moon Man's eyeball.

Moon Man moved. He jumped to the side and ducked his head. "Hey, man!" It was shrill.

In the front seat, Mad Dog laughed. "Hey, man," he mocked in a shrill voice. "All the bitch came out in this nigger."

"Hey, man, what's goin' on, man?"

"Shaddup. I'll tell you in a minute," Troy said, slamming the door. "Roll on," he said to Mad Dog. Diesel looked back over the seat. His grinning teeth shone in the streetlight they passed beneath.

As Mad Dog headed for the court bungalows, Troy played on the fear he heard. "Look here, man, you can live through this."

"You ain't even gotta snitch on nobody," Mad Dog said.

"We're goin' to get that stash of yours. We're gonna take you to the door, and you're gonna tell the dude you got inside to open up. If he opens up, cool. If not, I'm gonna blow your backbone outta your belly. Y'know what I mean, man?"

124

"Hey, man, I dunno—"

Before he could finish the denial, Troy backhanded him across the nose with the muzzle of the pistol. The crunch of broken nose bone was audible, as was Moon Man's gasp of pain. A broken nose hurts. "Ohh, man. Damn!" He held his head down. The blood ran down and dripped from his chin.

"You gonna do what I say, man. Right?"

"Yeah, man, yeah. Hey, I'm gettin' fuckin' blood all over my rag, man."

"You can buy some more tomorrow."

Moon Man said nothing, but he liked what he heard. It meant the head man expected him to be alive tomorrow.

"Look here," Troy said as they reached the neighborhood. "You can get more money and more coke. But you can't get more'n one life. So don't think you can fake me out. I will kill you. All three of us will kill you. Quick! You got it?"

"Yeah. I got it."

"Good."

The Chevy turned onto the ghetto street. The headlights flashed over the torn sofa abandoned at the curb, over the trash banked in the gutter, for the Sanitation Department seldom sent street sweepers down here. A wind had risen to drive the usual street loiterers indoors. That was good.

"On the right, those bungalows."

Mad Dog slowed and made the turn onto the driveway running between the bungalows. It had once been black-topped, but that had worn through in spots, so the car and headlights bounced as it moved ahead. Children scattered to the side and disappeared beside the bungalows.

Mad Dog stopped outside the bungalow. All three jumped out, Mad Dog with the pump .12 gauge, Diesel with a MAC 10 down low.

Troy reached back and pulled Moon Man from the car. It took too long for a handcuffed man to climb out unaided. Troy guided him to the door. Diesel and Mad Dog covered his rear, but they saw nothing except the kids peeking around a corner.

Troy banged on the door. "Tell him to open up," he said.

"Deuce Man," said Moon Man. "Open the door."

No answer.

"Tell him that we ain' gonna bust him if he opens up."

"He ain't gonna believe that."

"Tell him anyway."

"Hey, Deuce, these policemen say they ain't gonna bust you."

From inside came a voice: "What the fuck you bring 'em here for, man?"

"I ain' brung the motherfuckers. They done knew."

"Hey, Deuce," Troy called.

"Yeah."

"We're gonna let you go if you don't make us blow a hole in the door."

Behind him, Diesel and Mad Dog watched bungalow doors open. Faces peered out. The crowd was growing in numbers and hostility. "Hey, pig! Let the brother go!" someone yelled. Other voices took it up: "Let him go! Let him go!"

"He better open up," Troy said, cocking the pistol's hammer and putting the muzzle behind Moon Man's head.

"For God's sake, motherfucker! Open the door," Moon Man screamed.

"Okay, Moon! This better not be no bullshit!"

The lock clicked, the door opened. Troy shoved in, pulling Moon Man with him. Deuce stood there, a young African-American in baggy clothes with gold chains around his neck. He had his hands up. Troy grabbed him and shoved him out the door. "Hit it, man. You got lucky."

Deuce ran down the steps past the two uniformed deputies and disappeared into the night. It was great to be free. It was almost a miracle. His passage through the swiftly growing crowd seemed to galvanize it. Someone picked up a chunk of cement and hurled it at the bungalow. It crashed loud against a wall, making Troy jump.

"Get the car!" someone yelled. "Burn the motherfucker."

"Stop 'em," Troy said.

"Right," Mad Dog said, turning back toward the door with the shotgun.

"Don't kill nobody unless you have to," Troy said, sorry that he had to make the admonishment.

Mad Dog stepped onto the porch. Near the car, some teenage youths in baggy gang attire were trying to pull up a two-by-four from a bungalow porch rail. "Freeze on that!" Mad Dog yelled, and racked the pump on the shotgun. Only the remonstrance by Troy kept him from blasting them. At twenty feet he would have torn all of them apart with the double-ought buckshot. The unique sound of a shotgun being jacked silenced them. They looked at him, eyes white, and faded back into the darkness. "Gonna kill you, fuckin' pig!" a voice yelled from out of sight.

Inside the house, Moon Man said, "You dudes are in trouble."

Diesel stepped forward and smashed a fist into his face. It was a straight right-hand punch from a trained heavyweight prize-fighter. It cracked Moon Man's jaw and dropped him straight down onto his knees. "If we're in trouble, you're dead, nigger!"

"Give it up," Troy said. "Quick."

Mad Dog backed through the front door. "Hurry up."

"Where is it?" Troy asked.

"The bathroom."

A rock came through the window. The house was pelted with missiles. "Lemme waste a couple," Mad Dog said.

Troy shook his head. He held Moon Man's handcuffs in one hand and kept the pistol muzzle against his head. The drug dealer led them to the bathroom. It was tiny, and the stall shower door had a crack sealed with masking tape.

Moon Man indicated some built-in shelves. "Lift them all together."

Diesel pushed in, went to the shelves, and lifted. Jars and bottles crashed on the floor as the whole built-in section came up and out, exposing a niche the size of a large suitcase. It was piled high with polyurethane bags of white powder. They looked like two-pound bags of white flour.

Diesel reached into his hip pocket and pulled out a folded

shopping bag. He began filling it with the bags of powder. It quickly bulged. More bags remained.

Holding Moon Man in the doorway and watching Mad Dog at the front door and Diesel behind him, Troy said, "Grab a pillowcase from the bedroom."

"Right." Diesel ran to the bedroom and ran back with the pillow, pulling off the pillowcase as he returned.

"Where's the money?" Troy asked.

"Ain' . . . money," Moon Man said; it was hard to speak with the fractured jaw.

"Let's kill this lyin' fuck," Diesel said as he finished sacking up the cocaine. It was thirty kilos. The Greco had promised them twelve grand a kilo for all they got. It was too much for him to figure in the confusing circumstances, but it was a lot of money, any way it was counted. He squeezed out with the bags.

"You gonna jes hafta kill this niggah, 'cause there ain' no motherfuckin' money here, man!"

Was it true? Most dealers kept money separate from the drug stash. They'd ripped three hundred grand in cocaine. Why be greedy?

While he was thinking, six inches from his face a piece of plaster exploded, splattering pieces against his cheek.

He started and turned and saw the hole. A bullet had come through the outer wall and the kitchen wall and just missed his head. His heart jumped and missed a beat, but after that he was in control.

Moon Man had ducked his head. "Motherfucker!" was all he could say.

Mad Dog put his head into the kitchen. "Some asshole got a gun out there."

"No shit?" Troy said. Then he laughed and Mad Dog laughed, too.

Another shot tore through the front room. It wasn't even slowed down by the bungalow's outer wall.

"Put the light out," Troy yelled to Diesel, who was crouched behind a stuffed chair. Even a tough guy respected wild gunfire. He reached out and pulled the plug from the wall. The bungalow's front room went dark.

Another shot tore through the bungalow. Troy thought it must be a bolt-action rifle. Otherwise whoever it was would simply unload a volley of shots. Even a six-shooter fired faster than the guy outside.

It was time to leave. He released Moon Man and headed for the door. "Let's go," he said, touching Diesel on the shoulder and picking up the pillowcase. He went to the front door and pulled it open while staying back in the shadows.

When he saw the next muzzle flash, he started pulling the trigger at two-second intervals, aiming at the flash. He simultanously walked forward, out the door. Diesel came next, carrying the other bag while shooting the MAC 10 into the bungalows, but at a high angle unlikely to hit anyone. Mad Dog danced along at the rear, whirling this way and that with the shotgun. He would kill anything that moved—but he saw nobody. The firepower had driven them to cover.

Troy opened the driver's door and slid in behind the wheel. The key was waiting. He turned it as the others piled into the back. The engine roared. Troy rammed the shift into reverse and hit the gas. The tires spit gravel as the car leaped backward, weaving back and forth en route to the street, running over a trash can and knocking down a narrow fence post before Troy spun the steering wheel and turned into the street.

As he threw it into first gear and tromped on the gas, figures appeared next to a bungalow and began hurling rocks. Some banged harmlessly against metal; one cracked a side window.

Tires burned rubber and spit up gravel as the car fishtailed and gathered momentum, turned a corner, and was gone.

A block away, Mad Dog announced that nobody was behind them, and all three burst into the laughter of relief.

Later, however, when they had changed cars and were driving up the Harbor Freeway toward the clustered towers of downtown L.A., the adrenaline drained and Troy felt a great wave of melancholy wash through him. He'd taken off the biggest score of his life. It would buy what money bought: freedom and possibility. To be anything in this time and place necessitated money, unless one had inclinations toward monasticism. Troy had no other way to get money, so he did what he had to. Yet this left him empty. Still, he smiled when his partners laughed and slapped him on the back. In a few days they would cut up about $360,000. It was a lot of money even with inflation.

10

Even at four in the morning the Bicycle Club, a giant poker casino beside the Long Beach Freeway, was so full that erstwhile gamblers had to wait for a seat. Games included Seven-Card Stud and Lowball, but the most popular was Texas Hold 'Em, a wild and woolly poker variation that favored those who bluffed and played loose and relied on luck. The many gamblers were an ethnic stew, heavy on Asian, for awareness of chance in life was deeply imprinted on their culture. It inclined them toward gambling, unlike the stern Puritan streak still running through Protestant America. The Bicycle Club was the size of a football field filled with tables. Each table had seven seats, and every seat at every table had a rump in it, while a blackboard on the sidelines listed each game and had initials of those waiting to play. The humming roar of voices were a counterpoint to the rattling chips, broken by a cursing voice or exclamation of joy.

In the coffee shop booth sat Troy and his gang, drinking coffee and waiting for Alex Aris, who was late as usual.

The waitress refilled their coffee mugs.

"You don't think anything happened to him, do you?" Diesel asked.

"No, no," Troy said. "I told you how he is. He runs late."

"He wouldn't split with our money, would he?" Mad Dog asked. Troy's look of bemused disdain reassured Mad Dog. He thought about the money again. What to do with it? He'd send his sister a few thou. She had AIDS and was living in a ragged mobile home outside Tacoma. He could get high, too, when this was done and

131

he could get away from his partners. He had opened one of the bags and dug out a tablespoon of cocaine. He'd buy some smack and really get blowed out on speedballs—escape the torments of his life for a while. He might even get hooked with a hundred grand plus.

Troy wanted to fire up a cigar, but he'd seen a sign on the casino wall: Cigars not permitted on casino floor. No cigars in a gambling hall? What kinda shit is that? Vegas had probably changed, too. God, he loved Vegas. He could dive into the neon sea and forget the day, the hour, and everything else except the dice dancing across the green felt table. He could use a few days in Vegas after the scene at the bungalows. It had come out all right, and he had experienced no fear while the heist was in progress, but whenever he thought about it afterward, like now, nervous fear sent butterflies flying in his guts. He glanced at Diesel, whose glazed eyes bespoke distant thoughts.

"Hey, Big Man," Troy said. "How ya doin'?"

"I'm great, bro'. You know what I'm gonna do with my end, man, I'm gonna pay off most of the mortgage on my pad. Hey, did you ever think that I'd own my own fuckin' house?"

Grinning, Troy shook his head. It was as unlikely as anything in the world. "You're changing in your old age. One more score and you'll be rehabilitated."

"Yeah, ain't that true. I might vote Republican." He paused. "You know I don't like abortion. It's killin' babies to me."

Troy nodded, remembering his surprise at Diesel's vehemence on the subject in the San Quentin yard when the big man had been ready to fight after another convict cracked a joke about abortion. It contradicted everything else about him.

"Do you vote?" Troy asked.

"Oh, yeah. I registered when the kid came. The guys in The Face's local make sure everybody is registered."

In a way it surprised Troy; this was the first ex-con he knew who voted. On the other hand, it was obvious why the Teamsters Local made sure of registration. He looked to Mad Dog, whose eyes were blank and whose mind was far away. "What about you, Dog? You vote?"

Mad Dog snorted derisively. "Hell, no! Fuck a vote! That's shit for suckers."

A red flush rushed to Diesel's cheeks. Just then Troy saw Alex Aris enter. "There he is," Troy said, then stood up and waved.

Greco saw them and came over. As always, he was stylishly dressed, tonight in dark blue cashmere jacket and gray flannel slacks, cuffed and pleated in the latest style. He was smiling as he got close. Troy slid over to make room on his side of the booth.

"How you guys doin'?" he asked.

"Tell us," Troy said. "You got the news."

"You mean about those thirty keys?"

"Hell, yes, man. Damn!"

"The best I could do was twelve-five a key. I thought I'd get a little more, but the fuckin' market is flooded. They gimme three hundred grand and they'll give me the rest on the weekend."

"You got three hundred grand in the car?" Mad Dog asked.

"No, no. I'm too likely to get stopped. I got it at a pad. I'll take Troy and get it when we leave."

Forgotten was the anger of a minute earlier; both Diesel and Mad Dog grinned widely. Greco looked at them and decided it was time to mention other shares—without mentioning that he had actually gotten thirteen-five for each key, and so had thirty grand in hand already. "What about the lawyer?"

"Lawyer?" Mad Dog said.

"Yeah . . . the lip that fingered the score in the first place?"

"Oh, yeah. What do you think?"

"He should get twenty-five grand, and I should get five apiece from you guys."

"Outta what you got already?"

"No, no, out of what I get on the weekend."

The trio nodded at each other. "That's cool," Troy said.

"I'll give you the change next week."

The waitress arrived to see if Alex wanted anything. He shook his head. "I'm leaving in a minute."

When she was gone, Alex looked at Troy. "You know Chepe Hernandez?"

"I met him once. I know his brother better."

"He knows you. He wants to see you."

"Sure. What's he want?"

"You know he's in La Mesa."

"The joint in Tijuana?" Mad Dog asked.

"Yeah. He's doin' a dime. He could get out whenever he wants, but Uncle Sam has an indictment on him and they're pressing Mexico City to get him back. You know how they snatch suckers back from down there. Fuck an extradition warrant. But they can't snatch him outta La Mesa."

Troy nodded. He could appreciate Chepe's dilemma. Once the feds had him in Leavenworth or Marion, he would be history. High-security inmates never escaped from a U.S. penitentiary. Under the new sentences guidelines, an international drug smuggler would serve the rest of his life—case closed. Troy remembered that Chepe was fifty a decade ago. He was an easygoing guy with a sense of humor. He'd begun selling joints in Hazard Park on Soto. "You got any idea what he wants?" Troy asked again.

"Who knows? I don't think he wants you to kill anybody. He can get that real quick and a lot cheaper."

"I don't kill on contract," Troy said.

"I know that. I told him. It's something else. Somebody owes him, I think. Anyway, he wants me to bring you down to see him. I'm going next week. I gotta take a toilet bowl."

"They don't have plumbers down there?" Mad Dog asked.

"It's not for Chepe. Shit, he's got a suite like a Hilton. You ready for it? Shit, you can visit and stay all night."

"You guys go," Diesel said. "I'll visit my old lady and check with Jimmy the Face and meet you at the end of the week."

Troy looked at Mad Dog. "You and me?"

Mad Dog nodded and it was decided.

"I'll take Troy to get the dough," Alex said. "You guys wait at the hotel."

In addition to the fancy Jaguar, Alex Aris also drove a six-year-old Seville. It was nice enough to arouse no attention in Beverly Hills, yet old enough to blend into South Central. He was constantly on the move throughout Southern California. Nobody worked harder at being a criminal.

When they got underway, Troy wondered why he felt flat. The huge score would never be reported. Moon Man had big money and niggers to kill for him—but their underworld was as segregated as most of black and white in America. Moon Man would never know who got him. He probably believed they were rogue cops. Half the Sheriff's Department narco squad was under indictment for extorting drug dealers and stealing money and drugs during busts. Once upon a time a score like this would have thrilled him. What had changed? Why did he feel tired and depressed? Even if he knew, what could he do? It was too late to change. He had to keep playing or kill himself; he wasn't *that* depressed.

"How you gettin' along with Mad Dog?" Alex asked.

"He loves me."

"Watch his paranoid ass. He's got priors for turning on friends. Remember when he stabbed Mahoney?"

"I guess I do. I was about ten feet away. I spilled hot coffee all down my front getting outta there."

"Him and Mahoney were good friends."

"I know."

"Okay. I hope I don't have to kill him 'cause he kills you."

"Oh, no, that won't happen."

Troy looked out at the streets. They were crossing the southwest quadrant of the endless city. He'd once had a girlfriend who lived in the area. It had undergone a metamorphosis in the last decade. Developed after World War II and sold under the F.H.A. and the G.I. Bill, it had deteriorated from bright two- and three-bedroom ranch styles that could have been a Norman Rockwell cover to a world closer to the *colonias* he'd seen in Tijuana. The manicured lawns were weed-infested patches of brown. Torn and rain-soaked sofas were discarded at the curb. Trash filled the gutters and blew into piles against fences. Walls were defaced by graffiti in black spray paint. A pack of stray dogs had overturned a trash can and were

135

digging in the mess. This was not the Southern California of song and legend. It made him remember Chepe in Tijuana.

"What's the deal with Chepe?"

"I don't know any more than I told you."

"Why does he want me? He's got pistoleros running out his ears. Shit, he was tight with Big Joe and those dudes in the Eme."

"I think he wants somebody with more sense."

"Well, we'll see what he wants."

"You've never been to La Mesa."

"Uh-uh."

"You've got an experience coming."

Alex turned into a mobile home park: Narrow streets, mobile homes sited close together, DRIVE SLOW, CHILDREN AT PLAY signs. He parked on the road's shoulder. "I'll be one second," he said as he got out and went around a corner.

It was closer to a minute, but it was quick: Alex came back with a big suitcase. He put it on the rear floorboards. "Three hundred grand," he said.

Back at the Bonaventure, Troy carried the suitcase across the lobby and took the elevator. Diesel and Mad Dog were waiting in the room. The suitcase was opened and packets of currency were dumped on the bed. It was old currency, plucked from sweaty palms all over the city and gathered by denomination in packets fastened with rubber bands. The amount of each packet was written in pencil on jagged pieces of paper torn from a yellow legal tablet.

"Count it out," Mad Dog said to Troy.

"Take your own," Troy said.

The packets were in various amounts. Some had $1,000 in fives, others $2,500 in tens, but most were $5,000 packets of twenties. In less than a minute, each of them had $100,000. Diesel started to pack his share in an overnight bag. "While you guys are down there, I'm gonna go home for a couple days."

"Don't let that broad take all your money," Mad Dog said.

Diesel stopped packing and frowned. "What's that mean?"

"That means . . . whatever you think it means."

"Gentlemen, gentlemen," Troy said, stepping between them. "Take it easy. Don't start arguing over nothing."

"That was some kinda little dig, like I'm a trick or something."

"Man, you're paranoid," Mad Dog said, waving his hand in a deprecating manner as he turned away.

"*I'm* paranoid! Ain't that a bitch?"

"Hey, hey," Troy interjected. "Knock it off. What's wrong with you dudes? You're partners."

"Aw, man," Mad Dog said, "just 'cause this sucker weighs a ton and was some kinda halfass prizefighter, he thinks he's bad."

"No, I'm not bad—but I can keep bad motherfuckers off me."

"Cool it," Troy commanded.

"Don't tell me. Tell him. He started it."

"I'm telling both of you . . . freeze on that shit. It's not about nothin'."

Diesel swung his eyes to Troy. His face was red, but after a moment he turned away, muttering, "Crazy motherfucker drops a lug like I'm some kind of trick."

"Let it go, Diesel," Troy said.

"Hey, I was just putting you on a little," Mad Dog said. "Fuck you if you can't take a little ribbing." His voice was shrill.

"Hey!" Troy snapped, glaring at Mad Dog. Mad Dog was flushed, his eyes glazed, but then he snorted a half-laugh and shrugged. "I'm sorry, Troy. I don't wanna push your button." To Diesel, "Sorry, brother."

"Forget it."

Troy nodded, but he knew nothing was forgotten. He knew these men. Any wound to the ego festered in the mind. Mad Dog would chew on it and get paranoid. Diesel would feel the paranoia and get scared because he knew how dangerous Mad Dog could be. The only way to keep one from eventually murdering the other was to keep them apart. Diesel's going to Northern California was good. Troy would keep an eye on Mad Dog. He had mixed feelings about the maniac. He knew Mad Dog so well, knew the torture of his childhood and the torment of his youth. Whatever Mad Dog was, however insane and dangerous, he'd been made that way, and society had abetted the crimes against a child. His mother had burned him with cigarettes before she went into the nuthouse. When she got out, the juvenile court sent him back to her—and she tortured him some more for telling on her. He'd been ten years old and ran away; he was caught breaking into a neighborhood market. That got him into the juvenile justice system, where he was often punched and kicked by bigger boys because he was small and different—until he was once goaded too far and stabbed a bully in the eye with a fork. After that his reputation for being unpredictably dangerous got him a wide berth. Once he understood his situation, he exploited it by behaving with violent insanity, and in return got greater leeway from his peers. Even the toughest kids get nervous about the crazy ones.

When Mad Dog and Diesel and others of their reform school cohort graduated into adult crime and San Quentin, Troy was already a legend. He was chief clerk in the Athletic Department and controlled the lists for weekend and night gym. Coach Keller, who disliked being bothered, signed whatever Troy put in front of him. Troy okayed the gym work crew, one of San Quentin's better jobs. It had fringe benefits, a place to get off the Big Yard out of the rain, a chance to shower every day, access to TV for sporting events. Troy arranged for Diesel's job and played mentor to him for the next three years. Diesel was sure that listening to Troy had kept him out of trouble so he could get a parole. Now Troy had led him to a score that thieves dream about. What would Gloria have to say when he dropped a hundred grand on her pretty blond ass? That would shut up all her heckle and jeckle bullshit. Maybe he should get a new suit, too, a whole new outfit, a Brioni or Hickey-Freeman, and wear that when he arrived home. Diesel grinned to himself while he envisioned gloating and strutting as he pitched packet after packet of untraceable money on top of the kitchen table. How sweet it would be. "I think I'll leave tonight," he said. "Drop me at the airport and take the Mustang if you want. The Dog's car might not make it on Mexican highways."

"No, take the Mustang. I'm gonna buy a car tomorrow. We'll use that one." He turned to Mad Dog. "I'm not gonna buy a new one, so I need you to check it out. I don't know shit about cars."

"I'm your man for that," Mad Dog said. He liked that Troy had a favor to ask. It belied a feeling that Troy had pulled back from their friendship. Mad Dog usually sensed whatever anyone felt toward him; he had a kind of radar that he trusted completely. He knew the *regulars* thought he was paranoid, and maybe he was—but a little paranoia was a valuable tool if one lived in a land of snakes.

Late the following afternoon, Troy bought a five-year-old Jaguar with a Chevy 350 V8 under the hood, which juiced it to the horsepower of a stock Corvette. That part was hidden. The exterior was identical to the newest model, and was similar to what he'd driven twelve years earlier, which was partly why he bought it. Mad Dog checked it out and said it was in good shape. The odometer said it was low mileage, which was confirmed by unworn floor pedals. The seats still had the rich smell of new leather. Nothing mass-produced could compare with Jaguar coachwork.

"They're supposed to be trouble, but they're great cars, and this one is primo."

That's when Troy told the salesman, "I'll take it," and paid cash. They drove both cars back to the Bonaventure and Troy checked out. Except for a few hundred dollars, they hid the proceeds in the spare-tire well of Mad Dog's car; which they parked at the LAX long-term lot. It would be undisturbed for the few days they would be gone.

When they were underway in the Jag, Troy called Greco on the cellular phone. He would meet them at a Holiday Inn outside San Diego sometime that night. Tomorrow they would cross over. Nothing more was said. Talking on a cellular phone was to throw your words into the air; that was what the Supreme Court said in ruling that the laws against wiretap were inapplicable.

The Jag went east on the Santa Monica Freeway, then south on Interstate 5, which went straight to the border, passing through many Southern California towns en route.

East L.A., seen from the freeway, was much as it had been throughout Troy's life. He had come here from Beverly Hills when he was fifteen and sixteen, running around with Mexicans he'd met in juvenile hall. He remembered speaking English with a Mexican accent and smiled. Until he went to reform school and met tough white kids from Okie cities like Bakersfield and Fresno and Stockton, who could and would fight, he rather despised most white boys as weak and cowardly. The values of a macho ethic better suited his nature. The frame houses were older here, most from before World War II, and built more substantially, if not palatially. Everything was bleached to pastel by the steady desert sun, for that is what it was without the piped-in water from up north. Long before the blacks of South Central had Crips and Bloods, East L.A. had Chicano gangs—Maravilla, White Fence, Flats, Hazard, Clanton, Temple, Diamond, Dogtown, Eastside-Clover, Los Avenues, La Colonia de Watts, and others. Back then the fathers of the Crips were still picking cotton in Alabama.

The little towns of greater L.A., once described as thirty suburbs in search of a city, now blended into seamless sprawl. Once the factories of Firestone, Goodyear, Todd, and Bethlehem Steel provided the jobs. Now the factories were gone south in phrase and in fact. He had no idea where the working people of the little towns found jobs these days.

Los Angeles became Orange County—and the only way to tell the difference was a small sign beside the road. Billboards for Disneyland appeared.

"Ever been to Disneyland?" Troy asked Mad Dog.

"No. I never been to L.A. before."

"Let's go check it out."

"You're jiving."

"No, let's go."

"Why not?"

So they did, and seemed to be the only adults without a passel of excited children. They took no rides, the lines being too long, but it was an enjoyable hour just walking around. Mad Dog even had a cotton candy. "You know what," he said, "I liked it better as a kid."

Shadows were lengthening when they got back on the freeway. Even in Troy's memory, most of the landscape had been rural, orange groves and alfalfa, between the little towns. Now it was one urban sprawl for a hundred miles. Newport, Laguna, and the other beach towns were no longer separated by miles of empty shoreline and low hills. Expensive houses covered the seashore and rolling hills, so huge windows overlooked the sea at sunset. This was the land of milk and honey, of tanned bodies that expected the good life as their due.

When darkness came, they pulled off the highway to take a piss, look at the silver ocean under a harvest moon, and to smoke a joint. Looking for privacy, they went through an underpass and found a bumpy dirt road. It looked deserted. Then, without warning, the headlights flashed over an encampment of homeless Hispanics, probably all Mexicans, although there was no way to tell. Nearby were avocado orchards and melon patches. The Mexicans picked the fruit but could not pay for shelter on what they made. As soon as the headlights intruded, most of them ran off into the darkness. It might be the migra, so they couldn't take a chance.

Troy and Mad Dog turned around. Within a few hundred yards was the fence of a development where the houses started at $800,000. As they got back on the freeway, Troy was unsure of what he thought about the homeless farm workers.

They smoked the joint in the car. Troy still had to piss. It was dark beside the road. "Pull over," Troy said. Mad Dog did so and Troy got out. He was in pain from the need to urinate. In prison a urinal was always close by, so he was not conditioned to restrain himself. The embankment sloped and was dark. He went down; then slipped and slid five more feet, part of it on his hip, before his feet hit solid ground. He pushed himself erect and unzipped his pants. As he pissed into blackness, he looked up and saw Mad Dog standing atop the embankment while headlight beams flashed over him. "Damn," Troy said, realizing how stupid he'd been.

Mad Dog realized it, too. The stream of cars and trucks buffeted him with slipstream wind and the headlights blinded him. If a Highway Patrol car was coming, the police would pull over to see what was wrong.

Troy could climb partway, then his feet would slip and he would slide back.

141

"Here, man, try to grab this." Mad Dog took off his belt and got down where he could hold on to a root with one hand and toss the end of the belt down the slope. Troy grabbed the belt and, after a step, was able to take Mad Dog's hand. At the moment that their hands touched, Troy remembered that this man had murdered a seven-year-old child, and he wanted to pull away in revulsion. But Mad Dog pulled him up and they got back into the car. Under way again, Troy thought about his reaction on the embankment. It surprised him because he knew many killers, men who had slain cops or store owners or other criminals, men who came from the cellhouse in the morning without caring if it clouded up and rained dogshit, or if they killed somebody or died themselves before evening lockup. He felt nothing about whatever they had done—except the Zebra Killers, some crazy niggers (the term fit) who ran around San Francisco in a van, and whenever they saw a white person alone and vulnerable, they either murdered him on the spot or snatched her for rape and later murder. One of them had lived three cells away from Troy. Hundreds of times they passed on the tier, inches apart, without looking into each other's eyes or exchanging a word. It was the heat of obsessed hate that Troy felt, and after a while his initial bemused wariness turned to indignation, and then he saw that this nigger would kill every white person in the world, man, woman and child, if he could. Troy's hostility smoldered in response to the hatred directed toward him. It was Max Row in San Quentin, where they'd put him on arrival. He had several good partners on the tier, so he never felt threatened enough to require a preemptive assault. Eventually they moved the nigger away.

Troy had never murdered anyone, but that was as much luck as prudence or morality. Once, fresh from reform school, he had robbed a liquor store. The owner pulled a pistol from under the counter. Troy hesitated and yelled, but the owner was courageous and intent, so both fired simultaneously so that it sounded like one weapon. The owner's bullet passed by his eye like a buzzing bee; he felt the disturbed air. Troy's bullet hit the man's collarbone and tore straight through. He was out of the hospital in an hour—but it could have been robbery-murder. It was a crime now older than he had been at the time, sixteen or so. It was so alien from where he'd grown up. Such things were unheard of there, but rather common where he later found himself.

No, he had never killed, but he could have. In prison, too, there had been situations—and confrontations—where death could have resulted, his own or his antagonist's, but the disputes were settled short of murder, although not always short of violence. Such memories of reality made him hesitant to judge others. Still, murdering a seven-year-old child was a far cry from that.

Suddenly, red lights flashed ahead, all across the several lanes of freeway. Mad Dog hit the brakes and Troy lurched forward. It brought his mind back from reverie.

They began to inch forward. A helicopter went by above them. KNX News reported a multiple-vehicle collision with a "Sig Alert" near the Pendleton Exit. "We're gonna be late . . . late," Mad Dog said. Troy winked and reached for the flip-top phone. A sucker could quickly get used to this, Troy thought as he dialed. A minute later he was talking to Greco moving down a highway on the other side of California. "Don't sweat it," he said. "I'll be late, too."

"No, shit," Troy said. He was looking forward to seeing his friend and the trip across the border. He'd heard tales of La Mesa for many years. Now he'd finally see what it looked like.

11

That night the three men ate steak and lobster in the hotel dining room; then took in a topless bar a couple blocks away. They had business early, so they got back to the hotel early. Alex and Mad Dog used the twin beds. Troy was equally content on the hard floor: The thick carpet and a bedspread folded over made an adequate mattress for him to rest comfortably.

In the morning they left the Jaguar in the hotel parking lot and took Alex's middle-aged Cadillac Seville across the border. Tijuana, Mexico, was no longer a sleazy border town, half Old West and half whorehouse, but rather a shiny metropolis with a million or more residents. Corporate logos were everywhere. Still, a presidential candidate had been assassinated here, and a chief of police had been ambushed and gunned down. Federales had shot it out with the local police. The wealth of drugs was entwined with all of it.

Alex said he usually walked across. It was easier coming back and a lot faster. Driving back took an hour to get across at the best times. And there was always a chance the Border Patrol would motion him out of line for a search that tore the car apart and took several hours. They never found anything, but their goddamned dogs always barked at some residue of something. Today, however, he had the toilet bowl and his companions, so he drove into Mexico. Nobody looked at them. "Damn, man," said Mad Dog, "don't they wanna see something . . . a driver's license—"

"Hell, no! All they want is some Yankee dollars," Alex explained.

"They stop you for a visa about fifty miles inland," Troy explained. "The border is a wide-open game. That's what I read."

"Yeah, that's it," Alex said. "You can stay forever in Tijuana and nobody says anything. Shit, Chepe is from East L.A. He was down here fifteen years before they busted him—and they only did it because the U.S. State Department was putting pressure on Mexico City."

"If he's got a couple hundred million and all that power, how come he's in the joint?" Mad Dog said.

"I'm not a hundred percent about this, but this is what I think. I think his juice is the state authorities, the locals, but if they let him go, Mexico City will snatch him up and deport him into the arms of Deputy U.S. Marshals. But the U.S. Administration changes, the Mexican presidency changes, time passes, U.S. Attorneys come and go. Besides, you'll see, he's living pretty good, all things considered."

"I heard it was way out," Mad Dog said. "I heard the dope fiends down here line up at the joint."

"I wouldn't go *that* far," Greco said. "But when you can't score anywhere else in Tijuana, you can alway score at the penitentiary."

Troy half listened while looking out at Tijuana. At first it was what he remembered, the blinding Day-Glo colors of the taxis, the main boulevard, Calle Revolucion, with miles of businesses aimed at Americans on a day visit. Auto upholstery was cheap, medicine sold at a fraction of the cost across the border, shops sold Joy de Partou, Opium, and other expensive perfumes for half what they cost in L.A. On the streets the beggar women with their babies, the cantinas and strip joints, and the whores were abundant.

Suddenly it changed. What had been shacks and vacant land when he was visiting Tijuana for sex and drugs was now one factory after another, a compendium of the transnational corporations: Ford, Minolta, Panasonic, Smith-Corona, Olivetti, and more. Then the big, bright hostelries, Hyatt, Ramada, Holiday Inn. The visiting businessmen needed lodging.

"It changed, didn't it?" Greco commented.

"No shit," Troy replied.

"You ever been to La Mesa?"

"Uh-uh. I've heard stories, of course."

145

"Check this," Alex said. "It was built for three hundred. It's got three thousand . . ."

"Three thousand for three hundred!" Mad Dog said. "Talk about crowded jails . . ."

"That's some kind of cruel and unusual punishment, ain't it?"

"They don't play that shit in Mexico. I'll tell you the truth, though. I'd rather do time down here than anywhere in the U.S."

"You mean if you had some money," Troy said.

"Oh yeah. But it doesn't have to be no whole bunch of money. A hundred a month."

Troy knew about Mexican prisons because men in jail often talk of other jails. Mexican prisons operated on a different philosophy than those in the U.S. Incarceration was enough in Mexico; thereafter they let things approximate society as much as circumstances allowed. Wives visited for several days at a time, inmates ran businesses inside the walls. It was better preparation for society than an American penitentiary. Troy thought of Pelican Bay, California's newest nightmare, a world straight from Orwell and Kafka brought to life at the end of the twentieth century. Not clubs but tasers with fifty thousand volts of electricity, not beatings but Prolixin, one injection of which turned a man into a shuffling zombie for a week. What did society expect to walk out? Did they expect to sow hemlock and reap wheat? It made him angry whenever he thought of the sheer stupidity.

La Mesa had once been outside Tijuana, but the city had spread until the prison was surrounded by poor neighborhoods. The streets were dirt or rutted macadam. The parking lot was unpaved. The few vehicles tended toward pickup trucks and old Fords and Chevys. A dozen boys were engaged in a game of soccer. The ball bounced to Troy. It was stamped Los Angeles County Recreation Dept. He started to throw it back. "Give it here," Alex said. When Troy gave it to him, Alex beckoned to the biggest boy, who came up warily until he saw that Alex was holding an American greenback. Then he was very interested. "Watch the car," Alex said in English and pantomime. The message was clear. Alex then tore the twenty-dollar bill in two and gave one half to the boy, who grinned and nodded and went back to his friends to explain.

While Alex was unlocking the trunk to pull out the toilet bowl, Troy turned to look at the prison. They were near a corner. A long wall made of cinder blocks extended for several hundred yards. As prison walls go, it was not very high—but every fifty yards it was topped with a gun tower. Closer to them was a big sally port. The double gate was made of storm fence topped with concertina, with a gun tower looking down on it. The construction was haphazard compared to the expensive perfection of American prisons. It was effective, but it had a tenuous aspect to it, as if it had been built for today rather than for the ages. The fronts of some American prisons looked as if they wanted to last like the Parthenon.

A line of visitors, perhaps three dozen, waited outside the sally port. Most were women, many were children. Many carried large bags of groceries. Troy thought they were getting into the line, but Alex kept going, the toilet bowl on his shoulder.

In the wall beyond the sally port was a solid steel door with a peephole. It had a doorbell. A loud one.

An eye appeared at the peephole. Alex said, "*Los camaradas del Chepe.*"

The eye disappeared. "He's going to check," Alex said. "If you got any one-dollar bills, get 'em together."

"What?"

"For bribery. Never mind, I got it."

A heavy key turned in the steel door and it came open. They were in a narrow hallway with a dangling bare light bulb. A guard was beckoning them to the open door of an office. Alex and the toilet bowlled them to the door and inside.

A lieutenant sat behind a desk with his elbows resting on it. Still with the toilet bowl shouldered, Alex matter-of-factly extended a couple of twenty-dollar bills. "Get somebody to take this, *por favor, jefe?*"

"Sure . . . sure." Then he snapped fingers to the guard at the door. "*Venga aqui.*" The guard came, Greco gave him the toilet bowl, and the guard took charge of delivering it inside.

"Thank you, *pues,*" Alex said. "We're in a little hurry." He said that with another forty dollars extended.

The lieutenant came around the desk, took the money, and continued through the door, motioning them to follow. The next room had a trio of guards to process them in, to register them in the log and frisk them. Alex held out four one-dollar bills scissored between forefinger and index finger. They were snapped up, somebody wrote A, B, and C, in the log to keep the records straight, and the lieutenant banged on another steel door until it opened.

This was the last room, where the backs of their hands were stamped with something invisible to the naked eye. It wasn't a magic stamp to get them out again, but it was something the guards would look at. Alex gave the guard a handful of quarters. He nodded his head in gratitude as he hurried ahead to unlock the last door.

As it swung open, Troy stared out at a teeming mass of Mexican convicts on the yard outside. They were behind a red line ten feet from the doorway, and most of them were looking at the sally port and what was going on outside. It was possible to come to the outside sally port and yell across the twenty feet to the inside sally port.

As they stepped out into the human maelstrom, Mad Dog leaned close to Troy's ear. "I can't believe this joint," he said. "Two dollars and you could bring in a machine gun."

A few feet ahead of them, at the edge of the crowd, Alex was talking to a young Mexican sporting a big Zapata mustache. He had the flat nose and scars around his eyes indicating a prizefighter. Behind him stood another Mexican convict with the toilet bowl balanced on his shoulder. These two were at least part of the crew sent to greet them. Alex glanced back over his shoulder and motioned for them to follow as he set off through the press of bodies. The man with the toilet bowl was the point. As Troy kept close behind Alex and Mustache Pete, he became aware that a third man, a youth, was moving along beside him.

The mass of inmates gave way, stepped aside, for the retinue. Even then hands were extended and voices called, "Cambio . . . cambio . . ." Change, change. It was especially moving because Troy had never had a Mexican beg him on the streets of Los Angeles. Now he ignored the extended hands and kept moving.

They broke from the crowd onto a yard that reminded Troy of

148

an immense parade ground—a vast rectangle, two hundred yards by three hundred yards—surrounded by two-story buildings pressed together like rowhouses. At the ends of the buildings were roads that led to other parts of the prison. Off to one side, he saw what seemed to be hot dog or taco stands with picnic tables for customers. He looked back. The area around the sally port was like Times Square on New Year's Eve.

Alex motioned them forward and made the introductions. The Mustache was Oscar, Chepe's *segundo*. He introduced Wevo, who carried the toilet. The other two were flunkies with names forgotten immediately.

"Look here," Oscar said. "Chepe's mother is visiting him. She'll leave in ten or fifteen minutes. He wants you to wait until then."

"Sure. We're not in a hurry, are we?"

Mad Dog shrugged and shook his head.

"Want a tour?" Oscar asked.

"Sure," Troy said.

"You know what I'd like," Mad Dog said. "I'd like to score."

"Whaddya want?"

"A speedball?"

Oscar turned to one of the flunkies and spoke in Spanish; then told Mad Dog, "Go with him."

Mad Dog and the flunky took off, angling across the yard.

Oscar led Troy through a passageway between buildings. Behind the quadrangle was a two-tiered cellhouse, the doors solid steel with steel hasps for giant padlocks—but the doors were open. A woman was draping a throw rug over the railing; a man stood in the doorway holding a toddler. The family occupied the five-by-seven cell.

"Seven hundred for that," Oscar said. "Cheapest cell in the joint."

"What if you can't buy a cell?"

"I'll show you."

Oscar turned a corner. For a hundred yards was a grille of rusting bars with open gates every twenty yards. The bars were the front of a cinder block building. It was an immense space covered with bunk beds five levels high. Instead of springs the bunks had sheets

149

of steel. Some had mattresses, most did not. It was impossible to see the rear wall. It was a dark cave. Troy got close to the bars to look. He had to turn away; the stench of sour sweat and dry piss roiled his stomach. "Ohhh, shit!" he said.

Oscar and Alex laughed at him; then explained that those without a cell had to come here in late afternoon. Like all prisons, La Mesa had a count. When the count cleared, the gates of the Corral were opened. About one third of those who were counted there had a bunk; the others had to do the best they could. A friend could take them in for the night, or they could flop in a doorway, or anywhere else for that matter. "Looks like downtown L.A. at night around here," Alex observed.

From the Corral, Oscar took them down another road. It teemed with bodies like a back street in Hong Kong. Oscar obviously had power here. Prisoners stepped aside for the visitors. Several times Oscar exchanged nods and words of respect. The swarm was mostly male and Mexican, but mixed in were a few Americans and some women.

Through open doors, Troy saw workrooms where prisoners were doing leather or woodwork. Many of the cheap souvenirs of Tijuana sold in town were made here. Oscar explained that the prison once had an auto body shop with the main business of changing the numbers and the look of cars stolen in the United States. They were then delivered throughout Latin America.

Troy sniffed the air. He could smell frying onions. A moment later, Oscar led them around a corner. They had come upon the taco stands from the rear. There was also a café with tables under an awning. "Whaddya think?" Alex asked.

"It's damn sure not San Quentin."

One of Chepe's crew found them. Chepe was ready. They headed back across the yard. Below a ladder was a picnic table where a poker game was in progress. Troy was sure that at least some of the poker players were guarding the ladder.

Oscar went first, climbing the dozen feet to the roof. Troy was next. As he reached the top, he was surprised. It was a terrace with wrought-iron furniture, potted plants, including a couple of small

150

trees, and a well-built young woman in skin-tight Levi's. She was watering plants with a can. A muscular young man extended a hand. As he did so, his unbuttoned shirt fell open and exposed the butt of a .45 stuck in his waistband. Mexican prisons were sure different from the cold Calvinism found in the United States.

A bright red-and-green canvas awning extended out to shield the glass doors from direct sunlight. Chepe waited for them in the open doorway. A stocky man with almost cherubic face, his hair had grayed since Troy last saw him. He wore expensive slippers, cutoff jeans, and a T-shirt with *Harvard* across the chest. He extended a hand. "Hey, man, come on in. It's hot out there."

They entered the sitting room of a small suite. A giant TV screen dominated one wall. A small open kitchen was off to the side. "I thought there was another vato," Chepe said to Alex.

"He's here. He went on a tour."

"Not like Quentin, is it?" Chepe said.

Troy looked around the room. "Not hardly. How do you get this? I know it costs money, but how does it work?"

"I bought it. This one cost eighty grand. There's four or five like this. Some vato just came in and he paid a hundred and ten."

"You don't pay rent?"

"No, no, I own it. I can sell it, too—as long as the *Commandante* gets his cut. They got others that cost anywhere from ten grand up. We own a few, don't we, Oscar?"

"Yeah, what the fuck, we're real estate investors in the penitentiary."

"Come on down here," Chepe said, leading the way down a short hall. A bedroom had been converted into a combination library and office. A built-in bookcase covered one wall from floor to ceiling. The titles revealed an eclectic taste—Dos Passos and Dostoevsky, Conrad and Kafka, Steinbeck and Styron, plus a dose of history and biography. Troy had never seen evidence in San Quentin that Chepe had a bookish streak. Then, too, it was a trait scarcely valued among robbers, killers, and drug dealers.

Mad Dog came back and joined them, upon which Chepe called, "Stella!" The pretty girl in tight jeans stuck her head in the door and Chepe told her to make coffee.

"You didn't have her last time I was here," Alex said.

"I saved her from the Corral."

"Oh, man, she wasn't going to the Corral, was she?"

"Hell, no," Oscar said. "If the boss here hadn't rescued her, there's other dudes got money around here. A pretty ain' gotta worry . . . but an ugly fat bitch is in trouble. Ha, ha, ha, ha . . ."

And the men all grinned with understanding.

While they waited for the coffee, Chepe asked for news of mutual friends in California prisons and elsewhere in the California underworld. Everybody asked about Big Joe first; then Harry Buckley, Bulldog, Paul Allen, Joe Cocko, Huero Flores, Shotgun, Charlie Jackass, and Preacher.

"You could get outta here if you wanted, couldn't you?" asked Mad Dog.

"Oh yeah," Chepe answered. "The warden would hold the ladder for me. I pay him ten grand a month to feed his kids. That's about fifteen times his salary."

The girl brought them mugs of coffee on a tray. When she was gone, they got down to business. "You know Mike Brennan?" Chepe asked.

"I know who he is," Troy said. "I never met him."

"Who is he?" Mad Dog asked.

Alex answered: "He's a bigshot smuggler. He had an Irish daddy and a Mexican mama."

"He owes me a lot of money," Chepe said, "and he thinks he doesn't have to pay because I'm in here."

"We'll kill him," Mad Dog said from his drugged stupidity. "You want him killed?"

"No, he doesn't want him killed," Troy said. "If he wanted him killed, he has plenty of *pistoleros* for that."

"Smart, *ese*, smart," said Chepe, nodding approvingly. "If he's dead, he can't pay me. Besides that, he's a pretty good dude. I just want my money."

"Do you mind if I ask how much?" Troy said.

Chepe held up four fingers. "Million," he said.

"Four mil isn't what it used to be," Troy said, "but it's still a lot of money. Has he got it?"

152

"Oh yeah, he could pay if he wanted to. He thinks I can't touch him. I wanna teach him a lesson."

"What've you got in mind?"

"He's got a one-year-old kid in L.A. I want you to snatch him."

"Kidnapping?"

Chepe nodded. Troy's stomach sank. He disliked the idea—and he remembered reading that no major kidnapping for ransom had gone unsolved in the U.S. since the thirties. Of course, this would be a little different. Nobody would report this one. "You say the kid's in L.A.?"

Chepe nodded. "With his mother. They aren't married."

Troy thought about it, looked to Mad Dog, who shrugged and put the decision back on Troy.

"I'll guarantee you half a million, plus half of whatever he pays. If he pays it all . . ."

"Two million dollars," Mad Dog said; then whistled in soft appreciation. "It ain't chicken feed. It's up to you," he said to Troy.

Troy's furrowed brow and narrowed eyes reflected the debate in his mind. Kidnapping a child, even without hurting it, was a terrible thing. But this would give him the money to go away, and he knew that if he didn't go away, he would be lost. If he stayed, it was a matter of time before they got him. He was already a fugitive parole violator. That would keep him from making bail, plus he had two strikes under the new law (even if one was as a juvenile), so any bust would be life. Why not throw the dice, all he wanted in life if he threw a seven, the end of his life if he threw craps . . .

"We're not gonna hurt the kid, right?"

"Hell, no! I wouldn't even want you to do it if the kid was four or five, but the way it is, he won't even know."

"He's too young to snitch on you," Alex said.

"That's something to consider."

"Look here," Chepe said, "I'll guarantee you a million, *plus* half of what he pays."

"Make him pay interest," Mad Dog said. "Say another million."

"Hey, man," Alex said. "You keep throwing a million here and a million there, pretty soon we're gonna be talking about real money."

153

All of them chuckled about that, including Troy. But part of him stood watching the scene from outside. It was bizarre. The odds were good that Mike Brennan would pay what he owed. How could he abandon his child and still look in the mirror? The flaw in kidnapping was always the ransom; it was how the authorities nailed the perpetrators. This time, however, the police would have no idea a crime had occurred. It had the same advantage as robbing Moon Man: nobody could run to the cops. Mike Brennan couldn't even cross the border into the U.S. He, too, had a federal indictment pending.

"You got a deal, Chepe," Troy said. "I gotta talk to my other partner, but he'll go along with me—probably."

"Good, man," Chepe said. "I'm really glad it's you. I've got plenty of fools who do whatever I say. This time I've gotta have somebody with sense, y'know what I mean, *ese*?"

"I understand. You want it smooth."

"I want my money . . . but mainly I don't want this guy to think he can disrespect me. Wait a second." Chepe went to a wall with a bulletin board and many slips of paper pinned to it. He found the one he wanted and brought it back. "Here." It was an address on Virginia, in San Marino, California. Troy committed it to memory; then put it in his shirt pocket—just in case his memory failed him.

"Look here," Chepe said, "any message you got for me, you tell Greco. Right?" He looked to Alex and Alex nodded.

"Hey, Chepe," Alex said, "you know Troy's other partner, big Diesel from Frisco."

"Oh yeah," Chepe said with a grin, "a big tough kid. I bet on him when he fought that *miate*, what was his name, had a head like a loaf of bread."

All of them laughed; they knew whom he meant. "Dolomite Lawson," Mad Dog said.

"Diesel shoulda beat him."

"He went wild and ran out of gas."

The young woman stuck her head in the door. "*La cuenta*," she said. Chepe looked at his watch.

"You guys better hit it if you don't want to stay the night."

"The night!" Mad Dog said.

154

"Yeah," Alex said. "You can stay all night. Shit, you can stay a week if you want."

"Quit bullshittin'," Mad Dog insisted.

"It's true," Troy said. He'd known about it for years. "We better get outta here."

Chepe saw them to the terrace. He seldom went down into the yard and, when he did, he had several bodyguards around him. An international drug trafficker arouses enemies from unforeseen areas.

12

Diesel had been home for two nights and three days and was begging
God for Troy to call after the first night. As soon as he saw his kid
and got laid, Gloria's nagging got under his skin. He had to grin,
remembering it: He was on his back, still sweaty and getting his
breath, and she started on his case about the money: "Where did
it come from? Was anybody going to trace it? What had he done?"
He tried to tell her, "Gloria, goddamnit, you don't really want to
know . . . and I can't tell you . . . so get off my back . . ."

Ten minutes later, she began again. "You're going back to prison.
You've got a son. Don't expect me to wait." He noticed that her
recriminations failed to include an offer to return the money. By
the second evening, she drove him into the night, where he bought
watered-down drinks at $4.50 a shot, while seated beside an eye-
level ramp where young women danced naked except for high heels,
using a barber pole for a prop. He knew one of the girls; her brother
had been in the joint with him—and was back again, for heisting
the bank in the Fairmont Hotel. He was a gutty guy, and she was
fine—but just to look at right now. He was into serious business
and following his dick could fuck things up. He used to do things
like that, but three years outside prison had made him a lot more
cautious. Still, he would watch the young body and imagine the legs
opening for him. He filed her away; he would get to know her better
after this run of crime. By then he'd be halfass rich or dead. No
way he was going to jail, not with a third strike for life. That much
was settled in his mind.

When he got home on the second night, he was drunk and horny, and when Gloria came to berate him for making her worry, he grinned and his eyes had a gleam. He was thinking of the dancer. "Oh, no," she said, but he pushed her against the wall and cupped his hand between her legs while blowing and nibbling on her neck and ear. She tried to struggle without making noise that would awaken the child. It was her undoing. Within a minute her body took over and she stood on one foot while opening her legs and pressing up against him; she wanted his hand to touch her more intimately.

He carried her into the bedroom, both legs around him. He fucked her for a long time, and afterward she went to sleep without finishing her recriminations.

In the morning he awakened to a ringing phone and awareness that Gloria was getting up to answer it. He heard her coming back and kept his eyes closed to duck her. Instead of going to bed, she shook him. "It's Jimmy."

". . . the Face?"

"Yes. He called last night, too." She held out the cordless phone.

Diesel sensed that this was a setup deal between them. "Yo, boss, what's up?"

"Why don't you drive up today?"

"I'm waiting for a call."

"Tell Gloria to have 'em call here."

Diesel was trapped. She was watching him. He couldn't tell The Face that he didn't trust her to deliver the message. "Yeah, okay," he said. He would have to explain that Gloria was a bitch at times. The old mafioso was a hick about women and wives and shit like that. A snake in business, he was a squarejohn in family values. Diesel preferred Troy's attitude: "If you're a criminal, be a criminal twenty-four hours a day."

"I'll be here until seven," Jimmy said.

"I'll be there before that."

When he hung up, Gloria appeared in the doorway. "What'd he say?"

"He wants to see me."

"Are you going?"

"Hell no! Fuck that old dago cocksucker."

"Charles!"

He burst into laughter. "Bitch, you know you've been talking to him. Boo-hoo, crying about me."

"No, I haven't."

"Quit lying."

"I'm not."

"Okay, let it go. But lemme tell you this, when Troy calls, you be nice. Get his number. Tell him where I am and give him that number. If you play any games, I'm gonna go ape, y'know what I mean? I don't hit you—not unless you hit me first—but if you fuck with me on this, give your heart to God, 'cause your ass is mine."

Gloria started to spat back, but she felt the electricity in the air and gave an acceding nod. "If he calls, I'll tell him."

"Get his number."

"I'll ask him."

"Just don't play any games."

"You don't have to threaten me, Charles."

"If I don't have to, I'm sorry."

He decided to take everything he needed to go back to L.A. He could go direct from Sacramento. She could handle the hundred grand. She took good care of money. He had to say that for her.

Ten minutes later, he was on the road.

The setting sun sent rays through the old windbreak of eucalyptus. It reminded Diesel of sunlight through bars. He was on a secondary highway, two lanes built by the W.P.A. as part of the N.R.A. He saw the storm fence topped with barbed wire that he was looking for. Behind that fence was another fence, just like a jail. Behind that were the self-storage rooms covering a couple of acres. Nearly all the storage rooms were rented, and Jimmy planned to build more.

He saw the sign: ARROYO CARTAGE AND STORAGE.

He slowed for the entrance and made the turn. The driveway's asphalt was worn through, so dust billowed and was quickly blown away by the fast breeze that had risen. The only car parked outside the office was Jimmy's new El Dorado. Diesel parked next to it. As he got out, Jimmy came from the office. As usual, he had a big cigar in his teeth. He seemed hurried, and a bit surprised at the sight of Diesel. He recovered with a grin. "Hey, big fella, how ya doin'?"

"I'm good. What's up?"

"I wanna see you . . . Can you wait about ten minutes? I've got to pick something up before the post office closes."

"Yeah . . . sure." What else could he say to Jimmy the Face, the *capo* who looked out for him?

"Great." Then he was gone.

Diesel entered the empty office. A counter, a couple of empty desks, a glass-enclosed office at the rear. He remembered the first time he'd seen Jimmy Fasenella, pacing the yard in San Quentin. He'd known about Jimmy the Face, just as he knew about Lucky Luciano and Bugsy Siegel. Diesel was surprised at the mafioso's short stature. He was supposedly the mob's enforcer on the West Coast, supposedly "made" for blowing away Bugsy Siegel—nine shots through a Beverly Hills window. The underworld grapevine also said he'd murdered a man who thought The Face was a friend. Diesel would never make that mistake. He would laugh and jive with Jimmy the Face, but he would never really trust the little cobra—and if they ever had a dispute of any consequence, he would surely strike first, and without shooting in the head somebody who thought he was a friend. That was the fucked-up part about dago mafioso, even if the craziest of their killers were usually Irish and not even "made." Jimmy had told him that, and Jimmy knew about such things.

Diesel went to the rear office. It was unlocked. He sat behind Jimmy's desk and speculated on making a phone call. No. The odds were too good that the feds had it tapped. That was routine.

He put his feet on the desk and leaned back. Yeah, he could do this if there was money in it—sit with his feet on a desk. He spotted a newspaper folded in the wastebasket. He took it out. Sacramento *Bee*. SERBS SHELL SARAJEVO.

What was that? He was totally oblivious to the news of the last week or so, he never paid much attention anyway. Sometimes he leafed through a newspaper or watched the evening news, but he usually only kept up with sports, especially boxing. The word war caught his attention and he read that portion of the article on the front page. He snorted derisively. He believed America had lost its guts. It was getting soft—like Egypt, Rome, China, Spain, and England before it. None of those empires thought they would go down the drain. Troy had once given him an article to read, "The End of the White Man," that drew the parallels between the earlier mighty empires and the United States of today. Congress bought every weapon in the world, even the useless, but would not fight anyone. Oh my God, there might be a casualty. What the fuck were soldiers for? Blaaah!

He turned pages, read about the bust of a pot-growing operation in Grass Valley. Two men, two women, and a juvenile. The names of the adults were listed. Nobody he recognized.

He turned another page—and there was a quarter-page picture of Jinx, the girl who had been with Mad Dog in Sacramento. A second girl's picture was there, too. She was a friend of Jinx. Both were missing. Under both photos was the question: "Have you seen them?" A $20,000 reward.

Yeah, it was Jinx, no doubt of it. They had disappeared a week ago. The second girl's car was found at the County Airport. Beyond any doubt, Mad Dog had killed both of them and buried the bodies in the wilderness.

A weakness spread through Diesel's stomach. He believed Mad Dog had killed Jinx because Troy had reprimanded him about giving the girl their names. Oh my God . . . Forgive me, Father, for I have sinned . . . The knowledge was an awesome burden that he had to share with Troy.

He tore out the page and folded it. Then he heard a car engine and the crunch of tires on gravel. He went outside. Jimmy the Face was in a hurry. "C'mon, I got some dough for you."

Back inside, Jimmy opened a file cabinet and took out a fat envelope that he plunked into Diesel's hand. "A little thank-you. I got that contract."

Contract? Oh yeah, the trucks he'd burned up left no competitive bidder.

"Five g's," Jimmy said.

"Thanks, boss." Five grand was nice money for lighting a fire.

Jimmy looked at his watch. "I gotta go . . . but I wanted to talk to you about that maniac you're running with."

Diesel frowned. How did Jimmy know about Mad Dog?

". . . a smart guy," Jimmy was saying, "but there's lotta smart crazy people, y'know what I mean?"

"Uh-huh." Diesel realized that Jimmy was talking about Troy, not Mad Dog. Diesel was indignant, but he stifled the indignation with an acquiescent nod.

"Get away from that guy," Jimmy Fasenella said. "You don't need him. We've got things going. C'mon, walk me to the car."

On the way outside, Jimmy continued: ". . . got no sense of propriety. He's too loose. He takes risks. Crime is a game where you don't take risks you don't have to. One bad move, you know—bang, you serve a decade in the garbage can. They got no idea what kind of a maniac you can create in ten years. That guy is fucked up. You don't need him. You got friends. You've got a wife and kids. That guy . . . he's got nothing to lose."

"Thanks, Jimmy. You make sense."

"Great." He winked and gave Diesel a tap on the arm with the heel of his hand. "Take it easy. Keep in touch."

"Will do, Mr. J."

Diesel watched the El Dorado back out and spit gravel as it headed for the open gate. When it turned onto the road, he said aloud: "Gloria . . . you're a jive-ass bitch. I ain't going home now 'cause I'm mad enough to smack you for gettin' in my business."

When he got into his car, his anger surged. He slammed his hand into the dashboard. The glove compartment popped open. When he slammed it shut, it bounced open again. It made him laugh at himself.

He turned the key. The engine kicked in; so did the radio. He headed toward I-5. The interstate had very light traffic. A sign said it was patrolled by planes. They would have a hard time giving him a ticket. He pressed the accelerator and watched the speedometer climb quickly past ninety.

When he stopped for gas in Bakersfield, he used a pay phone to call home. He called collect.

"Yes, I'll accept the charges," Gloria said. "Charles, what're you doing in Bakersfield?" Her tone was querulous and aroused his ire.

"I'll call you when I get to L.A. See if you learned how to say hello." He slammed the receiver back on the hook and went to pay the gas station attendant. Back on the highway and beginning the climb over the Ridge Route, he remembered that he had Alex's phone number. Greco would hook him up with Troy and Mad Dog, so he had no necessity to call Gloria. That made him grin. Fuck her. "The bitch can stew for all I give a shit."

The KFWB News ("Give us twenty-two minutes and we'll give you the world") said that rain was falling in L.A. What would Troy say when told about the missing girls? Missing, shit, the *murdered* girls . . . That was four murders he knew about. How many more had Mad Dog killed? All four were women or children, but that didn't mean he didn't kill men. Everybody died with a bullet in the brain or a knife in the heart. It was scary being around a homicidal maniac. Sometimes the crime life called for icing somebody, but goddamn, not everybody, or anybody, for no good reason. Mad Dog was a mad dog. Jesus.

Troy was listening to the same newscast, but he already knew it was raining in L.A. The windshield wipers easily swept away the soft drizzle. He was careful. In another light rain, long ago, he had slid into the rear of a car waiting at a traffic light. The truck he'd been driving reeked from broken bottles. If he was still there when the police came, he would go to jail—so he told the other driver that he had to take a piss, went to an alley—and kept going. He got away, but caught pneumonia. Now he was very cautious behind the wheel, except when police sirens and flashing lights were on his ass. Then he drove like it was LeMans. A car cut in front of him and he had to hit the brakes. He grinned, but Mad Dog reacted: "That asshole don't know who he's fuckin' with. Pull up beside him." Mad Dog started to haul out his pistol.

"Hey, hey," Troy said. "Whaddya wanna do . . . shoot the fool for cutting you off? I can see you tellin' the dudes in the yard, "The motherfucker cut me off, so I shot him . . .'"

"Those dudes would never let me forget it."

"That's right."

"But the fuckin' punk—"

"You can't kill all the assholes in the world."

Ahead, the freeway sign announced: SOTO STREET, NEXT EXIT.

Troy eased over and got off. This was City Terrace and Hazard, in the shadow of the General Hospital. Troy knew the area. He had Chicano pals from around here, Sonny Ballesteros, Gordo, and Crow, among others.

He stayed on Soto as it followed the base of some low hills. On top of one was a radio tower with flashing red lights on top. The lights barely showed in the rain. As they passed the towers, Troy said, "I climbed that once. I was drunk, of course."

Mad Dog looked. He was a bit awed. It was a daredevil act if he ever saw one. There was no ladder, just the steel framework.

Soto became Huntington Drive, a six-lane boulevard with a wide median that had once carried the big red streetcars east across the county to Azusa and Claremont and Cucamonga. Troy thought of how the giants of the automobile and tire industries had destroyed the biggest public transportation system in the world—one that showed a profit every year of its existence. The money stolen from the public had not been returned; it was part of empire, "Ah, well, the fuckin' fools deserve it," he muttered. They give some dumb junkie twenty years if he runs into a bank with a note and gets $800 from a teller—and some financial executive can gamble away a billion dollars of taxpayer money, which the Congress borrows, and when the public finishes paying the interest, it is four billion dollars. The executive signs a consent decree and buys a five-million-dollar house in Florida before he files for bankruptcy. "Now why shouldn't I rip off a motherfucker like that?" he said, and looked playfully to Mad Dog as he said it.

"What's that?"

"Nothing."

Tiny ramshackle houses gave way to stores, and then again to houses, albeit nicer, as they crossed into Alhambra, and nicer still in South Pasadena. Now the median was lawn and tended bushes.

163

The sign said San Marino and the houses were nicer still. Troy had looked up Virginia Road in the *Thomas Street Guide*. They were getting close. He saw it. "Turn left."

Suddenly the houses were large and lovely, the dream realized. They sat back on wide lawns; their inner workings were modern American, the latest plumbing, the latest wiring, the latest central air. They were lath and plaster, but their looks were diverse copies of English Tudor and French Provincial, Monterey Colonials, brick Williamsburg, and sprawling modern ranch. Their grounds were manicured and flowers still bloomed despite it being December. A few already had decorated Christmas trees in big front windows framed with lights.

Mad Dog whistled. "This is *definitely* the high-rent district."

As the Jaguar continued, the road narrowed but the houses got bigger, now set behind high wrought-iron fences, hidden by thick greenery. The addresses told him they were getting close.

It was a two-story Mediterranean behind a brick wall topped with wrought-iron spikes. The lawn was the size of a football field. "Are you sure this is the place?" Mad Dog asked.

"We'll keep going. Lemme see." He turned on the map light and looked at the slip of paper. Unless Chepe had made a mistake, this was the place. "That's the one. Let's go back around . . . take another look."

They made two more passes along the front of the house. The corner pillar of the fence had no spikes. It would take ten seconds to go over there, and they could drop into bushes. The way the road was, they would see any approaching car at some distance. The only house with a view of the corner pillar was directly across the street, and it peeked out from behind a stand of trees.

"We'll come back in the daytime," Troy said. "Let's go."

They were on Monterey Road in South Pasadena when the cellular phone rang. It was Greco. "Your big man is on the Hollywood Freeway. I told him to get off at Highland and check into the Holiday Inn. We'll be waitin' for you."

"Thanks."

"Chepe's gonna call me pretty soon."

"Cool. There's a couple things I gotta see you about."

The Jaguar was now in South Pasadena. Suddenly there was a whole row of houses decorated with brilliant Christmas lights in front-yard trees and windows. One had a crèche erected on the lawn. This was the season that touches many, including Mad Dog McCain. "You know what, Troy," he said, "you're the only real friend I've got in the whole fuckin' world."

"C'mon, bro', lighten up." He said it with a grin.

"No, man. I mean it, man. I really do."

"You're my pardnuh," Troy said, and disliked the lie. In truth he was nervous around Mad Dog. Too volatile; too unpredictable. Yet there was an intoxicating power in knowing he could say, "Kill so and so," and it would be done. How could he know that murder would become a habit with Mad Dog? He imagined the Old Man of the Mountains, Hasan ibn-al-Sabbah, from whom the word *assassin* is derived. He hired his assassins out all over the world—gave them some hash to smoke and they cut throats, the ones they were sent to cut. Jesus, the world could use a few of them these days, instead of idiots ruling wholesale with their automatics.

After another half block, Mad Dog spoke again. "I gotta tell you, brother, I don't like that fuckin' Diesel."

Troy lied again. "I thought you guys were cool. He likes you. He thinks you're a little wild sometimes, but he just told me, 'That is a stand-up guy.'"

"Diesel said that?"

"Yeah. No bullshit."

"Maybe I'm wrong, but sometimes he acts like he's some kinda tough guy 'cause he weighs two-fifty and used to be a prizefighter. Motherfuckin' prizefighters bleed, too."

"He doesn't think that. He knows all the tough guys are in the grave." It was a convict axiom that tough guys ended up in the graveyard. "But if he really fucks with you, you let me know and we'll take care of it."

"That's cool. Thanks, Troy. You're the best dude . . ." His voice trailed off.

Troy felt misgivings about his deception. As a child, he had heard

165

special scorn for the deceitful, which had something to do with his choice of armed robbery as a crime. What was more direct and less deceitful than that?

Monterey Road came out of the hills of South Pasadena and crossed the bridge over the Pasadena Freeway and Arroyo Seco. Now they were again in the Los Angeles city limits. The area had been Italian and Irish working class, with a few second-generation Chicanos, ten years ago, but now it was totally Mexican. All the store signs were in Spanish. He knew about a ramp onto the inbound Pasadena. It was the oldest freeway, and instead of a lane that blended into the flow on the move, he had to jump in from a dead stop. He hit the gas pedal and the Jag accelerated like a rocket. Good old Chevy V8.

"I'm hungry," said Mad Dog.

"Me, too. Let's pick up Diesel and Alex at the hotel. It's close to one of my favorite restaurants."

"Oh, yeah. Which one is that?"

"Musso Franks on Hollywood Boulevard. They used to call it the Algonquin West."

"I never heard of either one."

"I'll run it down sometime."

At the Holiday Inn, a message was at the desk that their friends waited in the bar. Alex was sipping a screwdriver and Diesel was drinking beer. "Let's go eat," Troy said. "We can walk. It's only a couple of blocks."

While they walked, Diesel and Mad Dog followed the example of the many tourists and looked at the famous names of stage, screen, TV, music, and radio emblazoned with stars in the sidewalk.

In the restaurant booth, Troy told Diesel about the kidnapping. The big man's first reaction was a pained expression and a shake of the head. "Oh, man, I dunno. I don't like kidnapping a baby. I mean . . . damn . . . it's a fucked-up crime."

"Hey, we're not gonna hurt the kid. He won't even know he's been snatched."

"What about the Little Lindbergh law? That's life."

"*Anything* is life with three strikes," Alex said. "Shoplifting or defrauding an innkeeper."

166

"Maybe even mopery, these days," Troy said.

"Mopery. What the fuck is mopery?"

Troy and Alex answered in unison: "Exposing yourself to a blind person."

"What? Oh, man, quit jiving."

"Look," Troy said, "we're gonna split a lotta dough. Maybe two million. And ninety-nine out of a hundred it won't even get reported."

"You think it's okay, huh?"

Troy nodded slowly.

"Okay, I'm in."

The waiter arrived with their food. As Diesel ate, he began thinking about what he would do with his share. He would invest in something real safe, maybe rental property. That would put some security under Charles, Jr. He would ask Jimmy the Face about it. Jimmy had some real flophouse S.R.O. hotels in Sacramento and Stockton. About the kidnapping, so what if the baby's father was a kingpin drug dealer who would want to kill them? He had no idea who they were. Somebody had been trying to kill Diesel as far back as he could remember. His own crime partner, Mad Dog McCain, was scarier than any drug dealer. The thought reminded him to show Troy the newspaper clipping about the missing girls as soon as they were alone.

13

Mike Brennan, without disguise except for rimless glasses and a different hairstyle, blended perfectly into the torrent of U.S. citizens who walk across the international border from Tijuana to San Ysidro every Sunday afternoon. The day trippers pour north as the sun descends. The turnstiles whirl as fast at Border Patrolmen can glance at a face and maybe ask where they were born or where they live. A reply of San Diego or L.A. is less suspicious than some distant city. Mike had a wallet full of identification in an alias. As he had never been arrested, or been in the army, no fingerprints were on file. Consequently, he had no fear of being arrested on the warrant from the U.S. District Court of the Central District of California. He never told anyone he was coming, so nobody could snitch him off. He had no intention of going to jail; only fools went to jail. For him it was far riskier driving on a freeway. Even if there was a risk, he was going to take it. Christmas was close and he was going to see his firstborn son. The baby lived with the mother. While still sucking a nipple and shitting in a diaper, a baby needed his mother—but when the boy was older, somewhere between eight and ten, Mike was going to take him. The mother was getting four hundred grand a year to cooperate. She also knew bad things would happen if she stopped cooperating.

While driving the Hertz rental car half the two hundred miles of megalopolis that sprawled solidly from the border to Santa Barbara, and from the sea deep into the desert (the city went wherever water could be piped via aqueduct), Mike Brennan decided against calling ahead. She'd been told not to bring any men to the house. If. Mike found one, shit was going to splatter. Mike Brennan saw the world with an arrogance similar to that of the Spanish conquistadors five centuries earlier, which meant he was governed by no law except that of his own whim. Killing someone was trivial in the court of important affairs. When he thought of his son's mother, it was always as "the bitch," or "the broad." Forgotten was the interlude of affection and intimacy that had produced the child. He lived on momentary impulses; he had the emotions of a child and the power of a gang lord. Yes, he owed Chepe, but had no intention of paying the old man, who was now powerless and locked away. If the old man wanted to start trouble, Mike Brennan was ready for that, too. But Chepe was the furthest thing from his mind as he passed through the downtown interchange and went east on I-10: He was thinking of his son, whom he hadn't seen since shortly after the baby's birth. Christmas was close. Junior, he thought, was too young to know about Christmas presents, but soon . . . Visible from the freeway was a tall building dressed in lights like a giant Christmas tree. Should he check into the hotel in Pasadena before or after he went to the house?

He decided on the hotel first. As he exited the freeway and stopped for a traffic light, fat dark spots appeared on the concrete. Rain had started to fall on L.A.

The storm had continued off and on through the night and the next day. Troy went to the house in Highland Park that they'd rented to hold the baby and the nanny. Mad Dog had not wanted to take the nanny. "Man, she might identify us."

"Nobody's gonna call the police."

"I don't like it."

"So you know how to change diapers, huh?"

"I don't—but Diesel does."

"He doesn't wanna."

"Fuck it. Do whatever you want."

Troy playfully grabbed the thin little man by the nape of the neck and gave him a friendly shake—but the moment he touched Mad Dog, Troy remembered the newspaper clipping with the photos of the missing teenage girls and almost snatched his hand away. Mad

Dog had murdered four, and probably more. There might be a time to kill, but not all the time.

Troy went to the wine cellar. The house was ancient by L.A. standards, having been built in the twenties during Prohibition, and the wine cellar was as much for hiding booze as storing wine. It had been dug into a hillside and could be reached only by raising a trap door in a hallway. A mattress and blanket were on the floor, and Diesel had purchased a package of Pampers. Troy made sure no water from the storm leaked into the wine cellar and then came back up. His stomach was nervous. Time for the caper was getting close.

Outside, the rain still fell. He picked up the cellular phone and dialed the Roosevelt Hotel, where Diesel and Mad Dog waited. They changed hotels every two or three days. "I'll be there in twenty minutes."

"Right. We're makin' our move?"

"No use waitin', is there?"

"Uh-uh."

"Later."

The Jaguar was silent except for the rhythm of the windshield wipers; they became audible when the car stopped for a traffic signal. Each man was wrapped in his own thoughts and the struggle with fear. Mad Dog was the most excited. When Troy's call came and Diesel said they were going, Mad Dog ducked into the bathroom for a quick toot of cocaine for courage. Because it was the last one he'd have until after the score, he dipped more than usual, and now his brain was surging. He felt powerful, omnipotent. The 12-gauge pump at his feet made him lord of the world. He could kill, and that, to Mad Dog, was the power of God given to man.

In the backseat, Diesel was all too aware of the man in front of him. He'd seen the trace of white powder on Mad Dog's nose. Even without that, his charged-up demeanor was a giveaway. He thought of Troy's reaction on sight of the newspaper photo, a grunt of disgust, a moment of reflection, and then: "We'll decide what to do after the caper. Chill out 'til then, okay?" Diesel had nodded and maintained the façade of camaraderie with Mad Dog. It was difficult to take it when Troy was gone. His hostile contempt was mixed with a smidgen of fear. A 12-gauge shotgun was scary in the hands of a madman. Diesel would keep an eye on him.

They drove slowly past the house. A light was on in the rear.

"Somebody's up."

"There's nobody there but the nanny and the kid," Troy said. "The broad is out for the night. She goes out every Friday. Look, her car's gone."

As he spoke, the light went out, verifying his declaration.

Inside the house, Mike Brennan had turned off the light as he carried a beer from the kitchen to the family room, where ESPN was broadcasting a minor Bowl game. He was waiting for the bitch to come home with her boyfriend. It was delicious to imagine her reaction. She would shit her jeans. He smiled imagining it. The boyfriend better not open his mouth. Mike took the 9mm Browning from his waistband and put it on the coffee table in front of him. It signified that he would call the shots.

Meanwhile, outside the house, Diesel webbed his fingers to lift Mad Dog atop the brick pillar at the corner. Mad Dog jumped down into the bushes. Troy was next. When he was up, he reached down and helped Diesel. The big man had to grunt and strain, but he got a leg up and pulled himself the rest of the way. By then Troy had jumped down, his shoes sinking in the wet lawn. A moment later, Diesel was beside him. "C'mon," Troy said, leading the way.

All of them were soaked through. At least the rain muffles noise, Troy thought. When they came to a corner of the house, Troy pointed Mad Dog to a niche behind the bushes under an overhang. It was dry there. He was to keep lookout with a walkie-talkie. Troy had a receiver that looked like a hearing aid.

Troy and Diesel moved along the side of the house, passing the family-room French doors. The TV set was on, throwing out its jerky gray light. Both looked in as they went by. Because they weren't expecting it, and because human nature oftens sees what it expects, neither noticed that someone was in the big upholstered chair facing the TV screen.

Mike Brennan, however, saw the two shadows go by. He thought it was the bitch and her boyfriend back from wherever they'd been. Nobody but the nanny had been here when he arrived. Now he would give them a few minutes and catch them flagrante delicto, whatever that meant. He'd heard it in a movie and it seemed to mean what he thought it meant. He hoped he could catch them fucking . . . He would sure kick some ass then. The bitch was mother of his kid; he gave her *beaucoup* money. She had better keep her legs crossed.

Outside, the rain surged. Diesel and Troy were soaked. Dirt from a slope behind the house washed down stairs and over their shoes. They wore rubber gloves and hats pulled down. It would never come to a courtroom identification, but such precautions were routine.

At the rear door, Diesel pulled out the short jimmy bar. It would pop the door with one jerk. It proved unnecessary. The doorknob turned when Troy tried it. He always tried a door first.

"Bingo," Troy said, easing the door open and motioning Diesel to follow him inside. Not expecting trouble, neither had a weapon drawn. It was so easy that Troy felt none of the usual fear at the start of a caper. It was easy, a bird's nest on the ground.

The door between back porch and kitchen was ajar, as were the folding doors into the dining room. Beyond that was the family room with the TV still on.

Troy pushed open another door. It was a hallway beside the stairway. Ahead was the entry hall and the front door. The nanny and baby were upstairs. He motioned Diesel to follow and swung around the banister and started up the carpeted stairs on light feet. I don't like doing this, he told himself clearly—but instantly locked out the thought with *he who hesitates is lost.*

The dim glow of a night-light came from the partially opened door. The nanny, a chunky woman in her forties, spoke in Spanish. Diesel was to grab her while Troy took the child.

Troy pushed the door open and Diesel went past. The nanny was removing a diaper from the baby on a changing table. She turned to throw the dirty diaper in a basket, saw the intruders in a mirror, and gasped.

Diesel pounced like a cat. He had a fist clenched to hit her in the ribs, but instead grabbed her arm. "Shaddup!" he said.

"Watch the kid," Troy said. He was afraid Diesel would pull the nanny away and the baby would fall from the table.

"Got it," Diesel said, holding the nanny with one hand and putting the other on the baby's naked stomach. Startled by the sudden intruders and the tension in the air, the baby began crying.

"You speak English?" Troy asked.

She tried to speak; then nodded.

"Take care of him. Get him dressed."

By the time his words were out, he saw an unexpected man in the doorway. He looked like a Yaqui Indian, and Troy assumed he was related to the nanny.

Brennan frowned in surprise, for what he'd found was unexpected. Which of these jokers was the boyfriend and where was the bitch?

Diesel raised his jacket to pull his pistol—but Mike Brennan had prepared for confrontation: his 9mm Browning was in his hand down by his leg. He raised it and stepped forward before Diesel could get a grip. "Who the fuck're . . ." He didn't finish, but instead cocked the hammer with his thumb. The muzzle with the hole of death was three feet from Diesel's eye. He pulled his hand free, palm visible. "Take it easy."

The adults were frozen for several heartbeats; meanwhile the baby howled its plaint.

"Easy! Easy! *Usted's loco* . . ."

"Yeah, easy! I got the kid." As Diesel said it, he swung the baby before him and ducked his head. Unless Mike anticipated the motion, it happened too fast. The hand is not quicker than the eye, but it is quicker than the mind in such a situation.

Mad Dog, from his niche outside, had seen headlights through the wind-whipped bushes. Were they coming in the gate? The wind made too much noise to hear a car. He crossed the road and looked toward the gate. Nothing. When he turned back, through the family room window, he saw a silhouette rise from a chair and move out of sight. Who was that?

He moved fast to the back door and went through the kitchen into the front hall. His wet shoes squeaked; leaning against the wall, he pulled them off and put them down. He was silent going up the stairs two at a stride and at the top he saw the strange man in the doorway, facing the other way. Mad Dog raised his shotgun and pressed the safety button so the red was displayed. It was a ten-foot shot of double ought. Troy was beyond the man in the line of fire. Mad Dog moved forward and to the right on stocking feet. It gave him an angle.

"Nobody has to get hurt," Troy was saying.

The range was about eight feet when Mad Dog squeezed the trigger. The shotgun sounded like a howitzer and most of Mike Brennan's head was blown off his torso. It splattered across five feet of wall. The rest of the carcass dropped inert.

The nanny screamed until Diesel banged her head against a wall; then she whimpered and collapsed.

The baby wailed.

"Douse that light," Troy said. Had the nanny seen their faces well enough to identify them? Very unlikely. She was too distraught to see anything clearly.

Mad Dog hit the light switch. The room dimmed. Troy picked up the baby and carried him to the nanny. "Here. Get him quiet."

The nanny shook her head. "I can't."

Anger rose; Troy didn't have time for this kind of bullshit. He reached out with one hand, entwined his fingers in her hair, and jerked her around. "Take the little motherfucker," he said.

She took him. Years of conditioning made her do the right thing to soothe him.

Mad Dog was looking out the window. He began to laugh somewhat hysterically.

Diesel was looking at his own clothes. Was he splattered with blood? He could find none except on his shoes. He stood in a thick pool of it. Its smell was heavy in the room.

"Who was that guy?" Troy asked the nanny.

She shrugged and shook her head.

"A cop?" Diesel asked.

"Get his wallet," Mad Dog said.

174

"You get it!" Diesel came back.

Troy turned on him. "What's wrong with you?"

"I don't like this asshole telling me what to do."

Troy looked toward the ceiling with exasperation written on his face. "Man, get the fuckin' wallet. Let's find out who he is."

Diesel did so. Meanwhile the nanny was rocking the baby and trying to soothe him. "Take him outta here," Troy said; then, to Mad Dog, "Watch her."

Diesel opened the wallet and came out with a fistful of cards. "Joe Vasquez," he said, handing Troy the driver's license. He went into the other room and asked the nanny. She had no idea who he was. Troy was dubious. Should he put weight on her? No. She had to handle the baby. Who was Joe Vasquez? Never once did Troy consider it was Mike Brennan, although he did wonder if the dead man worked for Mike.

Was there anyone else? A moment of fear; then he decided it was most unlikely. How much time did he have? What about the blood on floor and wall? The buckshot holes? He'd think about that later.

Mad Dog motioned him to lean close. "We gotta kill this broad," he said. "She can identify us."

"Lemme think about it," Troy said. The statement had logic but was too repugnant. It was no time to tell Mad Dog, but he knew he could never murder someone so defenseless. The mother would be home in anywhere between fifteen minutes and two hours. He had to make decisions. They would move the body. They needed blankets, or something, to make sure it didn't bleed all over the car. "We need something to wrap him in," he told Diesel.

"The baby?"

"No. The body."

"What about trash bags?"

"Great."

Diesel went to the kitchen and returned with a package of lawn bags. Perfect. They went around the remains of the head; then they spread blankets and a bedspread on the floor and rolled the carcass on top; then folded the blanket and carried the remains to the front porch. Troy ran down the long drive to the gate, opening it as he went, and brought the Jaguar back. They stuffed the body in the trunk and slammed it shut. That was covered.

The plan had been to take both nanny and baby, but that was impossible. The mother would go out of her mind if she found blood and gore instead of her baby. Troy's adrenaline still pumped, stirring fear and fury, the emotions of survival, but underneath he could feel the keening anguish of despair. He had to play the cards that came off the deck, but down in his guts, he felt desperate fear. Things had gone awry, the unexpected man, the killing, having child and nanny and mother to decide about.

"Go get the kid and the nanny," he told Diesel.

"Mad Dog, too?"

"Yeah ... of course. Take 'em to the spot. I'll wait here for the broad."

"You won't have a car. You'll be here stranded."

"Go on, man."

Diesel shrugged and went inside. Soon the nanny came out, carrying the now quiet baby and followed by Mad Dog and Diesel. Diesel stepped forward, opened the back door, and motioned the nanny to get in. She hesitated. "No baby seat," she said.

"Never mind. Get in," he said. She did so. Mad Dog went to Troy.

"You really gonna stay here, man?" asked Mad Dog. "We can call and say what's happening."

"No, no. She'd call the cops. Here—" Troy handed over the cellular phone. You call here as soon as you get there. Have the nanny standing by."

"What about the ... the trunk."

"We'll dump that later."

Mad Dog nodded. He turned to Diesel beside the car. "Who's driving?"

"Go ahead. You know the way?"

"Well ... sort of. I mean, Troy was gonna drive."

They turned to Troy, who told them: "Down this road to Monterey, turn left and keep following it. You'll cross a bridge over the freeway. Keep going. Left on Figueroa. You know the street it's on, don't you?"

Mad Dog nodded.

"Turn right, keep going. You'll see that museum up on the hillside. Watch for the house."

"Got it.

"Keep her head down so she can't see where you're going . . . and keep the baby down low. You don't wanna get pulled over because he isn't in a safety seat."

"Right."

"Get going."

The Jaguar went down the driveway, the red brake lights flaring momentarily as it paused before turning onto the street. Troy went back into the house and looked at the murder scene. What a mess the shotgun made. Blood had run down in rivulets; then soaked in. There were tiny bits of flesh and bone and hair stuck to the plaster. Should he burn the house down? Could he burn the house down? He had nothing inflammable like gasoline or kerosene.

The headlight glare on the windows announced the woman's return. The car pulled into a porte cochere beside the house. Troy watched from behind a dining room drape as the woman got out, reaching for her purse before slamming it shut. She had driven and she was alone. Thank God for small favors.

She came in the side door from the porte cochere. She was coming through the house toward the stairs. "Carmen!" she called. "I'm back."

Troy stepped from the shadows. "Hold it, baby!"

She jerked and gasped. Her fright knocked out her wind so she choked instead of screamed.

He pounced on her, grabbed her arm. Her eyes were huge with terror in the shadowed light. "Be quiet. Your baby's all right."

"My baby! Where—"

"He's okay."

"Ohhh . . . ohhh . . . ohhh."

"Hey!" He squeezed and shook her. He felt queasy; he took no joy from this; it was terrible. "Settle down, baby."

He could feel her shaking. Oh, God, why had he done this?

For money, asshole, replied the Mr. Hyde of his mind.

"Where is he?" As she spoke, he felt her pull toward the stairs.

"He's not upstairs, baby. We got him."

"Please . . . don't hurt him. I'll do whatever you want. He's just a little boy."

"I know . . . I know. Shhh. Listen."

"Take me."

"Shaddup! Listen, goddammit!"

She stopped talking and nodded, although she still trembled.

"Nothing is going to happen to your baby . . . but the best way to get him back quick is to cooperate. You wanna cooperate?"

"Yes."

"What's his name?"

"Michael."

"After his father?"

"Yes."

"This is about Mike the father. Do you know where to call him?"

"I . . . I have a number in Ensenada. Sometimes I reach him, sometimes I leave word. He calls back or has somebody call for him."

"Good. He cares about his kid?"

"He might kill me over this."

"No, he won't."

"You don't know him. He's vicious."

Troy found himself thinking that she was not merely attractive, she had a clean-cut quality. She belonged in a sorority or something, not with a drug kingpin. He wanted to ask how she'd gotten involved with Mike Brennan, but stopped himself. He had to stay focused on the serious matters at hand.

"Does he have you watched?"

"Huh?"

"Does he have anyone watch you?

"I don't know. Maybe. Why?"

Should he tell her now about the gore upstairs? He had to tell her something sometime.

The phone started ringing. "Answer it," Troy directed.

She picked it up. "Hello." She listened for a moment; then handed it to Troy.

"Yeah."

"Everything's cool," said Diesel's voice. "They're down in the wine cellar. We need some baby food."

"Go get some . . . No, send the Dog."

"Okay. How's it going? I see the broad got home."

"Yeah. I'm running it down now."

"Want somebody to come and get you?"

"No. That's okay."

"How you gonna get outta there?"

"Never mind." He avoided saying that he planned to take the mother's car. He would park it half a mile from the hideout and walk the rest of the way. "Just hang until you hear from me."

"Good. Maybe it's gonna be okay."

"Maybe. Later." He hung up and looked at the girl. "Well, Mike Brennan had one of his *pistoleros*—"

"His what?"

"*Pistoleros* . . . torpedo . . . gunman . . . Anyway, he was watching you. He got killed."

"You . . . you killed him?"

"Upstairs."

"Oh God. Is he still there?"

"No . . . but it's messy up there."

"Oh, shit!"

Maybe she wasn't as soft as he had first thought. "Forget about that. You can clean it up later. Right now, I want you to call that number. If you get Mike, gimme the phone. If you have to leave a message, have him call you. When you talk to him, tell him that his kid is collateral on money he owes to an old man in jail. When he pays it, he gets the baby back. You got it?"

"What if he won't pay?"

"He'll pay."

"But if he doesn't?"

"If he doesn't, I'll give you the baby back. But if you tell him that, I'll blow *your* fuckin' brains out." He hardened the last few words for emphasis. Inside himself, he disliked the scene more and more. But hard times make hard people, and Troy felt himself extremely desperate. He, too, was fighting for life; that was how he saw it. "Here," he said, handing her the telephone.

She made the call. Mike Brennan, of course, was not available. He was expected tomorrow morning. "Be sure to have him call. It's urgent." She was looking at Troy as she spoke. When she hung up, Troy told her, "I need to use your car."

"Okay. Just . . . my baby." Her eyes welled with tears, and so did his. What the fuck was he doing? But what the fuck could he do this late in the game? "He'll be okay. Carmen's with him. You trust her, don't you?"

"Yes."

"The keys to the car?"

She got them from her purse.

"If you call the police—"

"I won't. I know better."

"I hope you do."

He made her walk him to the car. As he got in, she asked: "Will you let Carmen call me and tell me he's okay?"

"I'll do that. But I can tell if the wire is tapped."

"Don't worry. I swear I won't call the police."

Troy watched her through the mirror until he passed through the gate, the slight figure standing in the rain. He ached with pain for what he'd done, but he could not erase half a line.

He was passing giant houses brilliantly lighted for Christmas. That, too, added to his anguish.

14

The first dozen hours were as relaxed as such a situation can be. The nanny kept the baby quiet. Troy talked to Alex on the phone, and then they waited. By the following night the baby seemed to be crying for his mother and the phone conversations were tense. Troy even wondered if someone was playing games. Maybe he should call the girl and see if she knew anything. He decided against it.

On the third evening, Alex called. "That guy that walked in on you—"

"What about him?"

"You still got him?"

"He's starting to smell real ripe."

"You know what, bro', it might be Mike Brennan."

"You're jiving."

"I wish I was."

"This guy looked one-hundred-percent Indian. He didn't even look like a Mexican, much less half Irish."

"That's what Mike Brennan looks like."

"Oh, man, don't tell me that."

"Nobody's seen him over there. The old man has somebody in Brennan's mob, and nobody's heard from him since last Sunday."

"Oh, man, I can't believe it." But he did believe it. Indeed, the moment Alex described Brennan, Troy knew the body belonged to the drug lord.

"I never seen Chepe so fucked up. He's mad."

"At me?"

"At Mad Dog. He said to take him out or he's puttin' a contract on you."

Swelling anger was Troy's first reaction. "Fuck him in his ass . . . old motherfucker."

"Cool it. Chill out. Think about it."

"I don't let people tell me what to do. That's why I've been in trouble all my life."

"Yeah, well, I can understand that . . . but if you think about it, that guy deserves a goddamn good killin' anyway. It'll do everybody a favor."

"Oh, yeah?"

"You know it, bro'. He's a menace to everybody."

"Maybe I'll shoot myself in the head." Troy laughed as he said it. "At least that'd solve my problems."

"What about the kid and the nanny?"

"What about 'em. I'm not gonna waste 'em."

"At least you're not on the six o'clock news."

"Yeah, it won't be added to the crime statistics. Damn, homeboy, it's gonna be hard. That guy almost idolizes me."

"He'd turn on you in a hot second. He'd turn on anybody. He's nuts."

"It don't look like Chepe's gonna pay us, huh?"

Greco laughed into the phone. "No, I don't think so. If you let it ride, you'll be sorry afterward."

"I'll think about it."

"Lemme tell you, bro', that old man looks easygoing, but he's got Mexicans up the ass who'll kill anybody he wants for ten cents or less. I put all the weight on the maniac. But if you don't take care of it . . ."

"I got the picture." Indeed, Chepe had hundreds of millions, maybe a billion, and access to countless killers on both sides of the border. Some were idiots ready to murder for a couple of thousand dollars, and if some were too dumb to commit the crime, others were cunning, cold, and deadly. Troy was afraid of nothing that walked the face of the earth, including Chepe—but he preferred to keep the old man's friendship if he could.

As soon as Troy and Diesel opened the garage's side door, the stench of rotting flesh assailed and nauseated them.

"Good God, it smells bad," Diesel said, putting a hand over his nose and mouth. Troy turned away and pulled out a handkerchief. He had almost vomited. He hit the garage opener and the door rose. Outside the night was cool and fresh. Smog had been washed away by the recent rain. The storm had blown east across the southwestern deserts. The sky sparkled with stars. He breathed deep and thought: "Why can't life be easier than this?"

Diesel lugged the sack of quicklime to the car and slid it onto the rear floorboards. "Okay," he said.

"Go tell 'em let's go."

Diesel went into the side door. Mad Dog waited, holding the nanny's sleeve. She had a pillowcase over her head and held the sleeping baby in her arms. Diesel beckoned and Mad Dog told her, "Let's go. Watch yourself. You're going down three steps." He guided her with an elbow. Diesel waited ahead of her, backing down with his hands ready in case she stumbled.

Troy lowered the car windows, trying to blow away the stench from the trunk. When the nanny and baby were in the car, Diesel slammed the door and got in the front. Mad Dog ran across the street to his own car. When its headlights went on, Troy backed out and pulled ahead. "Don't lose him," Diesel said.

"No way."

Troy took back streets through Highland Park, crossed over a bridge above the Pasadena Freeway into El Sereno. With the windows down the moving car lost the nauseating odor, but the night was cold and the baby began to cry. The nanny cuddled him and soothed him in Spanish. Traffic was light, without pedestrians. Good.

He came out of the low hills and turned onto Huntington Drive and kept to the right, knowing what he was looking for, a bus bench by itself, without cars going by and with nobody likely to witness her getting out of the Jaguar.

Every few blocks found a bus bench, but for the first few, cars or people were around, so he kept going. At Fremont there was a cluster of businesses, doughnut shop, gas station, coffee shop. He had to stop for the light and wait until it was green.

A police car, black and white, crossed the intersection from left to right. Neither of the policemen looked over while going by.

The next bus stop was empty. Troy slowed and scanned the terrain with only Mad Dog behind him. Traffic coming the other way was a mile distant. He pulled to the curb.

Diesel was out quickly, opening the back door. "Come on," he said, leaning in to grab the nanny's arm for guidance and support. "Take it easy." They had her eyes bandaged in flesh tones, with dark glasses. It was impossible to see she was blindfolded unless you were up close. He had one hand on her upper arm, and the other over the forearm cradling the baby. It provided her the greatest sense that she wouldn't fall.

He guided her to the bench. "Sit. *Sienta se.*" She felt with one hand and sat down.

When her rump touched the seat, Diesel jumped back in the car as Mad Dog was just going past. Diesel slammed the door and Troy hit the gas. He watched the nanny and the baby in the rearview mirror until the night erased them.

Troy raised the remote telephone receiver and touched "send." The first ring barely started before she answered. "Hello."

"It's me. Your baby and the nanny are fine and are on a bus bench on Huntington Drive near the Pasadena Freeway."

"Oh, thank you, God, thank you."

"Did you go to the police?"

"No . . . no . . . I swear I didn't."

"Mike never called, did he?"

"No. I'm still waiting here."

"Give it up. Between you and me . . . he's history."

"What?"

"He's dead. So think what you're going to do now." Troy hung up without waiting for a response, hoping he'd done a favor by telling her; maybe she could get some dough by knowing fast.

He kept going down Huntington Drive. It was divided by a wide median and its three lanes in each direction were lightly trafficked.

He could head east, the way he wanted to go, without having to concentrate as if on the freeway. The kidnapping was behind them except for cleaning up the mess. That was what he had to think about.

"How you doin'?" he asked Diesel, after a couple minutes of silence.

"I'm okay, considering I'm not gonna be rich like I thought."

"Maybe we'll get a better one next time."

"Yeah . . . maybe." After a pause, he added, "When we get rid of this body in the trunk, I think I'm gonna go home for a while."

"Yeah. And we got one more thing to do."

"What's that?"

"Kill Mad Dog."

"That's your best idea in a long time."

"In a long time?"

"No, I didn't mean that. But it's good. Want me to do it?"

"No . . . he's my dog. I've got to put him to sleep."

"Suit yourself."

They drove along for a while. As they neared Rosemead Boulevard, he flashed the turn signals and watched as Mad Dog did the same. A ramp to the San Bernardino Freeway, Interstate 10, was a mile away.

"When're you gonna punch his ticket?"

"Why not put 'em in the same hole."

"*After* he helps dig, y'know what I mean?"

"You a big old lazy motherfucker, aren't you?"

"Shit, man, I don't like to dig ditches. They used to make us do that shit in Preston, remember?"

"Sure do." It was true, in reform school they'd been worked like slaves as a form of punishment. He remembered the blisters on his hands from swinging a mattock to tear up an asphalt athletic field. A hatred of hard labor had been planted simultaneously.

"You got shovels?"

"There's one in the back . . . on the floor."

Diesel leaned over and looked. "Just one?"

"We'll take turns."

"We need another one . . . and a mattock or a pick."

"There's nothing open. Maybe we could steal one."

"Right. We'd probably get caught doin' that and they'd find Mr. Smells Bad in the trunk."

"What're we gonna do?"

"Lemme think about it. I don't wanna wait until tomorrow night."

"I hear that. Shit, man, by then you'll never get the smell out."

"Yeah . . . like cat piss."

Ahead of them, the raised freeway was visible, cars and trucks flashing by. Troy eased into the lane to turn onto the ramp. Mad Dog followed.

The eye of the storm that had drenched L.A. earlier was now stalled somewhere over Arizona, but its trailing end was still causing occasional showers between Riverside and the state line.

The two cars were specks of flotsam carried along the river of Interstate 10. Cars, trucks, buses, all rolled flat out along the ribbon of multilane road. Anyone who stayed within the 55-mile-per-hour speed limit would be blown aside by the wind from passing Kenilworths. When they rolled through L.A. County's eastern towns, Cucamonga, Covina, and Pomona, the traffic was heavy. Big rigs formed caravans, like elephants nose to tail, while cars flashed past like whippets. Troy drove carefully, making sure nothing got attention from the Highway Patrol. If he was pulled over, the mess in the trunk would definitely be smelled. The stench of decomposing flesh would surely constitute "probable cause." He kept the windows lowered enough to blow the odor away without freezing themselves. It was cold at night on the desert.

Conversation was broken by long pauses. Diesel said, "After we take him out . . . you know he's got that hundred grand."

Troy grunted and pursed his lips, and answered after a minute passed, "We can't leave a hundred grand behind . . . but for some reason I feel kind of weird about taking it."

"Yeah . . . like we're killin' him to rob him."

"Uh-huh . . . We know it isn't that way."

"No, I'd wash him for free. Ha, ha, ha, ha . . ."

The full-throated laughter made Troy smile. God, what a thing to joke about! And what a mess. How many has he killed besides the three young women and the child? Men in prison told tales of crossroading con games, of safecracking and robberies, but very seldom did they talk of murders committed. They wanted to forget those for which they were convicted, and hide any others.

"Mad Dog reminds me of Nash," Diesel said. "Remember him?"

"Oh, yeah, who could forget that toothless monster. I was glad when they gassed his ass. He used to sleep all day and scream all night. I'd have killed his ass, he kept me awake for a year."

"Remember when he said that he had gutted that little boy under the Venice pier because he didn't want him to grow up and have the life Nash never had? Mad Dog is kinda like that."

"He sure is." Troy wondered if Mad Dog was haunted by conscience, like Raskolnikov in *Crime and Punishment*. Not likely. Killing seemed to soothe Mad Dog's demons, whatever they were. Troy thought it gave him a sense of power. Troy was going to kill Mad Dog, but it was going to be hard. Mad Dog idolized him. It's hard to kill someone who idolizes you, even if he's a homicidal maniac. It had been a bad idea, he thought, meaning the kidnapping caper. Too many things could go wrong. Unexpected things, especially like killing the goose with the gold. Jesus Christ, who could have anticipated that a drug kingpin with a federal indictment and a fugitive warrant would risk crossing the border on that one particular night? One thing was sure: no more kidnappings. He'd known better when he first heard the proposition—but, goddamn, the money was so big, maybe two million dollars.

"I'm hungry," Diesel said. "In fact I'm fucking starving."

Almost simultaneously they spotted a bright red sign: CAFÉ. It was on a pole raised high enough to be visible from the freeway.

"Smoking or nonsmoking?" asked the waitress who approached them when they entered. Diesel pointed to a booth with a vapor-coated window looking out on the parking lot. They wanted to keep an eye on the cars.

Diesel was the only one to eat a full meal, ham and eggs with grits instead of home fries. Mad Dog, full of methamphetamines, had no appetite and drank coffee. Troy tried milk and pie. The milk went down and soothed his burning stomach; the pie was dry and he nibbled at it.

Mad Dog asked, "You're sure this spot we're going to is cool? You ain' been there in a long time."

"What the fuck can change in the middle of the desert? It's a dry wash on the Cabazon Reservation. Nobody goes there but Indians. We pull off the road and there's nobody for miles."

"We better get rollin'. The sun's gonna be up pretty soon."

Troy left the tip and paid at the cash register. The other two were outside. As he went out the door, Mad Dog's back was to him. Troy looked at the flesh behind the ear. That's where he would put the bullet. He turned off the thought. It was not something he could dwell upon. He would put it out of mind until the moment arrived. The decision had been made and indecision had to be kept at bay. No reviews, no appeals.

Diesel stopped and waited for him. "We better get some gas," he said. Then lowered his voice. "He watches me pretty close."

"I told you I was doing it. I think I'll ride with him. You drive my car."

Now Mad Dog led the way, with Troy beside him and the Jaguar following. It was long past midnight and cars were few. Only the trucks carrying commerce rolled through the darkness. Mad Dog flashed his lights whenever he passed one. Beside the highway, a lot of the buildings were adorned in holiday lights. From the car radio came Christmas carols.

"So what's next?" Mad Dog asked. "Is the Greco gonna line us up another ripoff?"

"Ahhh, yeah, but not until after the New Year. Diesel wants to go home for Christmas. He's got a kid, y'know."

"He could stay home as far as I'm concerned."

"Don't be so mean, Dog. The big man is okay."

"He's okay with you . . . but I don't really like the dude. I put up with him because of you. The motherfucker thinks he's bad. Ain't nobody bad. All the bad motherfuckers are in the grave."

"That's what they say." Troy reached over and gave Mad Dog's shoulder a Judas shake. "Take it easy. It's gonna be okay, bro'." He despised his own deceit, but he knew what he had to do.

Across the desert were communities where none had been before. Troy remembered some things, but others were unfamiliar. Where was the side road? A sign said PALM SPRINGS NEXT TURNOFF. Suddenly another sign flashed in the headlights: CABAZON INDIAN RESERVATION.

"Turn here," he said.

Mad Dog hit the brakes and made the turn with a screech of tires. The headlights behind made the turn easier. Off the ramp was a narrow road. Had it been dirt before? Troy was unsure. It cut through the rough terrain, arroyos and low hills with huge beds of cactus, while against the skyline rose the saguaro like sentinels. If his memory was right—if this was the place—the reservation was five miles ahead, although their destination was short of that. He was a little worried until a pickup went by going the other way. Indians en route to town. Would they turn around to check on the two cars? He watched the red taillights disappear. Good.

The headlights illuminated the turnoff, the double groove from vehicle wheels heading into blackness. "Turn up there."

Now the car bounced and rocked and the headlight beams danced across the barren landscape. The car was filled with the glare of Diesel behind them. Beyond their narrow beams the world was total blackness, neither moon nor stars; it was a night without light. Troy knew there was nothing around them for miles.

They went on for about a mile when suddenly the tire tracks were cut by an arroyo turned into a swift stream by the recent storm. This was as far as they were going. It seemed as good a place as any. Troy's heart was racing. He forced himself to breathe slow and steady through his mouth. Take it easy, don't let your imagination race wildly ahead. It's an easy thing, just squeeze the hand and finger with a couple pounds of pressure.

Diesel had pulled up behind them and turned off the engine in the Jaguar. The sound of racing water muffled his footsteps until he was right beside them. "Is this it?"

"Unless you wanna swim."

"Does it make any difference?"

"Uh-uh. C'mon. You got the shovel?"

"Yeah. I'm ready to do some serious digging."

"Why don't we just leave the motherfucker?" Mad Dog said. "Won't the coyotes and the buzzards eat him up?"

"Sure they will . . . but somebody might see the buzzards and come to see if it's one of their cows."

"Not cows," Mad Dog corrected, "steers out here."

"Same difference."

Guided by the flashlight and carrying the shovel, they went over a rise where they would be unseen if someone should happen by. Maybe an Indian would want privacy with his girlfriend, or someone would want to check on the water in the arroyo. They would see the cars, of course, but it was best if they didn't see a couple of men digging a hole as well.

Diesel started to dig. Actually, he tried to start; the best the shovel would do was send chips flying like shards of concrete. He tried another spot. Same result. "Fuck this shit," Diesel said, throwing the shovel down. "We'll be here three days trying to dig a hole. A chump needs dynamite here."

"Look," said Mad Dog, "let's find an overhang, a ledge that sticks out. We put him up close and knock it down on him. A kinda landslide, y'know what I mean?"

"That's as good an idea as any," Diesel said. "Whaddya think?" he asked Troy.

Troy's thoughts were distracted, only half concentrating on the hole. He was fighting inside himself about what *he* had to do. "Yeah," he said, "sounds as good as anything."

They trudged down an arroyo. A hundred yards from the stream they found a ledge that angled out. It was as good as they would find. They went back to the car and opened the trunk. All of them turned their faces away from the stench. Diesel gagged and nearly vomited. "Goddamn, he smells bad!"

"You'll smell the same after three days," Mad Dog said.

"I might stink but I won't smell it," Diesel replied.

"Hold your breath 'til we get him out," Troy said, holding a

190

handkerchief over his nose and mouth while reaching into the trunk with the other hand. Through the blanket he grabbed an ankle. It had swollen large, and his grip sank deep. Fuckin' disgusting, he thought, and pulled the body up and out. It bounced off the rear bumper and plopped on the ground. "Gimme a hand," he said to Mad Dog. "You killed him. At least help me carry him."

"Don't be so mean, Big T," he said with humor—and it sent chagrin through Troy, who knew that within a few minutes he would murder the poor, tormented man. In Troy's view of the world, Mad Dog McCain was less responsible for his evil than the men of the Red Cross and blood banks who had let HIV-tainted blood go through untested because it would have cost a hundred million dollars, and because of that reasoned decision, seven thousand hemophiliacs were dying. *That* was truly evil. Mad Dog would die because he was a dangerous menace, but whatever he was, he had been made so by the tortured tragedies of his life.

"Here, lemme do it," Diesel said. "You lead with the flashlight."

The body was in a fetal position and still slightly stiff as rigor mortis evolved into decay. Mad Dog and Diesel carried it. Neither wanted to touch the flesh. Diesel lifted by the ankle through the blanket, but Mad Dog only held the blanket. It was a longer, harder walk than they had expected. Troy went ahead to use the flashlight to find the shovel. Behind him, Mad Dog stumbled and dropped his end. Diesel continued to drag the carcass across the hard earth, the headless torso bouncing and sliding along. "He don't feel it," Diesel said.

Troy used the flashlight to find what appeared the easiest place to make the ledge collapse. "Put him there," he said, indicating where with the flashlight. When the cadaver was against the embankment, he dug upward with the shovel.

He stopped. "We forgot the fuckin' lime," he said.

"Forget it," Mad Dog said.

"No, no. In a few months it'll erase this sucker. I'll get it."

"No, I'll get it," Diesel said. "I'm bigger'n you. Gimme the flashlight."

Troy gave it over; then watched the light move away, going on and off as Diesel flashed it every so often to orient himself. The light disappeared and there was silent blackness. Then, faintly, he heard a rustle . . . or was it the beating of wings? Creatures of the desert moved in the night when the burning daylight was gone, bats and coyotes and owls—and all of the things they ate. Troy could hear Mad Dog breathing somewhere close. Farther away, something disturbed some pebbles; maybe something attracted by the smell of physical decay. Troy's thoughts were only of killing Mad Dog. The moment was close and anguish made him weak. Whatever the mad-man had done, he was going to die at the hand of someone he loved.

"Damn, I'm cold," Mad Dog said. "How 'bout you?"

"I've got more clothes on than you."

"Where is that dude?"

"He'll be here."

Sure enough, a moment later the flashlight was visible. As he got closer, he was sputtering curses. "My fuckin' Ferragamo boots . . . seven hundred fuckin' dollars . . . all fuckin' scratched up. I'll be one dirty motherfucker."

"You can buy some more boots," Mad Dog said.

"Yeah . . . yeah . . . yeah." He reached them. "Where do you want this?"

"Over on the body."

Diesel used the flashlight to pinpoint the body. He dropped the sack of lime on top and Mad Dog plunged the shovel into the bag's side and the lime spilled out across the carcass.

"I'm gonna go up on top," Diesel said, handing Troy the flashlight. "You guys dig down here and I'll jump up and down up there. That should help, right?"

"Go ahead," Troy said. Ever since Diesel had gone for the lime, Troy had been holding the rough, checkered grip of the pistol inside his pants pocket, waiting for the moment to pull it and fire. He wanted it point blank at the base of the skull. Now his palm was wet with sweat. Looking in the direction that Diesel had gone, which was east, he could see the faintest hint of shapes. It was the false dawn that precedes the real. The knot of weakness in his gullet was spreading. Had he been alone with Mad Dog, he would have given up and lied to Diesel. He should have given the big man the job. He wished he was enraged; hot blood is far easier than cold . . .

"Okay, start digging up," Diesel said from atop the ledge.

"Here I come," Mad Dog said. Carrying the shovel, he passed close to Troy and began working on the bottom of the overhang. He grunted as he rammed the shovel at an upward angle. Diesel's silhouette jumped up and down. Troy moved closer to Mad Dog, at an angle behind his right shoulder. He had eased the pistol from his pocket and was holding it hidden against his leg.

Mad Dog paused and turned to look back. "A couple minutes and it'll fall. You better take over. I think I'm gettin' fuckin' blisters. Gimme the flashlight."

Troy handed it over. Mad Dog turned it on and dropped his gaze to look at his palm. Troy knew if he hesitated any longer the moment would be lost; he would be digging. He stepped forward, as if interested in the blisters. He was behind Mad Dog's shoulder. He raised the weapon until it was three inches from Mad Dog's head. He squeezed the pistol butt and the trigger evenly. The pistol jumped, the sound exploded, and a tongue of fire reached out and licked Mad Dog just behind his right ear. The bullet penetrated skull and plowed through brains. The hole coming out beside his left eye was the size of a half dollar. He dropped, instantly inert, on top of Mike Brennan. The flashlight fell to the ground and rolled a few feet, the beam dancing over the ground. The open sack of lime was sandwiched between the bodies. In a few months they would be fused together.

Troy put the pistol at the base of the skull and fired again. The body jerked. The shots echoed across the desert and a wild burro brayed somewhere in the bushes.

As Troy picked up the flashlight and turned it on his handiwork, Diesel came sliding down the embankment. Troy muttered, "I crossed the Rubicon."

"What's that?" Diesel asked. He, too, was looking at the dead bodies.

"I said we better finish coverin' 'em up." Inside, he was asking, how did my life get here? God gave no reply.

"That sounded like a fuckin' howitzer," Diesel said.

"Nobody heard it but some horned toads. Get back up there."

"You better go through his pockets. Get his ID and his car keys. That hundred grand is in the trunk."

"Damn, homeboy, you're startin' to think of things. I woulda remembered when we got back to the car."

"That's why you need me around. God, I'm glad that mother-fucker is dead. He *scared* me."

"He won't scare nobody no more."

They did a high five in giddy celebration. The relieved tension made them kind of borderline goofy.

It took twenty minutes to cause the mini-avalanche that hid both bodies. By then the sun's rim was peeking over the eastern horizon, heralding a bright, cloudless day. The storm had moved east.

Troy stared down at the false grave. The ledge that had extended out from the top now sloped the other way. At least a ton of dirt covered them. They might remain hidden to the world forever—and after a few months it wouldn't matter. The lime would make sure they were beyond identification. Perhaps they could be matched with dental records, but that would require someone suspecting who they were. With two bodies found together, the authorities would look for two persons who had disappeared together. That was all conjecture anyway. These were two murders that would certainly be unsolved, and most likely never even suspected.

They carried the shovel back to the cars and unlocked the trunk of Mad Dog's. Sure enough, the $100,000 was in a Nike gym bag. "We'll count it later," Troy said. "We'll put it in the Jag."

"We don't wanna leave this one here, do we?"

"Uh-uh. We'll leave it somewhere else."

"Where?"

"Anywhere. Maybe in the parking lot of that card room we passed. Nobody'll notice it there for a couple of days."

"It's registered under a bogus name."

"They'll just have another derelict car to dispose of. Here." He handed Diesel the keys and carried the Nike gym bag to the trunk of the Jag. Now the trunk had $200,000; three quarters of it was his money. Alex Aris still owed them money, too. That was good as gold.

As they turned from the dirt tracks to the narrow asphalt, Diesel said a silent Act of Contrition. Even though he would revile such things out loud, the imprint of the Catholic orphanage was still within him. Even as he did it, he was silently furious at what they had done to him. Done to him a long time ago.

Diesel followed Troy onto the main highway; then off into the parking lot of the card room. It already had at least a hundred cars. Troy turned in and signaled him to park on the other side.

They walked separately to the entrance. Nobody even looked at them. They walked back together and got in the Jaguar.

When they turned back on the highway it was 8:00 A.M.

"We'll be in L.A. before noon," Troy said.

"Call the Greco and find out about our money. I'd like to go home tonight, after I get some sleep."

"You can sleep?"

"I can really sleep after something like this."

15

Los Angeles sparkled after the rain. Air and sidewalks and green leaves had been washed clean, and the snow-topped San Gabriel Mountains were visible for a change. The wonderful winter afternoon reminded Troy of his childhood, when L.A. was as close to paradise as any city in America. Despite the day's beauty, a gray depression gnawed at Troy, an ache of the soul. Was it reaction to the murder or had that simply stirred sediments always deep within him? He glanced at Diesel. It had to be going through his mind, if not occupying it completely. Still, he looked placid enough. What about underneath? What effect had Catholicism had on him? They must have imprinted a belief in damnation. Troy wasn't carrying that burden. It wasn't God's judgment that bothered him, nor even mankind's, for one was nonexistent and the other would never happen. What bothered him was that his life had been reduced to putting a bullet in a maniac's brain. Wouldn't it be wonderful if he could wake in the morning with an entirely different life?

The self-pity lasted a few seconds before he sneered at himself. Wish, smish, fuck 'em, he thought. Deal the cards and play them as they come.

They were east of downtown. Ahead rose the clustered spires of the L.A. skyline. The first one had been rising when he went to prison. No city mirrored the changes of the twentieth century like the city of L.A. Southern California had gone from 90,000 at the start of the century to nine million at the end. L.A. was the world's first great city built for the automobile, but not for millions of them.

It was only a slight exaggeration to imagine running for sixty miles from car roof to car roof. He had missed it so much, but now he would be glad to get away. Where would he go? No, he had to make up the botched score before he planned his exodus from L.A. He had about $170,000, enough to party for a few months, but only a fraction of what he needed to emigrate.

Right now, he wasn't going anywhere. Ahead of him the brake lights flashed and the traffic slowed down. When the freeways worked, they were wonderful; when they didn't, they were a nightmare. More and more it was the latter. Right now they stopped, and then began inching forward. At least the left lane moved faster than the others. Troy picked up the cellular phone and punched in Alex's number.

"Yeah," was how Greco answered.

"It's me, you goddamned Greek fascist."

"Ha, ha, ha, ha, ha. Where are you, fool?"

"Gettin' near downtown. What's up? You see that guy?"

"Oh, yeah. I got that."

"Where you be?"

"I'm rollin', too. What about the P.D.C.?"

"Fifteen, twenty minutes?"

"Right on. Order me the Delmonico."

"Medium rare."

Troy hung up. Alex had the added thirty plus thousand and would meet them at the Pacific Dining Car—if Troy could get through downtown.

"Let's get off the freeway," Troy said. Diesel rolled down the window, waved, and looked drivers in the eye. They gave way and the Jaguar went up the ramp onto State Street, in the shadow of the gigantic General Hospital. Traveling east, he crossed the L.A. River and went through downtown on 5th Street, sometimes called "The Nickel." When he was young, it had been lined with S.R.O. hotels and open-doored bars. It had been junkies and winos back then, black and white. Now it was all black and all crack, which made heroin look like medicine for Little Orphan Annie. Junkies wanted to coast "on the nod." A junkie would do desperate things,

197

but a crack addict would do things too sleazy even for a Texas rooster. The eyes that watched them pass were wild with madness.

They stopped for a traffic light. A black man with clothes shiny from grime appeared with a spray bottle of water and a rag. He started wiping the windshield of the car next to them. The woman inside pushed down the lock and knocked on the glass and shook her head. He gave her the finger. Diesel laughed, and was still grinnning when the windshield wiper came toward them. Before he could start, Diesel reached under the passenger seat and produced a big pistol. Still grinning, he used it to wave the beggar away. The black man threw up his hands in mock surrender, grinning with gapped front teeth. "Awright, big man," he said. "You too mean for me."

The light changed and they moved away.

"Not too smart," Troy said.

"I know . . . but—" Diesel shrugged. "Everybody plays the fool sometimes."

At the Harbor Freeway overpass, 5th Street blended into 6th Street, one way westbound. Half a mile farther, the Pacific Dining Car was on the left at the corner of Witmer. Troy turned into the parking lot. Alex's car was ahead of them, being driven away by an attendant. Alex was heading toward the front door. He carried a flat attaché case.

Troy stopped and honked the horn. Greco turned; then came back to walk in with them. As they neared the front door, Greco said, "I see that other guy is missing."

"He's history."

"Is that right. Chepe'll feel better about that. Where'd you put him?"

"Where God might not find him," Diesel said. "Under the ground in the middle of the desert. I don't think I could find the place."

"Is that it?" Troy asked, indicating the attaché case.

"Yeah. Take it. You might as well carry it."

Inside the door, the maître d' knew Alex and, carrying menus, led them to one of the Pacific Dining Car's several rooms. It had three booths and two tables, none of which were occupied. It gave

198

them privacy to talk and for Alex to smoke, notwithstanding the new city ordinance to the contrary.

After the waiter brought them coffee and took their orders, Alex got down to business. "I told Chepe it was all that guy's fault. He was fuckin' mad. He was hotter'n I've ever seen him. Usually he's a sweetie pie."

"Yeah, I know," Troy said. "He's an easygoing guy."

"I put all the fuckin' blame on Mad Dog. The old man'll be happy when I tell him that crazy motherfucker is gone. One thing he worried about, he doesn't want this to get around. Don't be gossiping."

"Ahhh, man," Diesel said with hurt feelings evident in his voice, "what kinda guy do you think I am? I know better'n that."

"Yeah, sure I know—but human nature is human nature. They like to confide—"

Diesel was emphatically shaking his head, so Alex stopped the line of talk. "What now? You guys ready for another one?"

Troy looked to Diesel. The big man made a face of indecision. "I gotta go home for Christmas. I got a kid."

"I heard that," Alex said. "A little boy, right?"

"Yeah. I love him to death. Anyway, I wanna spend the holidays with him. After the first . . ."

"You'd be interested then?"

"Sure. What the fuck, I ain' never made money like this. And now that that fool is gone . . ."

"What about you?" Alex asked Troy.

"I think I'll go up to 'Frisco with my main man here. While he's with the family, I'll take a little vacation in Tahoe. Ski in the day, gamble at night."

"That sounds like a winner."

"Come on up, man?"

"Maybe I will . . . after Christmas. I got a family, too."

"Yeah, right. How old's your daughter now?"

"Sixteen."

"Good God, time flies."

"I'm gettin' her a car for Christmas. I'm gonna have it at the curb with a big ribbon around it."

"She'll like that."

With a smile of anticipation, Alex nodded agreement and shifted the conversation. "Okay, you got the rest of the dough in that bag. What else is there? You got my number. What about you, bro'. How can I get in touch with you?"

"You can call me," Diesel said. "You got my number?"

"No, give it to me." Alex produced an electronic organizer and punched in the number that Diesel gave him.

After dinner, Troy and Diesel said good-bye to Alex in the parking lot. When the attendant brought the Jaguar, Troy put the attaché case in the trunk. It already held his $100,000 and Mad Dog's $100,000. "We'll split it up back at the hotel," he said.

"Whatever you say, Big T. You call the shots in this mob."

The hotel was the Holiday Inn on Highland Avenue overlooking Hollywood Boulevard on one side and the Hollywood Hills on the other. Diesel had checked in for three days, and extended it for two more. The Mustang was in the hotel garage. It had an added layer of smog dust, but nobody had bothered it. They went to the room and divided Mad Dog's money and what Alex had brought.

As Diesel bagged up another $66,000, he envisioned his wife when he dumped it on the bed. Add this to the first $100,000 she already had, the bitch would never say another word about nothin'. God knows I treat her good. He found himself anxious to get home and see her, and especially Charles, Jr. "It's great having a kid, you know," he said.

Troy nodded. A father he would never be; he had given up the thought in the middle of his San Quentin term. "What're you gonna tell him?" he asked Diesel.

"Whaddya mean?"

"You know, about everything. Whaddya want for him . . . whaddya want him to think about your history."

"I don't know what I'm gonna tell him. I'm gonna kick his ass if he looks like he's gonna get in trouble. He's gonna be a fuckin' citizen. And a man. He'll be a man, for goddamn sure."

"I hope so, bro'. I wouldn't wish our life on anybody."

"No bullshit, man." Diesel zipped up the tote bag with the money

200

and grabbed the overnight bag with his clothes. "How we gonna do this? You gonna follow me? Want me to follow you?"

"Why don't you roll on up north. I'm gonna stay in L.A. one more night. I haven't had a chance to cruise the city and look things over. Maybe I'll pick up some chick . . . or buy some. I'll see you tomorrow evening up there."

"You sure?"

"Yeah. Maybe I'll go play some poker."

"Okay, I'll see you up there. Maybe we'll have a barbecue if you get there in time. I kick ass on a barbecue."

They went down the elevator and said good-bye in the lobby. Diesel went up Highland Avenue onto U.S. 101, the Coast Route. In Thousand Oaks, he stopped at a Denny's for coffee and two Dexamyl spansules. The amphetamine they contained kept his eyes wide and his mind racing as he drove north through the night, the sea often glowing phosphorescent on his left, the rolling hills black on his right—Ventura, Santa Barbara, Santa Maria, Pismo Beach, San Luis Obispo, and so on to south of San Francisco. It was between midnight and sunrise when he pulled up. A new Ford minivan was parked in the driveway. He had been thinking of buying her a new car, but now that she had gotten it without asking him, he was furious. He stormed down the hall into the bedroom and turned on the light.

"Goddamnit! Where'd that fuckin' new minivan come from?"

"Charles . . . Charles . . . wait a second! I can take it back. I swear. That's the deal I made. I'll show you." She jumped up, wearing panties and no bra, so her breasts bounced as she headed for the dresser. He knew what she said was true; he had no need to see the paper. Other thoughts had come to his mind. He went after her, put his arms around her and cupped her breasts. She trembled and the nipples hardened as he nibbled on her ear. He was carrying her to the bed when Charles, Jr., began to cry in the manner unique to a child. Diesel looked to the sky in exasperation and fell on his back on the bed. He had to wait for her to lullaby the child to sleep. He hoped he wouldn't have the same old afterward reaction, where he felt dirty and disliked what they had done. It was a lousy way to feel after making love; he knew it while unable to do anything about it. She wanted to cuddle and he wanted to get away. He vowed to hide the feelings this time.

When Diesel was gone, Troy packed his $170,000 neatly in the trunk of the Jaguar. The smell of death was gone—or at least suppressed by the mothballs he'd spread around. The carpets looked the same as when they came from the factory. Everything was neat. Nobody would ever suspect that a nearly headless corpse had rotted therein for several days. Troy wished it would leave his mind as easily as it did the trunk. He kept seeing the tongue of fire leap from the muzzle of the pistol and lick at Mad Dog's skull. He had just fallen, like a candlewick squeezed between fingers.

Before closing the trunk, he opened the attaché case and took out a packet of twenty-dollar bills. He debated a moment before also taking out a snub-nosed .38 Smith & Wesson and clipping its holster inside his waistband. It wasn't for the police or to commit a crime; it was for self-protection in his hometown.

As he pulled out of the subterranean garage, Troy called Alex. "You hungry, bro'?"

"I thought you went north for the holidays."

"Tomorrow. What about dinner?"

"I'm hung up on business, man. Damn!"

"Call me if you clear the deck. Otherwise, I'll see you when I get back."

Alex said something about good-bye, but it was unclear because the cellular transmission began breaking up. As Troy pushed the off button, he felt a mild letdown. He'd counted on Alex's companionship for the evening.

While eating at the Musso-Frank counter, Troy mulled over what to do with the evening. Maybe he should have gone with Diesel. What about a movie? No. What he really wanted was a woman, but not some hardcore streetwalker or a head job in a massage parlor. He wanted female conversation and laughter. He wasn't against paying a grand for the night, if he got value. Alas, he had no idea where to call a call girl. Then he remembered a cocktail lounge on the edge of the Strip. It had been a watering hole for high-class hookers.

When he walked in, he immediately knew he'd made a mistake. Instead of the dark wood and red leather and Frank Sinatra on the jukebox, it was now all mirrors, all male, and Judy Garland was singing. He beat a hasty retreat with red cheeks; then he began laughing at the absurdity of being embarrassed.

He then found himself heading east on Sunset, away from the glitter of the Strip and the wealth of Beverly Hills, toward seedy downtown and East L.A. beyond. Where Sunset Boulevard began was also where the City of Los Angeles had originated. When he got close to Union Station, he remembered a cocktail lounge on Huntington Drive in El Sereno. Ten minutes away, it was still a hangout for Chicano ex-convicts. Not two months ago Pretty Henry Soto had returned to San Quentin and, among other tales of life outside, mentioned that Vidal Aguilar now owned the Club Clover, with someone else's name on the liquor license, of course. Troy hadn't seen Vidal for several years, but for three years before that, Vidal had been in the next cell, and they had eaten breakfast and dinner together many times. They were friends and Vidal had gone out and stayed out, although stories came back. He had always been a high roller in the L.A. underworld. He and Alex Greco knew each other. The trouble with Mexicans really getting it together was that too many wanted to be top dog. Too much macho, not enough cooperation.

Beyond the bridge across the L.A. River, the graffiti marked the turf as "1st Flats." The nicknames replicated those of Troy's own youth. How many had he known named "Japo," "Grumpy," "Alfie," "Crow," "Wedo," or "Veto"?

He drove past the low, sprawling projects. Between the buildings he could see the clustered silhouettes of the homeboys hanging out. Some of the project windows had Christmas lights. Indeed, many of the small stucco bungalows had been outlined in bright-colored lights. They made him feel sad and alone. He was seldom envious, but as he thought about Diesel spending a Christmas morning with a son, he felt a pang of envy. He wished his life had allowed him to have a son.

He turned on Soto and followed it past Hazard Park and the rolling hills of El Sereno, most of which were still empty, and from which rose several tall radio towers topped with pulsing red lights. Once, when young and drunk, he had climbed one of them to the top. He would have quit halfway up except for a macho Mexican named Gato, who was climbing the next tower and refused to stop short of the top. What he would do at twenty-two, he would never do now. He then remembered he had told Mad Dog the story less than two weeks ago. His mind quickly erased the memory.

Soto became Huntington Drive at its origin. The green sign, clover club, stood out even though the "L" was a bare shadow of its original glow. Troy parked half a block down a side street and walked back. The evening was warm despite the late December date. He could hear the excited voices of children playing in nearby backyards.

The Clover Club's front door was opened, and the sound of mariachi music poured forth as Troy entered. The tables, booths, and bar were all full. A four-piece band was on a low stage at the other end. A few couples were on the tiny dance floor; they were pressed tight and swaying fast, doing the banda. Damn, Troy thought, fuckin' Vidal has a winner.

Troy made his way to the bar. A few eyes turned to look him over—a gringo in Aztlan—but nobody said anything or radiated hostility. At the bar the one open space was the station between brass rails used by the cocktail waitress. She was leaving with a tray of drinks. Troy noticed that she had a big round ass, the kind that Mexicans prefer, although it would be considered too heavy in Beverly Hills. Troy squeezed to the bar. The bartender, who was big for a Mexican, had the mashed nose and thick eyebrows of an ex-fighter.

"Yeah."

"I'm a friend of Vidal's. Is he around?"

The bartender looked him over. Just then the cocktail waitress returned and Troy had to step aside while she unloaded empty glasses and gave an order for "Two screwdrivers, two Buds . . ."

In the mix of English and Spanish that is the lingua franca of

East L.A., the bartender told the waitress, whose name was Delia, to tell Vidal that someone wanted to see him. The bartender turned to Troy. "What's your name, *ese?*"

"Troy." He found himself looking into Delia's dark eyes, and then watching her move across the room to the hallway with the restroom sign. His attention was pulled back when the bartender asked if he wanted anything. Troy shook his head.

A minute later, Delia appeared in the archway with a man. It wasn't Vidal. She pointed out Troy for the man. He beckoned.

As Troy crossed the room, he plowed through a layer of cigarette smoke. Secondhand smoke freaks would be in big trouble here; their eyes would water and if they complained they would get punched in the nose. The man awaiting him grinned. Troy knew the face but could not put a name to it. Delia went by, smiling at him. Was there anything in the smile? He turned his head for a glance at her swishing hips. When he turned back, the man in the arch was grinning at him. "You like that, huh?"

"You might say that. How many kids she got?"

The Chicano held up two fingers. "They all got two kids."

"Where's her old man?"

"Soledad Central. You wouldn't know him. He's a youngster."

They shook hands and the Chicano led the way down a narrow hallway with a closed-circuit TV camera at the far end. The restrooms were on one side. On the other was a door covered with sheet metal. The escort knocked. A buzzer sounded, freeing a lock. The Chicano pushed the door open. The room was combination storeroom and office, and along the walls were cases of beer and liquor.

Vidal sat behind a narrow, scarred desk. It had a wire basket, telephone, and a small TV monitor showing the corridor outside the office. Vidal grinned, his even white teeth showing against his dark skin and high cheekbones. His Indian blood was evident. Except that his hair was grayer, he had not aged in the six years since his parole. He stood up and extended his hand.

"It's good to see you, Big T," he said as they shook. "When did you raise?"

"Last month."

"Where the fuck you been? You need some dough?"

"No. I'm okay. How you been, bro'?"

"Chicken today, feathers tomorrow. Siddown, man. You want a drink? Whaddya want?"

"Bourbon . . . Jack Daniel's or Wild Turkey, with a little splash of Seven-Up."

"Why don't you do that, Tootie," said Vidal.

"Be right back."

Now Troy remembered: Tootie Obregon from Mateo. He'd worked in the kitchen and was a top handball player.

Tootie went out.

"How'd you wind up with this joint?" Troy asked. Vidal had been raised in the Ramona Gardens projects. His criminal career had begun in junior high school when he had started selling loose joints. He'd remained in the marijuana business because those he dealt with were far less violent and marijuana was far down the list of police priorities. Loose joints grew into ounces, then kilos, and finally truckloads. His one conviction was for a thousand kilos in a panel truck, although the drug agents turned in eight hundred and kept two hundred to sell for a thousand dollars apiece. Vidal's term was cut when the agents were indicted for skimming money and drugs from their busts. Indeed, half the Sheriff's Department narco squad were indicted. Vidal had changed his game when he got out. Word came back that he was a fence, buying and selling stolen merchandise. It was a crime with an even lower priority than marijuana.

"This joint was for sale and some *vatos* from Tucson hijacked a truck and trailer full of booze, six hundred cases of Johnny Walker and Jack Daniel's and whatever. They had it in three garages in East L.A. I gave 'em twenty-eight dollars a case and I bought this joint for the price of the license. Nobody else wanted it. I don't make what I made selling grass—but I'm doin' pretty good. Me an' Tootie, we run a football ticket, too. You sure you don't need a little dough, man? I can loan you five or ten grand, man."

"No, no, I'm good, Vidal. Thanks anyway."

"Yeah, you always did okay. You'd be surprised how many dudes come in here beggin' money. Some of 'em are scared to death because of that three strikes law."

"It's enough to scare anybody. They're givin' suckers life for nothin'."

"I know. You remember Alfie from White Fence?"

"Little guy in the *eme*?"

"Yeah. They're tryin' to give him life for stealin' a tire off the back of a truck. He's fightin' it like a murder beef. He says they may get him, but he's gonna cost 'em a million before they do. It said in the *Times* they're gonna build twenty more prisons in the next ten years. They oughta put a fence topped with barbed wire around the whole motherfuckin' state.

"Oh, yeah, you know Sluggo?" Vidal continued.

"I know three of 'em, two Mexicans and one crazy honky from Louisiana."

"The peckerwood—Sam whatever his name is. He was in here the other day. He's hooked on junk and been boostin'. He had one of those MAC whatever, those little stubby semiautomatics, not very accurate but they fire a lotta lead quick as you can pull the trigger."

"I know what they are."

"He said if they're gonna give him life for shopliftin', he might as well get it for robbin' banks and killin' cops. They changed him the wrong way. They took a shoplifter and made him a maniac. I love it," Vidal said. "I love the fuckin' chaos."

"What about you? How many strikes do you have?"

Vidal shook his head and held up thumb and forefinger in a circle denoting zero. "Where you staying?"

Troy shook his head.

"You ain't homeless, are you?"

"I don't have a spot, but I'm not homeless. I'm going up north and see Big Diesel Carson."

"The fighter?"

"Yeah."

"Man, I remember that fight in the lower yard on Field Meet Day . . . him and that nigger. What was his name? Spotlight Johnson?"

Troy nodded. Vidal rocked back and forth in his laughter. Then came a light knock on the door. In the TV monitor they saw Tootie and the waitress, Delia. She had a tray with their drinks.

Vidal pushed a buzzer under the desk and Tootie pushed open the door. Delia came in and put the tray on the desk. "Who gets what?" she asked.

"The bourbon's here," Troy said.

She had to lean over the desk to put it in front of him. Vidal was looking at her ass. "Oh, my God, so fine. I'm gonna have a heart attack!" He grabbed his chest in mock pain. Tootie laughed and Troy smiled. He was looking into her eyes. Was she saying something without speaking?

"Delia . . . Delia . . . oh, baby," Vidal said.

She turned and smiled and shook her head. "Vidal, stop it. You know Chita is my friend."

He threw his hands to the air. "What am I gonna do? What would you do?" he asked Troy.

"I dunno . . . but I can sympathize."

"I'm leaving," she said—but as she opened the door and it blocked Tootie and Vidal, she winked at Troy in a way that was either invitation or he was crazy. Then she closed the door and was gone.

"Hey, Troy . . . she asked about you," Tootie said. "She's interested."

"She's got a fine brown frame, no doubt of that," Troy said.

"She's got *tres,*" Vidal said, holding up three fingers and meaning three children.

"Damn, I only expected two," Troy said.

"I just thought I'd tell you."

Troy grinned and winked. The gesture said whatever Vidal read into it.

"What about Jimmy Baca?" Troy asked. "Have you seen him since he beat that murder beef?"

"Yeah. He's got cancer . . . in the liver."

The statement made Troy's heart jump a beat. Jimmy Baca! He was the toughest man Troy had ever met—and Troy had known many of the toughest men in America. None were tough as Jimmy. All men were mortal, but it was hard to think that Jimmy's body would betray him. His mind had never done so.

"He's not that old," was all he could say.

"I know," Vidal said. "It's a bitch. Sonny Ballesteros—"

"That's my pal," Troy said.

"Yeah, I know. He's got it, too, but they say he's gonna make it okay."

Death and cancer in friends were not what Troy wanted to think about, although they had taken his mind off Mad Dog for now, and when he thought of Mad Dog again, the horror would have slightly faded.

They were silent as they drank from their glasses. Through the walls vibrated the sound of banda.

"What's happenin' in the joint?" Tootie asked. "Give us some news."

"They finally killed Sheik Thompson."

"They got his ass, huh? Oh, man, what a fuckin' animal he was," Tootie said.

"Sheik Thompson?" asked Vidal. "Should I know him?"

"You should know about him. But I think he was in Folsom or Vacaville when you were there. He was some kind of throwback."

"A nigger?"

"Yeah . . . they made the word nigger for fuckers like him."

"How'd they get him?" Tootie asked.

"He was coming out of the coach's office. Slim and Motormouth Buford, they broke his leg with a baseball bat, and when they had him down, they cut his throat.

"Check this," Troy continued. "They busted 'em right away, and took 'em to the Captain's Office to question 'em. Later on, when it was time for lockup, every convict in the joint was lined up, and they bring Slim and Motormouth out of the Captain's Office, taking 'em to the hole. Every convict in the yard started cheering and applauding 'cause they killed Sheik."

"I know Motormouth," Vidal said. "Little black *vato*, used to be key man in the South Block."

"That's him," Troy said.

"How come everybody hated Sheik so much?"

"'Cause the fool wasn't human," Tootie said.

"Lemme tell you about him," Troy said. "He used to work in the stone quarry, up that road you can see from the lower yard. It's about two miles and it's got a little grade. He used to run to work with some little sissy on his shoulders. On Field Meet Day, when they used to have that, he used to run the four-forty, eight-eighty, and the mile . . . in the morning. Then in the afternoon, he would fight for the middleweight, light heavyweight, and heavyweight title. Sometimes he'd get a boxing lesson, but *nobody* ever knocked him out. He had the worst attitude."

"Yeah," inserted Tootie. "He used to spit in people's faces."

"That's dangerous in prison. And they stabbed him so many times. Mapa hit him in the head with a weight bar, hit him so hard it popped one of his eyes out—it was hanging by some kind of tendon. They tucked it back in and three weeks later he was on a fight card. Death Row Jefferson and a couple others jumped him with shivs. He beat the shit out of all three of 'em—and then went out and testified. Death Row Jeff went to Death Row for it. That's where he got his nickname.

"Then there was the fight he had with Johnson, in Folsom. It was around behind number-one building, and three gun-towers opened up on 'em. They were gettin' hit with thirty-thirties and thirty-ought-sixes . . . and they'd get knocked down by bullets, and jump up at the other guy. Johnson bit Sheik's ears off—and swallowed 'em. When they finally broke it up and got 'em to the hospital, the loudspeakers asked for blood donors. Not one dude in all of Folsom would give Sheik any blood. They went over and said they'd give Johnson some blood, but fuck Sheik Thompson. Except one guy who was HIV tried to donate, but after they checked him they didn't take it."

"It's funny I never heard of him," Vidal said.

"He was probably in Folsom when you were in Quentin."

"Yeah, that's probably it." Vidal glanced at his watch. "Me and Tootie gotta go take care of some business pretty soon. You can stay here and party, you can come with us . . ."

"No, no, that's okay," Troy said. "I gotta get on the road myself."

"Where you gonna spend Christmas?" Tootie asked.

210

"Up north, 'Frisco."

"You're coming back down, aren't you? This is hometown, right?"

"Uh huh. I'll be back next month sometime."

"Man, I'm glad to see you," said Vidal. "Lemme give you my card." From the desk drawer, he pulled a business card from a stack fastened with a rubber band; he passed it over to Troy, who put it in a shirt pocket, said his good-byes, and departed. As he came out of the short hallway into the main room, he stopped and looked around. Delia was at a booth, taking an order. Troy walked up and stopped. She looked around to see who it was.

"When do you get off?" he asked.

"About two-thirty," she said.

"Wanna get some breakfast?"

"I'll see you then."

"Good."

He went out. Thinking about her aroused him. What time was it? He thought it was about ten-thirty but he had no watch. Back in the car, News 98 said it was nine-twelve. Five hours plus. He would eat and go to a movie. He'd noticed *Pulp Fiction* on a downtown marquee. It was the only movie he had any real desire to see.

At 2:15 A.M., Troy turned onto Huntington Drive from Eastern Avenue. He immediately spotted the spinning blue lights atop the police cars—several of them, plus an ambulance, outside Vidal's club.

A uniformed officer was standing in the street with a flashlight. Flares were down. Part of the street was marked off and two officers were looking for spent cartridges on the asphalt. "So much for pussy tonight," Troy muttered, moving over to the far lane and following the car ahead. The policeman waved them to keep going. As Troy went past, a flashbulb went off. A body was lying on the pavement near the curb. A drive-by? Whatever it was, he wasn't going to see Delia tonight. "'Bye, baby," he said, and started thinking about the quickest way to a freeway. Any of them would take him to Interstate 5.

16

It was midafternoon of the next day when Troy turned down the street of small tract homes. The development was three years old and most of the houses had landscaping, although the trees were still small. Some had lawns turned winter yellow, while others were green with rye grass. Several houses remained unsold, their front yards still bare dirt.

In the middle of the street, half a dozen boys played touch football. They moved aside for the car. Troy saw Diesel's Mustang in the driveway. Troy pulled in behind it. Diesel had put in a lawn without subsequently caring for it. It was yellow brown except near a dripping faucet, where it was green and dandelions grew tall. The garage door was open; Troy could see the rear end of Gloria's new car, the one Diesel had told him about over the phone. Before exiting the car, Troy removed his pistol and clip holster and put them under the seat.

From the house, Diesel saw the Jaguar pull in. He went out to meet his friend. "I see you found it, bro'," he said, extending a hand. "Glad you're here. You're gonna spend Christmas with us."

"What's the old lady say about that?"

"Fuck her. I run this pad, y'know what I mean? When the bitch can whip me, then she can call the shots."

"Naw, naw, bro'. I don't wanna be the focus of a family squabble. I'll spend Christmas in the city."

"Suit yourself. That's tomorrow. This evening I'm gonna barbecue some sirloin for you. I don't want no bullshit about that."

"Okay, I'll go for that."

"We gotta go to the market. Wait here while I go tell the old lady."

Diesel went inside. Troy stood outside and watched the touch football game. A minute later, Diesel came out. They took Troy's car because it was the easiest to back out. As he started the engine, the boys playing football started to horseplay. The one with the ball zigzagged and cut back, finally trying to keep the car between himself and his pursuers. Diesel rolled down the window to say something when the two boys in pursuit went around both sides and the boy being chased had to take off across the street.

Wilson Walter Williams, night manager of the Safeway market, was in the upstairs office above the meat section. Down below, the market was filled with shoppers. His eye went to the two men as if to a magnet. The big one pushing the cart wore a short-sleeved shirt that displayed countless blue handmade tattoos. To the night manager, the big man seemed jittery and suspicious. The store had recently suffered an inordinate amount of loss from shoplifting, especially meat and cigarettes. The other man matched the description of someone the morning box boys had chased but had gotten away a few days earlier.

Wilson Walter Williams reached for the telephone. The number for the police station was under glass on his desk.

Down below, Diesel selected a big cut of sirloin and dropped it in the cart. He had a list Gloria had given him. "I gotta get all this shit, too."

"Do your duty, brother. I'm gonna go sit in the car."

"I won't be long."

On the way out, Troy picked up a package of mini-doughnuts. He also got some Pepto-Bismol for the heartburn. While waiting in the express lane, he picked up a *People* magazine to look at while he waited in the car. He paid the cashier and walked out to the car.

Behind the market, a police car with two officers, one white female, one black male, pulled up to the loading dock. The manager was waiting. "The big one is still inside. The other guy is out in the car, a burgundy Jaguar. I didn't get the license number."

"Did you see him take anything?" Officer Lincoln asked.

"No . . . but the one in the car was here last week. He got away with half a case of cigarettes."

The black male officer was on the passenger side. "I'll check out the big guy in the store."

Officer Melanie Strunk waited until the two men disappeared through the loading dock door. Then she drove slowly down the alley and turned toward the parking lot.

Inside the market, Diesel was pushing the cart piled high with Gloria's list and whatever else caught his eye. His pistol was working its way out of his waistband under his sweater. He looked around. So many people were shopping on Christmas Eve. Still, he couldn't have it falling out on the floor. He pushed the cart down the last aisle and looked around. Nobody was able to see him there, so he lifted his sweater and moved the .357 Python to a better position.

Up above, Officer Lincoln and Mr. Wilson Williams saw the suspicious movement. Officer Lincoln also saw the blue India ink tattoos on the big man's hands. The Training Academy had taught him that those blue tattoos were put on in reform school or prison. He unsnapped his walkie-talkie and flipped it on. "Say, partner, we might have a pair of boosters."

"Should I call for backup?"

"Naw, not for shoplifters. Find that burgundy Jaguar and run a make on the plates."

Out in the parking lot, Troy ate a doughnut and leafed through the magazine, wondering why he'd even picked it up. It gave no intellectual nourishment and he was only minimally interested in the soft gossip about movie stars, although he'd sure masturbated over a few during the years of prison.

His peripheral vision and the constant alertness of the predator made him aware of something behind the car. He looked in the rearview mirror and saw the black-and-white car parked across the rear of the Jaguar. His heart jumped. He started to turn and saw the uniform outside the driver window.

"Excuse me," said Officer Melanie Strunk, "could you step out of the car, sir?"

214

He hid his fear. "Sure. What's up?" He reached for the door, but she opened it for him and stepped back. He wished he could see her eyes. They were hidden behind dark aviator glasses.

He got out. "What's wrong, officer?" He wondered what had attracted her. Was there probable cause? The money and the shotgun were in the trunk. His pistol was under the seat.

"Why's your license plate covered?"

"What?"

He stepped to the rear (she backed up) and looked at the rear license plate. A newspaper had been draped over it at the fold. It was the kids horseplaying outside Diesel's house. That was the only possible explanation. He snatched it away. "Some kids must've been playing games."

"Is this your car, sir?" Her suspicion was less than it might have been because he was a well-dressed white man of thirty-five. A young black in baggy clothes would ring her alarm bells.

"Yes. I just got it."

"Can I see your driver's license?"

"Sure." He brought forth his wallet and extracted the license in the name of Al Leon Klein.

"Stay here," she said, taking his license back to run a make. She was on the other side of the police car, looking over it at him.

The police car blocked him from backing out, and in front of the Jaguar was a knee-high concrete barrier. Should he run? No. The driver's license and license plates would go through. He looked around. A few people were outside the market, watching the scene. No Diesel.

Melanie Strunk returned and handed him the license. "All right, Mr. Klein. There's been a lot of shoplifting here. Do you mind if I look in your car?"

Oh shit! The law said he could refuse; she lacked probable cause. But if he said no, she would never let it go. If he gave permission, he would waive his rights. "Am I under arrest?" he asked.

"No. Not yet."

Over her shoulder, Troy saw Diesel come through the glass doors. The big man cradled a bag of groceries in each arm. Troy thought of the pistol under the seat. Could he get it out and turn fast enough?

"Do you mind if I look?" she asked again.

"What are you looking for?"

"Do you have stolen merchandise?"

"No, of course not."

"Do you have narcotics or a weapon?"

"No."

"So what do you have to hide?"

"Not a thing."

"So . . . ?"

"Okay . . . sure. Let me get my sweater." It was on the other side of the front seat, above the pistol. He opened the car door. From the corner of his eye, he saw her unsnap her holster. He could never get the pistol in time. He whirled back to face her, desperation charging him.

"Freeze!" he said. "You're covered from behind." As he spoke, he moved forward so they were chest to chest. He loomed over her.

For a moment she froze; then she took a step back and reached for her pistol.

Troy threw a right-hand punch.

Melanie turned enough so her helmet took the blow and broke one of his knuckles. A bolt of pain ran up his arm.

Melanie fell against the adjacent car, her head ringing as she pulled her service revolver. Before she could raise it, Troy had grabbed it with his other hand and tried to twist it away. She grabbed it with both hands and wrapped both legs around one of his.

Down they fell between cars, struggling for the pistol. Troy would have easily wrenched it away except for the broken hand.

Diesel saw the sudden struggle. What should he do?

Before he could decide, Officer Lincoln and Mr. Williams rushed past, brushing against him as they ran to help the struggling officer.

Troy was twisting the pistol back and forth. Melanie was hanging on. She had a thumb in the hammer so it wouldn't discharge.

Troy heard the crunch of footsteps. Then a terrible pain and a flash of light shot through his brain. A rock?

216

Again the flash and pain. A nightstick bounced off his skull. Blood ran down into his eyes. A forearm went around his throat in a choke hold, dragging him away.

They rode him down, shoving his face into the asphalt. Hands twisted his arms behind his back. The steel bracelets clicked through the notches and fastened. Someone kneeled on his back. He went limp. Where was Diesel? Why hadn't he come to help? Troy wished he was dead. Then he heard the manager say: "There's the other one over there in the crowd."

Diesel didn't hear the words, but he saw the heads turn toward him. Until then he'd thought they didn't suspect him. They had touched him while going by. As he'd stood watching the melee, he had pulled his pistol and held it under the groceries. He tried to steel himself to go to Troy's aid. It happened too fast; he didn't have his mind locked. Neither could he bring himself to fade away and abandon his friend.

Now that was all moot. The two police officers were coming toward him, splitting apart to cover each other. All he had was the pistol, a minor felony, and a year earlier he would have surrendered and served the six-month-to-five-year term. Now, however, he faced a life sentence because it would be his third felony—no matter how minor it might have been. He knew what he had to do. It was better to kill or die than surrender the rest of his life. The female cop was coming right at him. The black cop kind of circled. The crowd parted for her. She was five feet from him.

"You," she said, pointing at him.

He looked around, feigning that he thought she meant someone else. Others in the crowd also looked around. Melanie Strunk moved another step closer.

Diesel turned back. He saw her freckled face framed by the police helmet. Her bulletproof vest distorted her uniform blouse, which was disheveled and dirty from rolling on the ground with Troy. She didn't see the pistol under the bag of groceries. She had a fraction of a second, which wasn't enough, when the muzzle appeared and exploded. The bullet hit her in the lower abdomen, below the vest. The force of the heavy bullet threw her hips backward and half turned her as she went down, a short cry of pain coming from her.

The crowd screamed and exploded away from him.

Officer Lincoln dove for the cover of a car and grabbed at his pistol.

Troy, his cheek ground into the asphalt by the manager's knee, jerked at the gunshot. He coiled and tried to rise. The store manager and a box boy jumped on his back.

Diesel fired one wild shot in the direction of the black officer, and ran toward the end of the building. Oh God, oh God, oh God, his mind chanted. The evening had suddenly become apocalypse.

Melanie Strunk rolled on the concrete, holding her wound and crushing her teeth together to keep from crying out. Blood seeped between her fingers.

Officer Lincoln waited until the big man had turned the corner before jumping up and running after him.

On a street behind the market, a retired deputy sheriff heard the shot and saw the figure come around the corner and head toward a fence and a road beyond. The retired deputy slammed on his brakes, jumped out, and yelled, "Hold it, buster!"

Diesel leaped onto the fence and vaulted over, landing clumsily, facing the fence and stumbling backward until he fell on his rump.

The retired deputy was right behind the big man. He spread his arms like a linebacker readying for a tackle. Diesel was back on his feet. He tried to run over the man, but when he felt resistance, he shot him in the leg. The hero fell down and Diesel jumped in the deputy's car.

Behind him, Officer Lincoln assumed a firing position and aimed. The range was thirty-five yards. As he squeezed the trigger, Diesel leaned to shift into gear.

The bullet went through the driver's window, missed Diesel by an inch or two, went out the passenger window, crossed the street, and made a hole in a barbershop window. Carl Ellroy was in a barber chair, unaware of anything except a shave—until the heavy slug smashed into his forearm, breaking the bone and his Christmas present wristwatch.

Diesel stomped on the gas. The car fishtailed getting underway. As it careened down the street, bullets tore into it—but it kept going. Diesel could feel them hit, but he was unaware of the two big holes in the gas tank, where a bullet had passed all the way through. Gas streamed onto the street as he sped away. He looked at the gas gauge: half full.

Back at the market, hysterical voices called for an ambulance. Motorcycle officers and police cars screamed up with sirens and lights going full blast. Policemen took over from the manager. Troy saw the legs in blue uniforms. As a cop stepped on his head and ground his face into the pavement, he could see the granite walls of Folsom Prison. Rough hands jerked him up by the handcuffs behind his back and dragged him to a station wagon with a wired-off rear compartment. His head banged into the door frame. Someone pushed his head down and they threw him in back. He could see the spinning blue lights outside. As the station wagon got underway, Troy heard the clackety-clack of a helicopter. Run, Diesel, run, he thought through his own despair.

The hijacked car covered a mile before it ran out of gas. It was in a neighborhood of older frame houses. Thick maples canopied the street, creating night before the sun was all the way down. As Diesel got out, a chill wind blew over his sweating body and he shivered. He had to get another car. He had to get away. He would snatch one. He ran down the block, went through an alley to the next street. He went up on a porch and rang the bell.

No answer.

He ran across the lawn. Light came through the front window of the next house. He pushed the doorbell and waited, shivering and looking over his shoulder. Footsteps approached and, as the door opened, the sound of TV from inside. A man in his sixties faced him. "Yes," the man said. Behind him was a Sheltie, barking loudly. "Shaddup," the man said, pushing the dog back.

The screen door was closed but unhooked. Diesel opened it and put the pistol in the man's stomach. "I need your car. Where's the keys?"

The man was speechless. All that issued was "Uh . . . uh . . . uh . . ."

Diesel grabbed his shirtfront and rammed the pistol in his stomach. "Where's your fuckin' car keys?"

"In the . . . the car."

The small dog was yipping at Diesel's leg. From somewhere inside came a woman's voice: "Who is it, Charlie?"

"Never mind, honey," the old man yelled back. "I'll take care of it."

Diesel feinted at the dog, which made him run off, as Diesel wanted.

The old man had been in the Marine Corps, and after the first bolt of fear, he had control of himself. "Take it easy, mister. I won't give you any trouble."

"Good. Move it."

The old man came outside and closed the door. Diesel pressed close, holding the pistol down by his leg on the side away from the old man—the way police are trained to do. He was going to take the old man with him. Two in a car might allay suspicion. He could imagine the hornet's nest of enraged police pouring through the streets.

They both came down off the porch, down the driveway beside the house, and went to the garage. It was unlocked and the old man lifted it, exposing the rear of a ten-year-old Cadillac Seville, the kind with the humped trunk.

As they stepped inside, the spotlight hit them from the street. An amplified voice bellowed: "*Police officers! Don't move!*"

Diesel looked over his shoulder. The spotlight nearly blinded him. He could barely see the outline of the prowl car.

"Be cool, old man," he muttered. "Don't say nothin'." Diesel's first bolt of despair and terror was replaced by a kind of indifference. If this was the end of the game, so be it. He'd gone too far to give up now. "What seems to be the trouble, officer?" he asked, looking through the glare to see if it was one or two.

"Stay where you are," said a different voice. Two of them. He heard their footsteps moving down the driveway. He could see the figures against the light.

The back porch light went on, and the back door opened. The

220

old man's wife stuck her head out. "What's going on out here, Charlie?" she asked.

The porch light illuminated the cops. One turned to her, swinging his shouldered shotgun away. It took Diesel a couple of seconds to lock his courage into place and raise the pistol.

"*He's armed!*" yelled the other cop.

The shotgun swung back.

Diesel shot first. The bullet missed. The policeman pulled the shotgun's trigger. Click. The hammer fell. He had forgotten to cock it. His partner shot with his pistol. Diesel felt the punch in the abdomen; then a hot poker in his guts, a weird sensation. The Python jumped in his hand again. This shot hit the first officer in the hip, breaking the bone and knocking him down.

The retired marine hit the garage floor as his wife screamed and fell back into the house onto the floor.

After he shot, the second officer ducked behind the garage wall. The spotlight beam from the street brought daylight to the garage interior. Diesel was half-blinded by the glare in his eyes as he crouched beside the car's front fender. The cop had him pinned. He would be duck soup if he tried to run out of the door. Yet he couldn't stay where he was. Where was the old man? He would be his hostage.

As if Diesel's thought was a trigger, the retired marine jumped up on the other side and ran out: "Don't shoot! Don't shoot!" he yelled, his hands up.

The officer held his fire. He could see his partner writhing on the ground, which was dark from the blood. He knew the suspect was on the other side of the car. "Give it up," he yelled. "You can't get past me. We got backup coming." As soon as he yelled it, he moved along the outside of the garage, using his flashlight to guide himself. If Diesel had run out in those few seconds, he would have had a clear path to the street. The officer came around the rear and up the other side of the garage. He was next to the opposite wall from where Diesel thought he was.

Diesel's body shook in spasms. Reinforcements would arrive any moment. He had to make a move. He watched the corner he thought the cop was behind, held his breath and creeped along the side of the car. He coiled himself and ran out to the right, charging around the corner, firing twice as he came. No cop.

"Freeze!" yelled the officer from behind him.

Diesel whirled. The cop's head and arm with the pistol were visible—he was standing in the spotlight glare. Diesel ran at him, pulling the trigger—but the .357 Python was a six-shooter, and six shots were gone. The hammer fell on empty chambers. Damn, he thought.

It was his last thought. The officer carefully shot him twice in the chest and once in the head. Diesel felt the impact as he tumbled through momentary pain and blinding light that flared and went out, taking his soul with it. He was meat when he hit the pavement, the hot pistol falling from his hand.

17

At the police station, Troy was dragged out of the station wagon. Officers were waiting with tight leather gloves and clubs. They beat and kicked and dragged him across the pavement and up the short stairway. Heavy boots kicked him in the head. Inside, someone held his head up by the hair and smashed a fist into his face. His nose crunched with every blow. His jaw fractured.

After he was booked and certified as okay physically, they handcuffed him to a barred gate beside the main hallway and anyone who so desired could kick and punch him until they were exhausted. True enough, the man who'd shot two officers and sent fear through all of them was dead, but here was his partner. When word came that Melanie might be partially paralyzed, the frenzy increased for a few minutes. Troy screamed hate and defiance as best he could.

When the shift changed, he had a fractured wrist so swollen that the blue-black flesh hid the handcuff. He was spitting out blood and pieces of teeth, his jaw was broken, and his ribs were broken. His broken nose and eyes were so swollen that he could barely see blurred movement. A drunk deputy who arrive late climbed up on the bars and jumped down on his handcuffed arm. The snap of bone was audible. The bolt of pain was so great that he fainted.

Before dawn, an hour ahead of the shift change, the watch commander came from his office for coffee and saw Troy still hanging from the bars. "Get this garbage out of here," he said, nudging the inert figure with his toe. "Take him to the county hospital before one of those Jew ACLU bastards sees him and starts crying police brutality. If anybody asks, he got hurt in the parking lot and was jumped by some niggers in the tank."

"Got ya, Cap'n," said the sergeant. "Them cocksuckers don't care about a paralyzed cop . . . just about a piece of shit like this. I'd take him out and shoot him if it was up to me."

"They got the right idea in Brazil. Due process there is a bullet behind the ear."

"We're gonna have to do that, too, pretty damn soon. Get him outta here. I don't wanna look at him anymore."

Thus was Troy put in the back of a police car with two police officers. "Patch him up and bring him back. The detectives want to talk to him before he goes to court."

While bouncing along in the backseat, Troy wished they would stop and kill him. They could say he was trying to escape. Had he been able to, he would have forced them to do it. He envied Diesel.

The emergency room staff tended whatever the police dragged in. Shot, stabbed, drugged out of their minds, what they saw was all the same to the doctors and nurses. They treated physical ailments and made no moral judgments or inquiries. On this occasion they knew who he was. The story had filled the local airwaves all night long, plus they had already treated two wounded officers and the citizen from the barber shop, so they knew why he was beaten up, but nothing more. The doctor insisted on admitting him. His hand, arm, and some ribs were broken, his cheekbone caved in, and he had a severe concussion. When they told the escorting officers, they called the watch commander. He disliked leaving the suspect outside the jail, especially when they weren't even sure of his true identity, but the procedure manual was clear: Medical personnel had the last word. "Make the doctor sign," the watch commander said, then designated an officer to stay at the hospital. The suspect would be leg-ironed to the bed frame. The hospital lacked a jail ward, but the room windows had flat bars. The watch commander had covered his ass. That was what concerned him.

When Troy came out of anesthesia after surgery, his wrist in a cast, his jaw wired, he no longer wanted to die. Morphine had worked its magic. It made bearable both physical pain and mental torment. He would withstand whatever happened without a whimper. He even managed snatches of sleep and pieces of dreams, one of them being Diesel's son, now grown, pointing at him with a finger of accusation, which made him feel terrible as he cried out his denial. Another dream awakened him full of fear and covered with wet bedclothes. He tried unsuccessfully to recall the dream, and then he laughed, which hurt his ribs. What the hell did he have to fear? The whole world had already fallen on his head. He thought of Diesel with mixed emotions—sympathy for Diesel's wife and son, and questioning anger as he remembered seeing Diesel in the crowd. Why the fuck hadn't he helped when he saw the cop? And if he wasn't going to help, why the fuck hadn't he gotten away when he had the chance? Troy ran the scene through his mind frame by frame and realized it was a question that Diesel would never answer.

The sound of rattling keys made him look at the door. It opened and a nurse ushered in three men. Two were granite-jawed detectives; the third a pink-cheeked youth with a briefcase who announced himself as an assistant district attorney. The detectives glared with hostility; Troy was the shooter's partner and equally responsible for Melanie Strunk being paralyzed. Troy ignored them and studied the baby-faced district attorney. His eyes were a flat blue, expressionless. Troy sensed that he was the dangerous enemy.

Out came a billfold and a badge. "Sergeant Cox," said the man who held it. "This is Detective Fowler and Mr. Harper. Mr. Harper is from the district attorney's office. He wants to ask you some questions."

Mr. Harper cleared his throat. "How do you feel?"

Troy's wired jaw impeded his speech, but he managed to slur out: "I'm okay. When do I go home?"

"Home! You think you're goin' home?"

Troy tossed a shoulder. "Di'nt do nuthin'."

Sergeant Cox sneered. "What about that money in the trunk? Where'd that come from?"

Troy shrugged.

"We know your name isn't Al Leon Klein. Who are you?"

Troy managed the semblance of a smile despite the wired jaw.

"We'll know in a few hours," Sergeant Cox said. "I'd bet my ass you've got a record."

"We're booking you on suspicion of murder."

"Murder! Whose murder?"

"Carl Johnson."

Troy sneered, but he felt sick inside. He'd thought of the felony murder rule whereby crime partners are legally responsible if anyone is killed during a crime. If the police drive up during a robbery, mistake the store owner for a perpetrator and kill him, the robber is guilty of murder. And if the police or store owner kill a robber with a partner, the partner is guilty of murder. But what was the felony being committed? Besides, he'd already been in custody, hand-cuffed and on the ground, before any crime started. Was there any other crime except the shootout?

"We're also planning to charge you with conspiracy to commit robbery."

"File it," Troy said. "Then prove it."

The detectives rolled their eyes. Mr. Harper produced a Miranda warning card and read it. "Sign this waiver," he said, "and we can talk about it. If you haven't done anything, tell us what happened so we can clear you."

Troy tried to ask with a look, "Are you insane?" Then he began shaking his head in disbelief and laughing. If he signed the waiver, there was nothing in the world to stop them from getting on a witness stand to recite a detailed confession, each corroborating the other. They might not do that, but there was no way to be sure. A friend of his had once gone to trial and had an LAPD detective sergeant swear under oath that the defendant had confessed to a safe burglary. If the defendant got on the stand to deny the confession, the prose-cutor would drag out his record to impeach him. Troy refused to risk it by signing a Miranda waiver. Rule number one when dealing with the police: Don't answer any questions without a lawyer on hand.

"You know what," he said between the wired teeth. "I think I better talk to a lawyer *now!*"

The detectives and district attorney looked at each other and shrugged. They got up to leave. The nurse opened the door. When the prosecutor and one cop were heading toward the exit with their heads turned, Sergeant Cox leaned forward as if to say something sotto voce. Instead, he glanced over his shoulder, made sure nobody was watching, and backhanded Troy hard across the face.

The splat made the others turn to look, but nobody knew what was going on. Cox draped an arm around each of them and said, "Let's go eat."

Later in the morning, the door opened. A deputy accompanied the doctor and a nurse with his chart. The doctor looked at the chart; then checked him, flashing a tiny light into his eyes, feeling the cast on his arm, poking a finger into the yellowish blue discolorations on his body. "You'll live," he pronounced as he wrote on the chart. He turned to the nurse. "We'll keep him another day." They went out. The deputy locked the door.

Ten minutes later, the deputy unlocked the door for the janitorial crew, a trio of blacks with mop and broom and rags. The deputy had to step out of the doorway while the wheeled mop bucket was pushed in. The black man who was wiping off the nightstand looked back to make sure the deputy couldn't hear. "Chuckie Rich is my cuz, man. He say tell you hello and what can he do?"

Chuckie Rich! Troy had known Chuckie since juvenile hall, and even though racial hostility permeated prison, they had been friends. Chuckie had been an All-City halfback at Roosevelt High School and had a scholarship to U.S.C. until he got busted with a gram of heroin. That was when he met Troy. Since then he played short con, boosted—and repeatedly went to prison for minor offenses.

"Where is he?" Troy asked. "Is he out?"

"Oh, yeah. He say what can he do for you?"

"I need a pipe wrench—about so big." He held his hands eighteen inches apart.

"I'll tell him, man. You be cool now."

The deputy had reappeared in the doorway. Chuckie's cousin finished wiping the bed stand and went out. The deputy locked the door.

Troy fought down his excitement. Nothing would come from this. Even if Chuckie wanted to help, what were the chances of

Chuckie's cousin risking jail? A pipe wrench would bend the flat window bars until they snapped, but how could he get it? The deputy stood watching when the door was opened for food and cleanup and medication. Even if someone did bring it, it would be tomorrow at the earliest. Tomorrow Troy was being discharged to the county jail. No, he knew how to delay that by at least one day.

He'd seen a rusty double-edged Gillette blade in the bed stand drawer. He opened the drawer and took it out. When the door opened for the lab technician, Troy had his legs drawn up enough to hide him nicking his thumb with the tip of the blade—just enough so pressure would squeeze out a tiny drop of blood.

The lab technician drew blood while taking his temperature; then did a blood pressure and, finally, handed him a urine specimen bottle. As he pissed in the bottle, he let the piss hit the tiny speck of blood on his thumb. Blood in urine could be many things, from kidney stones to cancer to internal injuries. It would necessitate more tests, perhaps even an X-ray. It would surely mean another day in the hospital. He had no faith in Chuckie's cousin, but he had nothing to lose by playing out the faint chance that maybe something would happen. Escape was his only chance of ever being free again. Escape from the hospital was more likely than from the jail, and escape from Folsom bordered on the miraculous.

When the door opened for the evening meal, the food on his tray, turkey and mashed potatoes and cranberry sauce, reminded him that this was Christmas. He had totally forgotten—and now was washed through with an ineffable sadness, fertile soil for self-pity, which was something he seldom indulged in. How could they charge him with murder? What had he done? All he'd robbed was a nigger drug dealer and a drug smuggler and killed a homicidal maniac. The kidnapping, well, that was bad, but that was to make a sucker pay a debt; it wasn't for ransom. And even if it was bad, it wasn't *that* bad; it wasn't justice that he spend the rest of his life in prison. That was bullshit.

Justice, that was what he wanted. Then he realized what he was thinking and began to laugh. He didn't want justice; he didn't even know what justice was. He wanted what he wanted, just like everyone else, and the rest was bullshit, verbiage.

To escape its anguish, his body demanded sleep. It pulled him down. Maybe he would awake in another world.

Before daylight, the door opened. Troy heard rattling chains. Two deputies entered, one pushing a wheelchair; the other had his torn and stinking clothes. "Wanna wear 'em?" the deputy asked.

Troy shook his head. He felt sick. He thought they were transferring him to the county jail. They pushed the wheelchair to the back door into the parking lot; then told him to get up and walk. One deputy told the other that they had plenty of time, the judge never appeared before ten-thirty. Troy felt hope ignite. He was going to court, not jail. He might get one more night in the hospital. Maybe Chuckie Rich and his cousin would come through.

The Municipal Court was across the street from the main courthouse. While they were still several blocks away, they got a call that television news cameras and reporters were waiting at the front entrance, so they parked in an alley and took him in a rear door. The courthouse hallway was already filling with lawyers and litigants, cops and defendants on bail and bail bondsmen. A bailiff unlocked the door to the still-empty courtroom. They took him down the aisle and past the high bench. Even a runt becomes a giant when he wears black robes and sits on a courtroom bench. The courtroom was paneled in dark wood and had the look of a manor. The bailiff opened a door into the bullpen next to the courtroom, which looked like an outhouse, with graffiti-marred concrete walls, the stench of a plugged-up toilet. At least he was alone. He'd been in courthouse bullpens where fifty prisoners were jammed in an eighteen-foot room.

As the bailiff and deputies unlocked the leg irons and handcuffs, their eyes showed their special hostility. He tried to radiate a haughty indifference in return.

Through the door, he could hear people gathering in the courtroom. At ten-thirty, the court was called to order, and a minute later the door opened and the bailiff motioned him out. The courtroom was empty of spectators, but it had a full complement of prosecutors, clerks, armed bailiffs, and a judge who remained looking small and bald even in robes on the high bench. Everyone took their places and the court clerk called the case: "The People of California versus John Doe Number One, Criminal Number six, six, seven, four, eight dash ninety-four."

Troy lowered his head and smiled to himself. They still didn't know who he was. They had to charge him with something in forty-eight hours or cut him loose.

"I serve the defendant with the complaint," the clerk said, handing the bailiff several pages of stapled legal papers, who handed them to Troy.

"Let the record reflect that the defendant has been served," said the judge, looking through bifocals at copies of the complaint. Then he looked at Troy. "What is your name?"

"John Doe, I guess."

The judge, who was bald, turned red at the answer. "Do you have your own lawyer?" he asked.

"Not at the moment, Your Honor. I haven't been allowed to make a telephone call."

"Is that true, Mr. D'Arcy?" The judge looked at the assistant district attorney.

"I have no idea, Your Honor. I understand it's standard procure to allow everyone a phone call."

"Not me, Your Honor."

"Could that be because you wouldn't give your name?"

"I don't know. I just know I haven't had a chance."

The escorting deputy stood up. "Your Honor . . ."

"Yes."

"I'm transporting Mr. . . . uh . . . Doe. If he hasn't had a phone call, I'll guarantee that he gets one as we leave here."

"You're Deputy—"

"Bartlett, sir. Senior Deputy Bartlett."

"Very good. I'll leave it to you." To Troy. "Are you going to have your own lawyer?"

"Yes. I hope so."

"You have funds to hire one?"

"Well, I did have some money in the car."

230

"Your Honor," inserted the prosecutor. "I believe the defendant is talking about a hundred and fifty thousand dollars found in the trunk. We believe it's proceeds from a crime—"

"What crime?" Troy said.

The judge raised a hand. "Restrain yourself, Mr. . . . uh . . . Doe."

"We're investigating where it came from," the prosecutor continued. "It's booked as evidence."

"Well . . . we won't deal with that issue at this proceeding. I'll appoint the public defender until you retain your own lawyer. What about bail? What's the position of the people?"

"We think a million dollars is appropriate. The defendant hasn't revealed his identity. The charges are extremely serious and there's a great likelihood of flight to avoid prosecution."

"Mr. . . . Doe. What do you have to say?"

"I think you're overrating me."

"No, I don't think so. A man who won't give his name. I'm going to set bail at one million dollars. We need a date for a preliminary hearing."

The clerk carried the big book to the bench and put it in front of the judge and pointed a finger. "We'll set preliminary hearing for Friday, January fifth, at ten A.M."

The arraignment was over. The judge ordered a ten-minute recess. The bailiff and deputies took Troy to the door and put on the leg irons, plus one handcuff attached to a wide leather strap around his waist; his other wrist was in a cast. The arraignment had taken four minutes after six hours of waiting.

Back in the bullpen, he waited another five hours for transportation back to the hospital. It was dark outside. He looked through the mesh on the station wagon windows at the lighted store windows. In one of them a clerk was taking down a Christmas tree. The sight triggered a pang of inchoate longing. He had given up hope of Chuckie Rich sending him a pipe wrench via Chuckie's cousin. His shift was over; he was long gone from the hospital. Even if he was still there and had the pipe wrench, there was no way to get it through the door. It was way too big to hide in his food tray. Could he bust the little observation window in the door and pass it through there? Not hardly.

He stared longingly through the screened window at the free world, while in the background of consciousness he heard the deputies talking about mortgage rates and marriage.

The sheriff's van pulled to the emergency room entrance. One of the deputies went inside and returned with a black attendant pushing a wheelchair. They legironed him to the wheelchair, put a blanket over his lap, and pushed him down a hallway that gleamed from fluorescent light on pale enamel paint. In his room, they had him strip off the court clothes and put on hospital pajamas.

Even while he watched the steel teeth clicking through the slot, he was aware of the lump poking up from under the mattress. He started to lift the edge of the mattress and reach beneath to pull out whatever it was, but his instinct made him decide to wait until the deputy and attendant left.

As soon as the door closed, he reached underneath himself and pulled out a large plastic shopping bag. His heart skipped and raced as he felt how heavy it was. As he pulled it onto his lap, through the bag he felt the handle of the wrench. It banged against something else. He opened the bag and reached in; his fingers felt the hammer and cylinder of a revolver. Using his raised knees to shield any view through the observation window, he pulled out an older .38 Smith & Wesson with a long barrel, a pistol once called a "police special" before they went to .357 Magnums and fast firing 9mm automatics. The blueing was faded on the barrel and the handle was chipped, but it was oiled and loaded. He put pressure on the trigger; the hammer started to rise and the cylinder started to turn. It damn sure looked workable.

Next the pipe wrench. It was hefty. Okie Bob had told him about snapping the same kind of bars in Soledad with a pipe wrench. Put the wrench on the bars and work them back and forth until the metal fatigued and the bar snapped. Troy would wait until things settled for the night, probably after the midnight count—then he would make his move, or see if it could be made.

The deputy and attendant returned with a tray of cold food. He had the pistol and wrench under his legs beneath the blankets. He was too excited to eat. As the hours passed with excruciating slowness, he realized what Chuckie's cousin had done. The room door had either been left open because nobody was in the room, or had been opened temporarily for a cleanup, and not watched during that interlude because the room was empty. It had to have been like that. There was no other way. Who the fuck said a black man and a white man could never be friends? Chuckie Rich was a better friend than many of Troy's white homeboys. Too bad the bag had no address or phone number.

The lights went out at ten. For another hour he could hear voices from a TV in a nearby ward; then that went off, too. He heard footsteps in the hallway. A flashlight beam came through the observation window. He feigned sleep and made sure his body was easy to see. He didn't need them coming in to check him out.

After the next count, it was time to start work. The first order of business was to get out of bed. The pipe wrench made short work of the hollow vertical rod at the foot of the bed. It was made out of pot metal and snapped with a couple of twists. The leg iron came free. True, it was attached to his ankle and the chain dangled, but he could move free.

He got out of bed and went to the door, looking both ways down the hallway. Nothing moved. The deputy on duty obviously preferred sitting in the nurse's station where he could watch movies all night.

Troy went to the window and removed the screen. He had to break a couple of small panes of glass to get a bite on the flat bar. As he fastened the wrench and pushed, his spirits sank. It seemed unyielding. He pulled hard; then pushed with all his might. It moved a tiny fraction of a millimeter. That was enough. If it moved at all, he could eventually snap it off. He pulled as hard as he could; then pushed again.

Rattling keys, footsteps. He dove into bed, clutching the pistol. If anybody opened the door, he wouldn't go out the window, he would walk out the front. He didn't want it that way. He would have no head start whatsoever. He turned his head away and closed his eyes. From behind his eyelids, he saw the glare of light. It disappeared and the footsteps receded. Another routine bed check. My God, how did the guy miss the screen off the window?

Once more, Troy slipped to the floor and looked up and down the hallway. Empty. Back to work.

The bar gave a little more—and yet once more. Suddenly, it snapped. The sound was loud. It seemed like a small pistol.

Oh shit! Jesus Christ! Somebody had to hear that. He replaced the screen and hurried to the door. If someone came his way, he would jump into bed and hold his breath.

Nobody responded. He began to get excited. He was going to get away. True, a barefoot fool in loose pajamas, dangling a chain and wearing a cast, was still a longshot—but what had already happened was almost miraculous, that one of the few black men who was his friend would have a cousin who worked in a hospital and had enough guts to smuggle him a pipe wrench and a pistol. Thank God Chuckie Rich wasn't a white-hater like so many brothers in California prisons.

Now was the time to make his move. He tore a bedsheet into strips to wrap around the length of chain and so tie it to his leg. He had socks and cloth slippers. At least he wouldn't be barefoot, although it would damn sure hurt when he dropped into the alley.

With his arm in a cast, it was impossible to hold the pistol in one hand while climbing out. He used more bedsheet strips to put through the trigger guard, tied the ends, and made a pistol necklace to dangle around his neck underneath his pajama top.

Using the pipe wrench, he bent the bars out enough so he could climb through. It was a tight squeeze, but he went headfirst, wriggled his torso out, then pulled the rest of himself free. The jagged end of the broken bars gouged a ribbon of flesh from his chest. He didn't give a shit about that. His feet were on a tiny ledge just big enough for a toehold. It was eight or nine feet to the alley below, too high to risk jumping without shoes.

He worked himself down the window until he could grab the tiny ledge with his fingers. He let himself dangle. He planned to hold himself and drop, but his momentum was too strong. As his body extended, the weight pulled his fingers loose and down he went. He fell back onto his ass with his legs up in the air, but nothing was broken. He reflexively threw back his arms to catch himself. The pain from the broken wrist was a bolt of lightning and sent instant sweat from his whole body. Great geysers of pain leaped into his brain.

He had to move fast, and keep moving to get out of the small town. When the sun came up, every citizen in town, and every cop for a hundred miles, would be looking for him. Anyone who saw a man running in hospital pajamas would sound the alarm. He had to go fast and far before the morn.

He moved to the end of the alley. Which way was what? It was a scene of surrealism, the empty stores, the deserted streets with the traffic lights going through their cycles for nobody. On the street there was nowhere to hide if headlights approached—but he had no choice and had to chance it.

He sucked in a deep breath and sprinted on an angle across the boulevard toward the next intersection. Darkness beckoned down the cross street. He went a block and was on the edge of a seedy residential neighborhood. It had trees and bushes and shadows to hide him. When headlights approached, he pressed against a tree, and eased around it as the car went past. Another car appeared, and he dove facedown next to a ficus shrub, which elicited a frantic barking from a backyard dog. The passing car went by, and Troy moved on the other way. Lights came on behind him and he heard the dog's owner yelling for it to "shaddup."

He knew very little of the town, but the street sign said he was heading west. The interstate lay a mile—or two, or three—in that direction. It ran north and south, to San Francisco and L.A., three hundred plus miles away. It made no difference to Troy which way he went—he had to get away from here—although San Francisco was much closer.

He turned down an alley that ran between houses. Instantly a tabernacle choir of dogs began to howl and bark and jump at gates and fences. He hurried forward. The dogs seemed to pass him along, from behind one house to the next. The roadbed was rough dirt and rocks. The cloth slippers provided no protection when he stepped on rocks. Each time he winced and limped a few steps. His feet were starting to wear through the cloth; gone were the barefoot days of youth when he spent most of summer without shoes. He estimated that he'd walked about three miles. Pretty soon, his feet would be raw and bloody. Maybe he should find a hole and go underground. No. The hunt would be too intense. They might even use dogs. The town was too small. He had to get many more miles away.

At the end of the block the houses stopped. Beyond that was a park. He was unable to determine its size, but it was more than a square because he was unable to see through to the other side. He went in. Thank God, the wet grass soothed his feet. Through the trees, he could see a sliver moon low on the horizon. The last traces of morphine wore off; pain throbbed through him from several sources, but he kept going.

First came the whoosh, whoosh, whoosh sound—and thirty yards beyond, he came around a hedge and saw the raised interstate. All that was visible above the ivy-covered fence were the tops of huge diesel rigs rolling through the night. Desperation made his next decision: he would hijack a car. He was a man alone in the most primal sense imaginable.

Moving along the edge of the park, veering around bushes, he watched the raised highway across the narrow parallel street. At the end of the park, the cross street led to an entrance ramp onto the highway. There was an underpass beneath the highway. There would be a ramp there, too, but that one would be heading north toward San Francisco. It was closer, but L.A. was where he had help. A sign said U.S. 101 South with an arrow. Next to the intersection of the ramp and the road beside the park was a stop sign. Good.

Not so good was the forty yards of open space between the greenery and the stop sign. The big light on the freeway turned the lawn into the Dodger Stadium outfield. First, he would have to charge across the open space and hope nobody spotted him—and then hope that their doors were unlocked.

As he moved into a hiding position, he remembered nature films with the lion crouched in the grass, tail twitching.

Headlights. A stake bed truck with Mexican farm workers paused; then proceeded up the ramp. Damn, they went to work early. Not even a rooster was up yet and they were en route to the fields already.

Another car appeared. It passed in silhouette and had one occupant. It slowed and stopped.

Troy leaped forward, the pistol banging against his body under the sweatshirt, which was now soaked with sweat. He needed his good hand to open the car door.

He was still thirty yards away when the bright brake light went off and the car started to move. He closed for another few seconds; then it quickly opened the distance. He stopped. He was panting. For some reason he remembered that the prey escape the charging lion most of the time.

Had the driver seen him? No, his acceleration had been slow and even.

He walked back, sucking cool air into his lungs. He sat down on the wet grass behind the bushes. After a minute's rest, he refastened the leg iron chain, several times wrapping the strip of bed sheet around his leg and pulling it as tight as he could. He was hot and sweaty and the chill predawn air gave him goose bumps. He took the pistol from around his neck. It slowed him. He would carry it in his hand until he reached the car; then he would tuck it under his arm during the second he needed to reach for the car door. He practiced the motion a couple of times. Please, God, let it be unlocked.

Another car, an old Cadillac Seville with the humpback. It went by. Two figures.

Troy started the moment it passed, running behind it, hoping that neither looked over their right shoulder.

The Cadillac's brake lights went on. It was stopping ahead of him. He ran to catch up.

The car stopped as he arrived. He lunged, tucked the pistol in his armpit, and reached for the back door. The handle went down, the door opened. Troy dove into the back.

At that moment the car started moving. The driver hit the brakes. Troy crashed into the back of the front seat. Pain shot from his wired jaw to his brain. The pistol fell on the floorboard under him.

The woman screamed. The driver turned his head, the movement pulled his foot from the brake. The car rolled into an embankment of iceplant and stopped. He was a black man with a thin mustache and the scent of aftershave.

The woman kept screaming as Troy rolled and twisted and pushed himself up; he could feel the pistol under his knee.

The car filled with brilliant light. The blast of an air horn. A giant truck rolled by, the disturbed air buffeting the car.

Troy's fingers closed around the pistol. "Shaddup!" he yelled.

She twisted around and pressed her back to the door frame.

"Tell her," Troy said to the man, raising the pistol.

"Shhhhh," the man said, reaching out to give his wife's arm a hard shake. "Quiet down."

"Back up . . . move this car," Troy said.

"Okay . . . okay . . . just don't hurt us."

"I'm not gonna hurt you . . . as long as you do what I say. Now back the motherfucker up and let's roll."

"Up on the freeway."

"Yeah. Where the fuck did you think—"

"You said back up."

"Let's go. C'mon."

The Cadillac backed off the iceplant; it was still across the lines off the ramp itself.

More headlights, two cars, one honking to warn them as it blew by.

The Cadillac soon gathered momentum up the ramp and moved onto the freeway. He was rolling. He had a chance. It was hard to believe that he had gotten this far. It was enough to light the candle of hope.

"Take our money and the car," the woman said. "Let us go."

"Naw . . . I can't do that."

"Why not?"

Her husband answered for her: "Because we'd call the police right away."

"No, we wouldn't—"

"Charlene!" the man admonished. "Don't lie."

"If we gave our word . . ."

"He wouldn't believe us."

"I can't afford to," Troy said. "But I'm not going to hurt you if you don't try anything. If you do, well . . ."

"What do you want us to do?" the man asked.

"Right now I want you to turn on the news."

"You got it."

Because the sun was nearing the eastern horizon, the all-news stations from L.A. and San Francisco were thick with static, but neither had anything about the suspected killer on the loose in central California. At least his mug shot wasn't flashing on TV screens. He was tired, too, and had several spots with throbbing pain. They beat counterpoint to each other.

Troy snapped awake. He had started to doze. He moved over to the corner on the right and pressed the button to lower the window. The chill air was sucked in against his cheeks. That would keep him alert. Something was under his butt. He raised up and reached.

A zipper attaché case. Papers and a Bible, its soft leather binding worn and frayed. Pages were loose. It was a Bible often studied.

Troy could see the back of the woman's head and a partial profile of the man, who seemed about sixty. It was hard to be sure. "Look here," he said. "I'm sorry about this . . . and I don't want to hurt you . . . but I'm desperate . . . and I'll kill you if you try anything. Got it?"

"We won't try anything," the man said.

"Just let us go—" She was trembling visibly.

"Charlene!" The man cut her off. "He won't do that . . . so don't demean yourself."

After a long pause, Troy leaned forward. "I can't . . . I can't take the risk, y'know what I mean?"

The man nodded.

"I am really sorry." He had started to say "fuckin' sorry," but the Bible and the rectitude made him drop the vulgar. "What's your name?"

"I'm Charles Wilson . . . and this is my wife Charlene."

"The Reverend Charles Wilson," Charlene added.

Troy smiled. Despite everything, Charlene was making sure that her man got his due recognition. How long before they were missed?

He saw no luggage. That meant they weren't planning to be anywhere overnight. "Where you going?" he asked.

"We're coming back," Charlene said. "We've been visiting in Berkeley. We saw our son's baby girl for the first time."

"Anybody expecting you?"

"No . . . but—" she stopped, as if remembering.

"But what?"

"Never mind. I . . . I forgot."

"What's she talking about?" Troy asked the reverend.

"We're supposed to call our son when we get home."

"We'll call him. Tell him you decided to take an extra day."

"Another thing," the reverend said. "My wife's a diabetic. She needs to eat something real soon."

"Get off on the first ramp that has services."

Daybreak simply turned the black sky to pewter, and vague shapes acquired substance. At the first ramp the Cadillac turned off—a truck stop, several gas stations, one with a small motel and a McDonald's that competed with a small coffee shop. The gas station restrooms were off to themselves, and the parking lot was empty except near the coffee shop.

Troy and the minister went into the men's room with the reverend's suit bag. Troy kept the door ajar so he could watch the car while he changed. The pants were a little big in the waist and a couple of inches short to the cuff. If he let them hang loose on his hips, they were long enough to avoid absurdity. An overshirt also worked. The sleeve was big enough for the cast to go through. He left the cuff unbuttoned and rolled it up. He left the shirttail out to hide the pistol in his waistband.

At the McDonald's he repeated the m.o. He left Charlene in the car, which he could watch through the window, and took the reverend inside. He waited while the minister called his son and lied: "Mom's feeling a little tired, so we're going to stop a night in San Luis Obispo . . . Yes, sure . . . We'll call tomorrow."

Phone call over, they stood in the line to place an order. In the line beside them, a pair of truck drivers were talking and Troy heard "road block . . . San Luis . . ." It wasn't where he had been, so it had to be ahead. If he had doubts about what he'd heard, they were dispelled by the expression on the reverend's face. He, too, had heard the conversation.

Back in the old Cadillac, while Charlene drank orange juice and ate an Egg McMuffin, Troy looked at an Auto Club map from the glove compartment. California had mountain ranges running north and south, and major highways paralleled the mountain ranges. Smaller two-lane highways went east/west through the mountains. He would head east almost to the Nevada border and take the farthest north/south highway toward L.A. The odds were greater against them blocking that highway—and if they wanted him that bad, fuck it, they deserved him.

Troy had the reverend turn around and head north for twenty miles to a state road through the mountains. It was narrow, its curves tight, and in places the recent storms had washed rocks down the cliffs. It was slow going, but it was also safe. In an hour the only vehicle they saw was a pickup truck pulling a horse trailer. Going the same direction, it was even slower than the Cadillac. They had to follow the horse's ass for nearly an hour before they could pull around and away. Then the gray sky slowly opened and the rains came down. Radio reception was poor down between the mountains, but by afternoon they were out of the first range of mountains in the long Salinas Valley. By then the manhunt was not only mentioned on the all-news stations, but was on the five-minute hourly news carried on nearly every station. The first time it came on, the Reverend Wilson and his wife immediately exchanged a glance that Troy saw from the backseat. "Turn that up," he said. ". . . addition to the charges pending from the parking lot shootout, the fugitive is wanted by Corrections as a parole violator. He has a history of extreme violence and is known to be armed. Events leading up to the present manhunt began last Tuesday in the Safeway parking lot . . ."

Troy listened with an eerie detachment, as if the grim tale being recited was about someone else. Damn, he told himself, they sure do overrate a sucker. It was gallows humor. He knew the power of the state was focused against him. His mug photo was being printed for thousands of police car dashboards—and probably flashed on countless television screens across California. He'd known men who'd had this kind of heat—*everybody* looking for them. None had gotten away for long. Files and computers combined to mark everyone in the industrialized world, and most of the Third World, too. Gone were the days when a fugitive could disappear forever into South America or the Far East.

In bits and pieces. Troy got to know Charles and Charlene Wilson. They had been married for thirty-four years and were still in love. Each was more concerned about the other than themself. And after their initial terror diminished, they were concerned about him, too. Troy despised most of America as hypocrites, professing a code of virtue while living by one of expediency. The herd went along with the herd, and what might have been wrong when done by an individual was acceptable, even moral, when done by all. Charlie (as she called him) and Charlene followed their own consciences and what they thought Jesus would want. "We judge not," she said. "That is for God. We try our best to walk in Jesus' footsteps."

"And we fall short much of the time," the Reverend added. It was mild rebuke for her sin of vanity. She nodded; she understood. Their words and demeanor toward each other—and toward him once their fear subsided sufficiently—made Troy feel scorn for their ignorance, and painful guilt for their simple goodness. No hypocrites here. Such innocents as these were a large part of his decision to prey on drug dealers. Remorse mixed with anger (what else could he do, give up?) and made his stomach burn.

Without warning, on a tight curve, the car started to skid. The reverend hit the brakes. The back end broke loose and came around so they were hydroplaning sideways, a hill on one side and a precipice on the other.

The car went into the hillside instead of over the cliff.

"I can't . . . drive anymore," the reverend said. "I just can't." He held up his hands. They were shaking.

"I'll drive," Troy said. "You two ride in the backseat together. You won't try anything, will you?"

242

They shook their heads. Still, he put the pistol between his legs on the driver's seat.

The road map showed another pass through the mountains east of the Salinas Valley. Near the summit the rain turned to snow, slowing them more. It took the rest of the day to zigzag through the mountains. By nightfall they were near Tehachapi and the rain had been replaced by a thick fog that filled the canyons between the peaks. Troy had no idea what was beyond the headlight beams that bounced back from the wall of fog. He now felt hopeful of reaching his sanctuary of Los Angeles.

Ahead in the fog he saw a pulsing red light. It hung high over the middle of an intersection and flashed red in every direction. He braked, then wondered if he should continue straight ahead or turn. Still undecided, as he rolled into the middle of the intersection, he hit the brakes and peered out for a road sign.

He decided to turn. As he let the steering wheel come straight, the car was filled with flashing blue light. A police car had come up behind them. He had been looking ahead and was unaware of its presence until the flasher went on, sending fear and despair through him.

Should he punch the gas and run?

No. He had no idea where he was or where he would be going.

"*Pull over!*" a policeman bellowed through the amplified bull-horn.

The light came from directly behind, so bright that he could see nothing else. Had they come forward immediately, they could have taken him without a struggle. He was too drained; he had to put his mind in a state to shoot it out. It wasn't an attitude one could maintain constantly.

Seconds ticked away. He squinted and looked at the glaring lights in the mirror. They were radioing in the license number.

"Stay where you are," he told the hostages; then reached between his legs for the .38 and opened the door handle with his elbow. They had waited too long. He was ready in his head. He slid out, holding the pistol next to his thigh.

"What's wrong, officer?" he asked as he stood up. He could only see the headlights and grille. He raised his left hand to block the glare. His breathing was fast and shallow; he felt drained and enervated. Thank God he wasn't shaking visibly.

"Don't move, mister," said the amplified voice. Now Troy saw the shape outside the open driver's door.

Troy took a step forward. "We're kinda lost," he said.

"Freeze!" yelled a new voice. It was to his left. He looked and saw a second officer on an embankment across the road, a shotgun braced against his shoulder, aimed at Troy.

"What's wrong with you? Don't point that—"

"*It's him!*" echoed the amplified voice.

Troy reflexively turned to look at the police car. That officer was pulling his pistol.

Troy raised his .38 and fired in one motion. It was a dozen years since he'd practiced, but it was twenty yards and he'd once been really good with small arms—plus the officer had neglected to put on his bulletproof vest. The lead slug hit him just below the collarbone and angled down through a lung and out his back. It made him drop his weapon and go down on his knees.

Troy turned and squeezed. He didn't hear the shotgun, but he did hear what sounded like a handful of pebbles striking the car trunk. It tore into his cheek and shoulder and knocked him sideways but failed to knock him down. Not buckshot. That would have torn him apart. It was—bird shot.

He righted himself and fired three times to a pattern. His shots were drowned by a second blast from the shotgun. This time it hit him head-on, chest and stomach and neck. It knocked him down on his back. He was torn up by the bird shot, but none of the wounds was really serious. He was unaware of the fact, but his third bullet had nicked the officer's chin, went through his throat and out the side. He fell backward over the embankment.

Troy's brain spun. Through his daze, he heard a pistol firing. The shots were rapid and many. Troy opened his eyes. The officer beside the police car was sitting down; he had his thirteen-shot, nine-millimeter semi-automatic pistol in a two-hand rest. He was emptying it through the backseat of the Cadillac. The bullets tore through trunk and upholstery and buried themselves in the bodies of the Reverend Charles Wilson and his wife, Charlene.

Troy felt around and was unable to find his pistol. He crawled from the glare to shadows and fog. Near the edge of the road, he lost consciousness.

Now he felt it, he was moving; he was on a stretcher. He kept his eyes closed. If they discovered him awake, they might work him over or tighten the chains, as if they weren't too tight already.

They stopped. He heard doors being opened; then he was sliding inside. From the babble, Troy heard an occasional word and fragments of sentences: ". . . no pulse . . . in the irrigation ditch and drowned . . ." ". . . two in the car look like Swiss cheese . . ." "Madigan's gonna feel terrible when he finds out he killed two innocent citizens . . ." "He thought they were perps." "Let's roll."

The doors slammed; the ambulance started to move. Then it stopped. Troy opened his eyes and looked. He could see the intersection full of police cars, their flashing lights eerie in the fog.

Footsteps approached. He could see a figure at the driver's window. A new voice: "How's this scumbag? Is he gonna die on us?"

"Naw. He'll live to go to the gas chamber."

Derisive laughter. "Fat chance of that. Okay . . . move it . . ."

The ambulance began to move. It gathered speed. Its siren began to wail. Troy closed his eyes and went out again. His dreams this time were terrible.